THE
GATEKEEPERS

THE GATEKEEPERS

Susan B. A. Hofmann

TATE PUBLISHING
AND ENTERPRISES, LLC

Published by Tate Publishing & Enterprises, LLC
127 E. Trade Center Terrace | Mustang, Oklahoma 73064 USA
1.888.361.9473 | www.tatepublishing.com

Tate Publishing is committed to excellence in the publishing industry. The company reflects the philosophy established by the founders, based on Psalm 68:11,
"The Lord gave the word and great was the company of those who published it."

Book design copyright © 2016 by Tate Publishing, LLC. All rights reserved.
Cover design by Bill Francis Peralta
Interior design by Mary Jean Archival

Published in the United States of America

ISBN: 978-1-68254-892-9
1. Fiction / Religious
2. Fiction / General
16.02.12

I tell you that, if these should hold their peace,
the stones would immediately cry out.

—Luke 19:40

LIST OF CHARACTERS

Allocen—duke in hell
Amon—fallen angel; head of legions of fallen angels and other
    evil spirits
Angelo de Fuego—guardian angel assigned to Joe Austin
Ann—Joe's first cousin

Backbiter—Amon's demon spy
Belial—fallen angel, which means without worth
Brittney Mueller—one of the Daughters of Amon

Charlie—the college janitor
Christine—one of the Daughters of Amon
Chulda—a.k.a. Sara Cunningham, the first Gatekeeper
Coach Saunders
Courtney—one of the Daughters of Amon

Damian Tingly
Deceit—demon assigned to Joe Austin
Denial—assigned to help Deceit

Enepsigos—fallen angel who appears as a human female
Eras—fallen angel who possessed Peter Warren at play

Gusion—fallen angel who can discern the past, present, and
future

Heady Stiles—Damian Tingly's housekeeper and Sara
Cunningham's sister

Ingrid Riggs—Skyler's biological mother
Jason Riggs—Skyler's biological father
Jessie Langford—manager of records at Austin Robotics
Joe Austin—back-slidden Christian
John Langer—co-conspirator of Damian Tingly
John Pollard—attorney for Austin Robotics, Heady's friend
and lunch companion

Julie Warren—Peter Warren's mother

Laura Parson—Joe's girlfriend
Lee Warren—head of the Warren Group

Mary Riggs—Skyler's stepmother
Mia Allred—one of the coven members
Mr. Delmore—Laura Parson's boss

Paul Miller—under cover for the Warren Group
Peter Warren—son of Lee Warren

Rover—Joe's Saint Bernard dog

Samantha—one of the coven members
Sara Cunningham—the first Gatekeeper
Skyler Riggs—used by Deceit to help bring down city
Snowball—Joe's Siamese cat
Widow Claire Deaton—earthly prayer warrior

1

Joe can see his parents' house as he stands alone on top of a small, grassy hill. The full moon helps illuminate his path, but also casts many shadows. As Joe draws closer to the house, he feels a brush of cold air across the back of his neck and right cheek.

He raises his right hand to his cheek and rubs it, as if to rid himself of what might have touched him. He keeps his head straight forward as his blue eyes search for whom or what has touched the back of his neck. His well-defined, dark brows furrow, and the muscles on his strong, square jaw tighten as he clenches his teeth. Picking up his pace, he nervously runs his hand through his thick hair.

Joe, you idiot, you're making a mountain out of a mole hill. I wonder what would Ann think if she saw me now? She'd probably think of me as the "pretty chicken boy."

Well built and well defined, he has earned a nickname around campus as "pretty boy."

"God, how I hate to be called that. There's more to me than meets the eye," he says angrily.

Being tall, dark-haired, and handsome is only the icing on the cake. Math and science come easily to him, which is why his major is electrical engineering and minor is in medical science. He is a man of many interests, some of which run wide and deep. One being the occult.

His science project and everything else he is working on has begun to wear on him. He is only halfway through creating a device which aids the physically disabled to stimulate the nerve endings to grow and reconnect, allowing physical mobility once again.

Thank god for his best friend, Angelo de Fuego. He is always there to encourage and support him. Angelo always seems to be there just when Joe needs his help the most. On occasion, Joe hits the fashion runway to pay for school and the few dates he manages to work into his busy schedule.

Joe feels a cold breeze pass across his cheek again, making the hair on the back of his neck stand up. He picks up his pace and nervously looks round. His shadow seems to move slightly ahead of him.

"That's weird. I know my shadow should be behind me, not in front of me," he says aloud. *Joe, you're letting your imagination run away with you.*

Reaching the front door, he fumbles with his keys as he unlocks the door. He gets a sense of someone standing right behind him. Nervously, he inserts the key into the lock and flings the door open. Rushing in, he slams the door with a loud bang. Leaning against it, he closes his eyes feeling safe and secure in his childhood home.

It seems like only yesterday Mom and Dad were here. I can already smell the pot roast cooking on the stove, and Dad breathing in lungful of baked potatoes and, of course, fresh, homemade, hot, apple pie. Nostalgia hits him like a sucker punch.

"Get it together, Joe. They're in a much better place now."

Five months has passed since a drunk driver plowed into his parents' car, killing them both instantly.

A loud hissing and low growling snaps him back to the present. The hissing is coming from the left side of the living room and a low growling sound seems to be coming closer, directly in front of him. His eyes strain to adjust to the darkness. His heart pounds faster as the growling draws nearer.

Unable to move, Joe remembers an incident when he was five years old. Joe and his father were walking home at night. The moon was full and the air warm. He recalls vividly just what happened and what his father had said to him.

"Hurry up, Joe, or the demons will catch you and take you with them."

"Daddy, wait for me."

"Look, there's one now! See him? He's right behind you."

"No, Daddy, that's my shadow."

"Joe, demons like to pretend to be shadows. You have to keep your eyes sharp so you can tell which ones are demons and which ones are shadows. If you're fast enough, you can catch them when you turn on the lights."

Joe feels fear come upon him like a wet, clammy shirt. Barely able to move, he slowly runs his hand across the wall searching for the light switch. Upon finding it, he doesn't turn the light on right away. Remembering his father's words, he prepares himself to see if all the shadows will disappear all at once. Taking a deep breath and being keenly alert, Joe turns on the lights.

Movement to the left of him catches his eye. He quickly turns just in time to see a black, transparent figure slip behind the grandfather clock. Turning his attention to where the low, hissing and growling sounds are coming from, he sees his old, beloved dog, Rover, a Saint Bernard, walking slowly and steadily toward the clock. The hissing is coming from Snowball, his Siamese cat, which is perched on his favorite chair. Her back is arched and fur is standing on edge. Joe's heart pounds like a drum as he stands looking at the clock.

"Joe, you know what to do. Now just do it."

With a shaky voice, he says, "Get out of here."

Nothing happens. As quickly as Joe can remember, he runs through his mind what he said the last time the same thing occurred. Scriptures pop into his head.

"The Lord is my shepherd; I shall not fear what man can do unto me."

Calm comes over him, as if warm water is being poured into the top of his head filling every inch of his body with peace.

"Think, Joe, think. You can do this. Remember, you've done this before," he says calmly.

His eyes are fixed on the shadow which seems to be moving out from behind the clock, slowly advancing toward him. Joe searches his heart again for what he has kept dormant for much too long.

"Lord, forgive me. I have sinned against you. I repent now for not totally forsaking my dealings with the occult. Amen."

As soon as the last words leaves Joe's mouth, the shadowy figure steps out from the wall and says in a high-pitched voice which sounds like nails dragging across a chalkboard, "Traitor!"

"Get out of here in the name of Jesus," Joe says with great authority.

The demon shoots up through the ceiling and disappears. Joe feels his heart beating now more with exhilaration than with fear. His hands are shaking badly, but the relief he feels in knowing that he can send a demon packing strengthens his spirit and greatly lessens his fear.

"And don't come back!" Joe yells up at the ceiling as he walks with newfound confidence to his favorite chair. Sitting down, he opens his Bible and starts to read.

Shooting skyward, the demon turns its back and spits out curses at Joe. He heads back across town. Slowing down, he alights on the roof of a small, Spanish style house. The warm glow of yellow light falls gently across the flower bed which is now in full bloom.

The newly cut grass gives off a fresh scent which mingles with the scent of honeysuckle. Together, the scents drift up his nostrils. Snorting loudly, the demon tries to clear the fragment scents of the spring night from his black, turned up, rubbery nose as he paces across the red clay tiles. Wringing his clawlike hands, he thinks of what excuse he is going to give his commanding officer.

"This was such a simple assignment. How hard is it to seduce a mere human into returning to his old ways? He should have returned to muttering his old mantra," he says with a hissing sound.

His long talons click against the red clay tiles as he paces. Abruptly, a sinister smile forms on his black, batlike face.

"I will go and tell the commander that I was attacked by two, no, ten mighty warrior angels of the Most High. That fool should believe me. After all, my name is Deceit."

With a determined look on his face, Deceit bends his spindly legs and pushes up from the roof at an incredible speed. He flies skyward passing through layers of clouds and into the cold darkness of outer space.

2

Joe is awakened by something warm and heavy against his leg. With a jerk of his head, he sees his old pal Rover pawing at him.

Looking at his watch, he says loudly, "Nine o'clock? Don't tell me I've been asleep for two hours. I don't even remember closing my eyes or even feeling sleepy. Okay guys, I'll feed you. Come on, let's go."

Joe pushes himself up off the dark green leather wing chair. He fondly remembers the hours he spent as a young child sitting on his mother's lap while she read the Bible to him.

"I miss you, Mom," he says with a soft sigh. The rustling of the large bag of premium dog food causes Rover to sit impatiently at this master's feet.

I think I've spoiled you guys.

As Joe pours the large cup of dog food into the large, silver dog dish, a soft meow can be heard as Snowball stares up at Joe.

"Snowball, sorry, sweetie, I'll get your food next."

He walks to the refrigerator and opens the door. His heart begins to beat faster as he is reminded of the evening's encounter.

Pushing down the small knot of fear that is starting to form, he says to Snowball, "So that's what you were hissing at."

She looks at Joe as if to say, *Yeah, yeah, now feed me.*

Snowball daintily begins to eat her food. As Joe leans against the sink, his stomach begins to growl. He turns and walks toward the refrigerator, stops and is reminded of the cold brush against his neck and cheek from just a few hours ago.

"I know what, I'll eat some nice, hot chicken soup," he says cheerfully, as one who whistles in the dark.

He opens a cupboard, pulls out a small pan, and places it on the stove. A loud pop sounds as he pulls the lid off the can of soup. After pouring the soup into the pot, he refills the can with water and pours that into the soup as well.

"Hey guys, in all the excitement, I forgot to lock the doors."

Joe turns and walks into the living room where he proceeds to lock the doors and windows and closes the blinds. Next, he goes into the kitchen. The blinds are still open. A pair of red eyes peer into the kitchen and scan the room. Quickly, the black, transparent figure passes through the window, the sink, and into the wall of the back bedroom.

"Good, no lights on in here."

Silently, the shadow moves to the head of the bed and hides behind the headboard.

3

Feeling better after his humiliating defeat at the command of a mere mortal, Deceit flies toward the compound at a leisurely pace. He decides to circle around the vastness of dark, cold space surrounding the impressive compound where he has been assigned for centuries, before reporting to his commanding officer, Amon.

The lights from the millions of stars shine brightly as Deceit draws closer to headquarters, where he can see the buildings stretched across one hundred miles in all directions. *What a beautiful sight, I must admit.*

The walls of the compound shimmer and sparkle from the lights which come from the many fires, street lamps, and other sources of lights. They even come from the magnificent creations, the fallen angels. Though they are now in a permanent state of disgrace, they still remain beautiful and shine brilliantly. They still have the powers they were endowed with at the time of their creation by the Most High God.

Groups of evil spirits and demons of all sizes can be seen communicating with each other. Some before reporting to their superior officers, others just sharing conversation with their comrades.

From Deceit's vantage point, he can see the powers and principalities around the world giving orders, while others are seen in fierce battles with the angels of light.

All the angels, both fallen and of the Most High God, are bright, masculine, powerful, and very beautiful. They vary in size. Some have wings and others do not. But they are all loyal to one or the other, the Most High God or to Satan.

"I must admit," he says to himself, "They are all beautiful to behold. If I were a mere human, I would be deceived and think they were still angels of light and not angels of darkness."

Deceit focuses on battle closest to him. As the battle rages on, the fallen angels are starting to gain ground.

"I see the saints are taking a break from praying," Deceit says aloud. "Good! Slumber and take a rest, you fools, you deserve it."

Suddenly, a stream of profanities spew out of Deceit's mouth as the angels of light receive strength from the prayers of the saints and continue to fight with vigor, turning the tide of the battle against evil.

The rank and order of fallen angels and evil spirits that Satan has under his rule is impressive indeed. But truth be told, they cannot renew their strength as the angels of light of the Most High God can, not to mention Satan has copied the rank and order of the angels of the Most High God.

Here at headquarters is where Satan has some of his vast array of powers and principalities stationed to rule over the western hemisphere. The compound, as it is referred to by all, is more like a large city rather than a military compound. It is made of topaz, marble, and various other semiprecious stones and materials. He can see legions of fallen angels, demons, evil spirits, and imps of all sizes coming and going down to earth. Others are seen sparring with one another, no doubt, honing their skills.

One would think Satan would rule from the pit of hell, but he has not, as of yet, been cast down there. He is, after all, called the prince of the air, and this is where he rules and reigns through those assigned here. Deceit has heard of the palace Satan has made for himself, but has yet to have the privilege of going there.

"There will come a time when I, Deceit, will rule and reign alongside Satan, the prince of the air," he says arrogantly.

The smell of sulfur is getting stronger as Deceit flies effortlessly above the lights. He draws closer with each spiraling turn. The shrieks and howls of demons pierce his ears, as some are struck with the broadside of a long, glowing sword held by a tall, brawny fallen warrior angel.

"Idiot," cries Deceit, as a demon flies by him. The demon howls from the backhanded slap given him by a large, ugly demon whose way he was in brings a sneer to Deceit's thin, black lips.

"The fool must have failed at his assignment no doubt. You're lucky that's all you got," he yells, as he watches the smaller demon fly out of sight.

Deceit decides to go to the south side of the compound since he has never been there and is in no hurry to report to his commanding officer. Curiosity gets the better of him, and he heads toward the sound of clashing swords. There, he sees two fallen, warrior angels fighting. Deceit alights behind a large, six-inch-thick wall made of smoky topaz. Unable to see through it, he pokes his head around the corner to get a better view of the action.

The two angels are quite a sight to see. They each stand about twelve feet tall. Both are wearing intricately ornate helmets. Deep, orange crests about two feet long hang from the top of each helmet. These magnificent creatures are strong and masculine. It reminds Deceit of the Roman soldiers he was once assigned to. Their beautiful faces are partially obscured by their helmets.

The only thing he can see of their faces are their green and gray, glowing eyes and the tops of their cheeks, lips, and chins. Their chests are covered with custom made, ornate, metal breastplates. Attached at the shoulders are short, deep orange capes which come down to their waists. The white, pleated, mid-thigh tunic, which they wear underneath their armor, moves gracefully as they fight.

They swing with great force, the six-foot-long, broad swords. Their powerful, muscular legs move swiftly as swords clash, sending a blaze of fire and sparks in all directions. They move nimbly, even though legs are fully clad up to their knees with ornate metal shin guards.

Deceit steps in for a closer look. Excited over seeing these angels in action, he does not realize he has gotten too close. The tip of one sword cuts superficially into Deceit's left cheek. Stunned, he turns to fly away and gets cut again, this time on his backside. Shrieks of pain and terror are heard as he flies out of harm's way. Spinning out of control, he leaves a trail of black smoke spewing from his rear end.

Slowing down, Deceit looks around for somewhere to land. A small piece of space junk floating by catches his eye. He darts toward it, landing roughly. Whimpering, he gingerly touches his left cheek. By now, the pain of his wounds have subsided. Turning his head to the right, he takes a look at his backside.

Profanities flow freely as he yells out, "They will pay for this indignation. How dare they strike me! Don't they know who I am?"

Quietly, he says, "Oh, that's going to leave a mark."

Licking his scrawny, boney finger, he touches it gently to his still smoking backside. *Next time, I'll watch from a safer distance.*

Taking flight again, he continues to circle the compound. Scores of legions of fallen angels, demons, and imps come

SUSAN B. A. HOFMANN

in an orderly fashion as they return from their assignments. Others leave with a scroll secured safely to their backs.

Deceit has heard that Gusion, one of the fallen angels, has the ability to discern the past, present, and future. He has been stationed here for the last three hundred years.

He will be a great help to me in my plan to rise in the ranks of the dark forces. While my wounds are still fresh, it will be a good idea to talk to Amon. This will certainly give credibility to my story. But first, I think I'll take another look at the fallen angels.

He lands a short distance from them, making sure they are not able to see him. They have ceased fighting.

"That was quite a move you made. Where did you learn that maneuver?"

"I learned that move in my last confrontation with Adria of the Most High God. He almost had me. I turned and left as fast as I could. Mathias must be training them for the final battle," replies Eligor, who appears to humans as a good knight with a lance.

Standing tall, they are elegant and glow with a fire from within which makes all the metal they are wearing look like burnished bronze. Both have removed their helmets and have placed them on the floor. The angel on the left has long, dark, wavy hair. His muscular arms show the scars of previous battles.

He has the profile of a mythical, Greek god of ancient times. But the heaviness of the rock-hard heart he now possesses taints his beautiful face. He leans on his badly nicked and scratched sword, as his dented and gouged breastplate gleams with the fire within. His name is Belial, which means without worth.

Deceit notices the angel's tunic is frayed at the hem. Turning his head, the angel sees Deceit and looks straight into his eyes. The sheer hate and hardness in those beautiful, green eyes makes Deceit shake with fear.

Okay, I've seen enough for now.

Quickly turning, Deceit shoots upward heading toward Amon's station. He goes over in his mind the story he is going to tell his superior.

"Yes, he'll buy it or my name isn't Deceit."

Spotting the main gate, Deceit lands gently and close to a group of smelly, ornery-looking imps. With an air of superiority, he walks past them. As he reaches the double doors to Amon's office, the eighteen feet high and twelve feet wide doors open dramatically on their own. Stepping inside Amon's office, Deceit confidently strolls up to his commanding officer and bows his head in a show of respect.

Amon's massive desk is made of solid, white marble. It has a plaque given to him many centuries ago by the people of Babylon. It is made of pure, solid, yellow gold and is inscribed with in-laid gem quality emeralds, which is fastened to the front of the massive desk with four six-inch gold screws which reads, "To the God Amon."

On the top of his desk, there is one gold tray to the left, which has twenty-five scrolls laid neatly in its holder. In the middle of the front edge of the desk are three separate scroll holders, evenly spaced. Each holder contains scrolls with assignments that have been given to Amon to complete. This is where he keeps them until they are completed. One has been there for five hundred years, others for fifty years, ten years, and one for a day.

To the right is another gold tray which contains one-hundred-forty neatly stacked scrolls. These are the assignments which Amon has completed with the help of the demonic forces assigned to him. The assignments come in continually. Some are simple assignments which are completed almost immediately, and others take years, even centuries to complete.

Unseen by Deceit, Backbiter quietly listens in on the conversation between Amon and Deceit, as he stands behind Amon's large, ornate shield. Next to that is a stand made of gold, which is used to hold Amon's very sharp, very heavy, and very large broadsword.

"Well, how did it go?" says Amon with a deep voice, which carries through every inch of his office, giving both Deceit and Backbiter a chill that runs down their spines.

Trembling inside, Deceit answers, "It was going very well until I was attacked by the mighty warrior angels of the Most High God."

Amon leans back as he glares at Deceit with his rich, brown, glowing eyes.

"How far did you manage to get the human to backslide?"

"I lied to him, telling him all he needed to do is to call on his spirit guide for help and guidance. Soon he started chanting his old mantra. The human slipped back into his old ways as soon as he saw me. He couldn't remember what to say. He stuttered and started asking his spirit guide to help him. Just as I whispered into the human's ear to encourage him to fall even further, he called out to Jesus and ten of His warrior angels surrounded and attacked me. I had to break away and flee for my life. They chased me clear across town. I stopped on the roof of a house to make my stand, but they were too many for me to fight off. I fled to fight another day. You can see by my wounds on my face and rear, I fought valiantly."

Deceit turns and bends over to show Amon the wound on his backside. A couple of puffs of black smoke escape from his partially healed bottom.

Backbiter places his hand over his mouth to prevent himself from laughing out loud. Standing too close to Amon's sword, Backbiter's pointy head hits Amon's sword which is precariously lying on its holder.

With a loud crash, the sword falls to the floor barely missing Deceit's feet. Without so much as a blink of an eye, Amon pushes his chair away from his desk and stands up, calmly walking to where the sword lays and picks it up, placing it properly back on its holder.

If looks could kill, Backbiter would certainly be dead. Amon turns his eyes away from Backbiter and returns back to his desk.

SUSAN B. A. HOFMANN

Taking his seat, he leans back in his large wooden chair, which is comfortably upholstered in green silk and tastefully adorned with gold. He looks Deceit in the eye. Deceit lowers his eyes trying to avoid Amon's. Feeling his insides churn, he looks around Amon's office while waiting for his reply.

The ceiling resembles one of the magnificent Roman cathedrals with arched, wooden beams, like the ones Deceit has seen during his frequent assignments on earth in the ancient city of Rome. The walls and floor are made of white marble and have large, emerald-green rugs, which match the upholstery on Amon's chair. In front of the desk are elegant, twin, wooden chairs adorned with gold that match the upholstery of Amon's chair and face Amon's desk. A large, sparkling chandelier hangs from the ceiling right in the middle of Amon's office.

Suddenly, Amon says, "Well done. Next time, take a couple of imps with you," says Amon, as he sits down at this desk. "They can act as decoys giving you time to manipulate the human."

I don't need any help to accomplish this assignment. Deceit bows his head slightly. *What a fool.*

"Go into the north end of town from where you came. There you will seek out a young man by the name of Skyler Riggs. He should be on the football field. Convince him he is going to be dropped from the team. Report to me when you accomplish your task," says Amon in a calm voice.

"Yes, Commander. I will certainly take some imps with me. They will be of much help," says Deceit, keeping his emotions in check.

Amon lowers his head and waves Deceit away.

Right, take some imps with me. As if I needed any help. Just who does he think I am anyway?

He turns on his feet and makes his way out the double doors of Amon's office. As Deceit leaves the building, he looks at several imps standing around and says softly, "Hell will freeze over before I ask any of you for help."

Deceit turns on his clawlike feet and leaves. Like a shot, he flies up into the atmosphere and dives down to earth heading directly into town.

Amon turns to Backbiter, his favorite spy, despite his occasional clumsiness and says, "Follow Deceit and report back to me when you have news of his progress."

"Yes, Commander," says Backbiter, still shaking behind Amon's shield.

"Go!" yells out Amon.

"Yes, Commander."

Backbiter walks out from behind Amon's shield and bows deeply. He leaves as quickly as possible from Amon's office. His ungraceful departure draws stares from the others who are still waiting outside the beautiful, two-hundred-story building.

4

As the team is finishing up practice, Coach Saunders picks up a towel on top of the large cooler and wipes his face.

"Good workout, guys. Now hit the showers."

"Riggs, come here a minute."

That kid is going places. That's if he can leave the ladies alone.
He opens the cooler and grabs the last Gatorade.

Skyler Riggs looks over his shoulder and smiles a wide, toothy smile and yells back, "Okay, Coach. Be right there." Riggs turns from the group of cheerleaders and jogs over to Coach Saunders.

"Hey, Coach. Want to talk to me?"

"Riggs, you'd do well to leave the ladies alone for a time."

A frown appears on Riggs's face as he says, "What do you mean, Coach? I always make practice. And you did say it's always good to take time out for a social life."

"Social life yes. A break yes. But you seem to pay more attention to the cheerleaders than the calls I make."

Riggs smiles sheepishly and looks away.

"You missed the last three calls I made. Lucky for you, Zelinka didn't. He made the plays you should have."

"Coach, I'll do better next time, promise."

"You'd better. Now hit the showers."

Deceit stands next to Riggs intently listening to the conversation. *Here's my opening.*

Riggs walks to the showers tightly holding his helmet. As he turns the corner, he sees his teammates in various state of undress. As soon as they see him, they go silent. Riggs looks round and says, "Don't stop talking on my account."

His teammates quickly resume chatting as if they were caught doing something wrong.

They know something I don't. I bet Zelinka opened his big mouth and told Coach I was partying last night. He should talk. I had to drive him home. So what if I do some drugs now and again. Everybody does it. There's nothing wrong with that.

"That's right," Deceit whispers in Skyler's ear.

Who is he to talk? I'm the one who makes most of the points and takes all the crap Coach dishes out. Not all of us come from rich families. Zelinka can come and go whenever he wants. Unlike my parents, they have to know where I am every second of the day.

Deceit continues to speak negative words into Riggs's ears.

"You need to relax. You deserve it. Look in your gym bag in the left pocket. See if you have a little coke left. Take it, no use letting it go to waste."

Deceit is amazed at how little urging this human requires to be encouraged to do wrong.

"You make my job almost too easy," says Deceit. "Your ear gates are so wide open, I could easily come and go at will and possess you should I desire to. But for right now, I'll have to wait for the right time when it will benefit my plans the most."

Deceit steps back and lands on the lockers. He watches and waits to see who else he can deceive in order to help him accomplish his plan.

The locker room is almost empty as the players leave accompanied by Lust, Liar, and a few other demons who follow them out as they go their separate ways.

A sense of impeding corruption hangs in the air, mixed with excitement and longing.

Skyler, now dressed in his shirt and jeans, stuffs his soiled football uniform into the gym bag. He thinks about what he has overheard.

True, I didn't understand most of what was being said, but they sure seemed guilty of something.

"That's right," says Deceit, as he stands next to him. "They were talking about you and what you've been doing after school. Zelinka is behind all this. He wants to be captain, but the guys still want you."

Yeah, that's right. Zelinka still wants to be captain. I bet he thinks he can buy his way in. Well, I have news for him. Coach is a decent guy in that respect and so is the team. He'd never be bought. I wonder what else Zelinka is doing to get me out.

"Remember, he took the whole team out on the town when you played a game out in Vegas. I'm sure he has most of them on his side. They're all in on it and you're the target. They all want you out. You're going to have to think of a way to bring Zelinka down," Deceit says to Skyler.

That's right, thinks Skyler as he closes his gym bag.

I'll think of something. I'll get them all. But I'll have to think of some way to do it so nobody will know I'm behind it.

Riggs is the last one to walk out of the locker room. He takes one last look around and yells out, "Is there anyone left in here? I'm leaving and turning out the lights."

The sound of the door as it closes echoes through the hallway. Riggs walks at a quick pace through the deserted building.

He waits for a few moments then says softly, "Okay, I'm outta here."

He turns and opens the door to the locker room and reaches for the light switch. A handwritten sign on a square, fluorescent—orange paper is taped to the wall right beside the light switch.

It states the last one leaving the locker room must turn off the lights and is signed by Coach Saunders. It glows eerily as the lights are switched off.

A chill runs down Riggs's spine as Deceit lands gently on his left shoulder and digs his black, sharp claws into

Skyler's shoulder. Riggs looks at his watch, six o'clock right on the button.

Better hurry. Don't want to be late again tonight. Remembering what happened a few nights earlier, when he had gotten home late from a date, he doesn't care to repeat the experience.

Backbiter passes easily through the closed doors and out the gym. His beady, dark eyes watch Deceit closely as he flies high and at a distance from Deceit. As Skyler reaches his car, he pulls his keys from his jacket pocket.

Skyler turns the key, and after a second time, the engine comes to life.

"Well, old girl, it's time to give you another tune-up," he says, as he pats the dashboard of his old Ford. Putting the car into gear, he backs out and unknowingly smacks into Deceit. Startled, Deceit jumps into the backseat of the car as Skyler drives off, slowing down, but not stopping as he approaches a stop sign.

"You're ten minutes late, Skyler. You know how we worry about you," says his father, as he slowly removes his belt.

"Dad, I'm sorry. There was an accident on Main Street. The cars were being detoured through Copper and down to Elm. You know how many lights there are on Elm."

"No excuses, Skyler. Curfew is 10:00 p.m. sharp on a school night."

Skyler remains motionless as the color slowly drains from his face. He turns to face the living room wall and places his hands high above his head and spreads his legs apart. Lowering his head, he braces himself as he closes his eyes, dreading what will come next.

His father stands a couple of steps behind him. Jason Riggs lifts up his right arm, and with a practiced move, he brings his belt quickly across Skyler's clenched backside. Again and again, the narrow, brown leather belt, which is held tightly in the strong right hand of his father, comes down striking Skyler. In the kitchen, Skyler's stepmother, Mary, hears the sound of the belt hitting the well-worn Levi jeans.

A concerned look crosses her fair, finely lined face. Her blue eyes fill with tears as she drops the green, plastic cup into the sink. The deep dark, red liquid splashes against the sides of the sink and flows down into the drain. She quickly picks up the half full bottle of Santa Medina California Port which she has just filled her cup with and quickly opens the soft, gold-brown, kitchen cabinet door below the sink and drops the bottle in. It wobbles precariously and then stops. Mary turns and hurries into the living room. She takes a deep breath and places her left hand on Jason's left shoulder while she gently, but firmly, holds his right wrist in mid-strike.

"Honey, that's enough, don't you think? I'm sure Skyler didn't mean to be late. No one can predict a traffic accident. Besides, he just went to the football practice."

Jason Riggs slowly turns his head and looks straight into his wife's eyes. The look of disgust, anger, and self-hatred that covers Jason's face disappears. She lowers his right arm and pulls Jason toward her as she says in a soft, gentle voice, "Come on, let's go to bed. Tomorrow we'll talk about this."

Jason and Mary Riggs slowly walk to their bedroom. She loosens her grip on his right wrist and slips her hand over the belt, pulling ever so gently. For a moment, Jason keeps a tight hold. Slowly, he releases his grip on the belt.

Skyler remains with his hands still up on the wall of the living room, tears streaming downs his face. He doesn't know for sure who he's shedding his tears for, himself or his stepmother. She has been the only mother he has ever known.

Mary has always protected him from his father. Even as a toddler, Jason Riggs would find any excuse for spanking Skyler. She was not aware of the anger he had hidden from her prior to their marriage. Jason was a good husband and father except when he was stressed out from work. Unfortunately now, with the current recession and layoffs at work and the possibility of him being next, he increased the "disciplinary action" to become more frequent and more severe.

Jason Riggs had a good life growing up with a father who was a military career man. That is, until the day his father had a skiing accident that ended his career in the military. Consequently, he began drinking and took out his frustrations on his own son, Jason.

Skyler slowly moves away from the wall and gingerly makes his way into his bedroom. He closes his bedroom door and leans against it. Closing his eyes, he thinks.

Mom, I wish you were here. What I wouldn't give to have you here. Then Dad wouldn't blame me for your death at my birth. There has to be ways of making Dad understand it was not my fault.

He brushes away the tears from his face with the back of his hand. The determined look on Skyler's face delights Deceit.

"Things are shaping up quite nicely," Deceit says aloud. "With just a little more pain and discouragement, I should have this human right where I need him to be. Then I can complete my plan and show Amon just how valuable I am. He will have to promote me to a higher station with more power and many others under my command. Eventually, I will have a legion of fallen angels and demons under me to do my bidding. No longer will I have to put up with Amon and his stupid ideas."

Deceit lets out a high-pitched laugh. Backbiter remains unseen by Deceit. He has hidden himself behind the black, lacquered chest of drawers.

So that's what the pompous, little jerk is up to. It will please Amon when I tell him about Deceit's plans. If anyone is going to be promoted, it will be me.

Backbiter slips stealthily from the chest of drawers and heads up through the corner of Skyler's bedroom ceiling. He makes his way through the trees and heads back to camp where he will report to Amon.

Skyler steps into the bathroom and slowly removes his clothes. He turns his back to the full-length mirror which is attached to the back of the bathroom door. Turning his head to the right, he sees a multitude of narrow, long, red marks starting just below his shoulders going all the way down to his calves.

He steps into the shower and turns on the water. The cool, soft flow gently falls on his face. It makes its way down his body, helping to alleviate the sting and thereby helping him to clear his mind.

Who do I know that can help me? I remember Jenna telling me about some girls that are trying to start a witch's coven. What did she call them? Come on, Riggs, think. Oh yeah, they call themselves the Daughters of Amon. Yeah, that's right. I think I'll ask around to see who these girls are. Maybe they can help me. I've heard there are some people who can talk to the dead. That's what I'll do, I'll call them. Then maybe I can get dad to listen to reason.

Skyler relaxes under the water.

5

Joe finally calls it a day and puts away the diagrams and paperwork into his backpack. Turning off the lights in the lab, he closes the door behind him and swings his backpack over his shoulder as he walks down the hall. Turning the corner, he almost bumps into Charlie, the school janitor.

"Almost ran right over you," says Joe apologetically.

"It's okay, no harm done," says Charlie.

"Have a good weekend," says Joe, as he makes his way down the hall and out the double doors.

"Yeah, you too," says Charlie with a sigh. "Enjoy your life now kid 'cause it ain't always going to be so easy."

Joe reaches the door and steps out into the early evening. He goes over the day's events in his mind. As he makes his way to his car, he is quite happy at the progress he has made on the project that he has been working on for months. He reaches his car, unlocks the door, and slides in.

"First stop, the supermarket," he says with a smile. He drives the speed limit the few miles to the store and parks at the first open space he finds. At a brisk pace, Joe crosses the parking lot in short order. The doors open automatically allowing a rush of air over his face.

He picks up a small plastic basket by its handles. He notices there are two other baskets stuck to the one he is holding.

Two little children are watching him as he struggles to separate the baskets. The two newly freed baskets clatter to the ground, bringing a fresh new wave of laughter and faces from the two children standing next to their mother who is too busy chatting on the phone to care how her children are behaving.

Bratty kids; doesn't anyone discipline their kids anymore? thinks Joe, as he makes his way from aisle to aisle, picking up more items than he had planned on. He finishes shopping and places his basket on the checkout counter. The cashier deftly and expertly pulls out each item and scans them, placing them in the plastic bags which are open and ready to be filled.

"That'll be twenty-five, fifty-four please," says Sara with a big smile. Her braces glisten under the bright fluorescent lights. Joe smiles back, as he slides his debit card and punches in his code.

"Thank you. Have a good night," he says, as he picks up his bags and heads toward the door. Her eyes follow him out. Joe can feel her staring at him. He is used to having girls flirt with him, but this one in particular gives him the most uncomfortable feeling.

Let it go, Joe, she doesn't mean any harm. She's just trying to be nice.

He makes his way out the doors of the supermarket and out to his car.

After unloading his groceries at home, Joe pulls a Coke from the carton and places the rest into the refrigerator. Standing in front of the kitchen window, he takes a long, deep, satisfying drink.

Joe's thoughts begin to drift back to the simpler days when his parents were still alive. Outside, the breeze begins to pick up rustling the leaves. Joe recalls the times he and his dad would mow the lawn during the long hot summer days.

He remembers how his mother would come out to join them with a tray of freshly made lemonade and sandwiches. They never seemed to taste as good as they did then.

Rover starts to bark, breaking Joe's train of thought. He downs the last of his drink and tosses it into his recycle container he has in his kitchen. It is a green-colored, tall trash can with a lid. The can makes very little sound as it lands softly on other recycled material.

Joe opens the screen door. The sound of squeaky hinges alerts Snowball. Both Rover and Snowball make a beeline for the door which Joe holds open for them. With ears pinned back and a determined look on her white, furry face, Snowball runs ahead of Rover. She just nearly misses being stepped on by Rover's big paws. Both run straight into the kitchen. Joe stands holding the door open for a few moments more as he looks at the clouds that are forming.

"Hmm, looks like it may rain after all," he says softly, as he let's go of the screen door and closes the wooden door behind him, locking it securely. Both Rover and Snowball eagerly await their meals. Joe pours each one his share of food and then turns to get a second Coke and takes the pizza still in its carton into the living room. He places the pizza on the coffee table and his drink on a coaster. Lowering himself on to the sofa, he pulls out his first slice of pizza. *Mmm, that's good.*

Joe looks for his TV remote control; he finds it and turns on the television and looks at his watch. It is six thirty on Friday. Half an hour more and his favorite show comes on. Finishing the remainder of the pizza, he stretches out on the couch and is soon asleep.

The living room becomes dark with shadows as the sun sets. The only light is coming from the television. Rover walks in and sniffs the pizza box. Not liking what he smells, he walks to this favorite spot, circles around, then lies down. Not wanting to be left out, Snowball jumps onto the sofa and curls up at Joe's feet. No sound can be heard, but that of the three of them breathing deeply as they sleep and the voices coming from the television.

A dark form crosses the room and makes its way toward Joe. A pair of long black fingers begins to gently stroke Joe's head. He frowns deeply, as his sleep is now being disturbed by the unpleasant dream he is having.

In his dream, a black cloud forms in the east. Joe stands facing it. He is aware of an evil presence that is coming in the cloud. A strange, yellow glow begins to form in the mist of the cloud. As it draws closer to him, a wind starts to blow. Soon it is so strong, Joe must brace himself against it. The wind blows hard enough to make his hair go straight back and his clothes stick to him.

Deeper and deeper go the strange, long, dark fingers into Joe's head. Suddenly, there appears a greenish round face with sharp, pointy teeth and round, black eyes in the midst of the cloud. It somewhat resembles an iguana. As it opens its mouth, it growls and tries to claw at Joe's face. Joe starts to pray and rebuke the demon, but it continues to come at him. He realizes he must fight harder and with all his strength. Joe raises his right hand and prays against the demon with all his might. He does not fear what might happen, for he knows he will win this fight. Suddenly, the face and claws begin to ripple as if it is water. The wind, clouds, and the demon disappear as quickly as they appeared. The dream is over, and Joe's sleep is again restful and peaceful.

Deceit lets out a howl as he withdraws his fingers from Joe's head. The smell of sulfur whiffs past Joe's nostrils. Deceit swiftly makes his way out through the living room window and into the night, all the while licking his smoldering fingers. He flies toward town with hate and anger in his heart for Joe.

The rising sun shines brightly across Joe's face. The warmth of sunlight soothes him as a warm gentle hand. He opens his eyes slowly and watches as the sunlight paints the morning sky the color of rose, yellow, and pink with wisps of white clouds, making their way lazily across the sky. Remembering the events of the night, Joe's spirit lifts along with grateful and heartfelt thanks to God.

He gazes over to where Rover is lying on his right side, with his legs fully extended, still deep in sleep. Then he turns his gaze toward the front window and sees Snowball licking her paw carefully.

Joe savors the next few minutes of complete peace and quiet. Through the curtains, the sun is already hailing him good morning with long, soft, warm rays of sunlight. Joe stretches out and then relaxes again. But the bitter taste in Joe's mouth gets him up reluctantly. He makes his way through the house and into the bathroom where he pulls out his toothbrush and carefully applies toothpaste to the brush. Afterwards, he showers and shaves.

Walking to the kitchen, Joe feeds Rover and Snowball. After finishing his breakfast he begins to clean up the entire house. After several hours the only thing left to do is the laundry. As he finishes up folding and putting away his clothes warm from the dryer the phone rings.

"Hello?"

"Hey, Joe, how you doing?" asks Ann, his favorite first cousin.

"Oh, I was just thinking of you," says Joe in a genuine tone.

"I hope it was good," answers Ann cheerfully.

"Yes, it was."

"Well, yes, knowing you, I'd say so."

"What can I do for you?" asks Joe, as he puts away the last of his clothes.

"I wanted to know if you're free to go to a play next Saturday at Brinkman Hall. It starts at 7:00 p.m. and finishes at 9:00. Mr. Tingly wrote this particular play, and he directs it as well. You know how fond he is of you. I'm sure he would be pleased to see you afterward and hear your opinion of what you thought of it."

"Next Saturday, right? Well," Joe pauses as he mentally checks his calendar. "Sure, I'll go. When do you want me to pick you up? Maybe we can go to dinner before and catch up on what's been going on with you."

"Sure, that would be great. How about five thirty?" replies Ann, already thinking of what she will wear. It's not often she is seen on the arm of such a good-looking man, even though he is her cousin.

This is going to be fun. I always have a great time when we go out together, thinks Ann as she says good-bye to Joe.

Joe and Ann had grown up on the same street and had become more like brother and sister, than first cousins. Joe still looks out for her. Her big, brown eyes and her long, dark brown hair and olive complexion easily give her a look of innocence.

Ann heads to the mall and parks in front of her favorite store. Walking briskly to the escalator, she gets on. From this vantage point she quickly scans the area to see which direction she will head to.

Hmm, I believe I'll wear my favorite pair of jeans and just get a new top. As she rounds the corner, she accidentally bumps into Sara Cunningham, the cashier from Joe's favorite supermarket.

"Oh, I'm sorry," says Ann, as she backs away from Sara.

"No harm done," replies Sara, as she walks toward the checkout counter.

"Did you find everything you needed?" asks the cashier.

"Yes, yes I did," says Sara with a smile.

Ann picks out several blouses and heads toward the dressing rooms. She tries them all on and decides on two blouses. One is deep purple in color, with long sleeves and a ruffled neckline and the other is a pink, tailored shirt that covers her backside. Ann carefully checks herself out in the mirror while wearing the purple blouse. She loves the way the purple color complements her complexion, but wants something less frilly for the occasion, so she settles on the pink blouse.

Carrying her new blouse to the cashiers, she decides she could use a new belt as an accent. After paying for her blouse, she heads off to ladies accessories. There she picks up a wide, black belt, a pair of silver hoop earrings, and a silver bangle bracelet.

Her stomach begins to rumble. She looks at her watch.

Wow. Too late to go home and make dinner, might as well eat something here.

Happy with her purchases, Ann heads for the food court. She passes Sara who is sitting alone nursing her Coke. Sara watches Ann carefully as Ann takes her food and begins to look for a table. Sara stands up and says cheerfully, "You can have my table, I was just leaving."

"Gee, thanks," says Ann, as she places her bags close at her feet and her food on the table. Sara smiles mischievously as she walks away.

6

Mary pours a second cup of coffee for Jason and herself. With cups in hand, they sit quietly at the kitchen table.

Skyler stops abruptly at the kitchen door when he sees his parents. He was hoping not to run into them before he left for school.

"Good morning, Skyler," says Jason in a soft tone.

"Morning, Dad, Mom," replies Skyler as cheerfully as he can. "I didn't think you'd be up so early. It's only 6:00 a.m."

"Son, I, we, want to talk to you before you leave for school," Jason says with a little more force.

"What about?"

"Honey, sit down please," says Mary, as she motions to the chair next to her. Skyler reluctantly walks over and pulls out a chair and slowly sits down at the edge of it.

"Son. Skyler," says his father, as he clears his throat, "I'm sorry for hitting you last night. I was wrong. You weren't responsible for the car accident. But if you would have left a few minutes earlier, you would have been on time," he says, as his voice rises in volume.

Mary places a firm hand on his forearm. Jason turns his head quickly and shoots an angry look at Mary. Surprisingly, Mary stares right back at him without backing down.

After a moment, Jason turns his head toward Skyler and says, "Your mother and I have decided to go to counseling. We've made an appointment for Monday at 9:00 a.m. with Maxine Smart. I realize I have to take care of my problem before it gets out of hand."

Out of hand? What do you call what you did to me last night? A slap on the wrist? Skyler's face shows what he is thinking.

Jason looks down at his cup while Mary sits up straight in her chair and looks into Skyler's eyes.

"Skyler, this is hard for your dad to talk about, so please, have patience with him. I should have intervened a long time ago. I am sorry, but we're going to work on it now. So please, let's work this out together."

A heavy silence hangs in the air. So much so, that it takes Deceit by surprise.

"Okay, Mom," Skyler says, then pauses, turning his head toward his dad and says, "Okay, Dad."

"Good," says Mary, as she stands up, pushing her chair away with the back of her legs.

"Honey, more coffee?" she asks, turning to her husband Jason.

"Oh, no thanks, I'm good."

"Skyler, what would you like for breakfast?"

"Just a bowl of cereal. I'll get it myself."

"No, no," says Mary. "Just sit right down, and I'll get it for you."

—∿∿—

"Hi, guys!" yells Brittney, as she crosses the grassy area between buildings on campus.

"Hi, Brittney. How do you think you did on the math test yesterday?"

"Oh, I think I passed it. I didn't study all week for nothing, you know."

"How about you, Courtney?"

"Oh, I aced it."

"Always bragging," says Brittney with a sneer.

"Can I help it if I have a high IQ?" she asks slightly wounded.

"How about you, Christine?"

"I think I got a C plus or B minus."

"Oh, that's not bad," says Britney and Courtney one right after the other.

"Court, Chris, we're having a meeting tonight at the Coffee Cart at 6:00 p.m. Sara introduced me to a guy who's interested in meeting with us. He wants to know what we're about, and he thinks maybe we can help him."

"Who is he?" asks Courtney, looking hopeful at meeting a new guy.

"Courtney, it's business, you know? His name is Skyler Riggs. He's the captain of the football team."

"I hear he's really cute."

"Okay girls, calm down. We have to keep our cool here. Don't want to scare him away or worse, have him shut us down."

"Yeah, you're right," says Courtney. "We better get to class."

They hug each other good-bye. Courtney reminds the others to meet at 6:00 p.m. that evening at the Coffee Cart.

7

Skyler is awakened by a soft knock on his bedroom door.

"Skyler, its nine o'clock," says Mary, "May I come in?"

Skyler jumps at the sound of Mary's voice. He sits up in bed and softly says, "Mom? Is that you, Mom?"

"Honey, may I come in?" says Mary, as she opens the door and peers in.

"Oh, yeah, sure," Skyler replies, as he swings his legs over the bed and stands quickly to his feet.

"Oh honey, I just wanted to let you know your dad and I are going to the country today. We should be back by seven tonight. That is, of course, unless we decide to stay for the weekend. If we do, we'll call you and let you know."

"Oh, yeah sure. Have a great time, Mom," he says, hoping she does not notice his rumpled clothes.

The sound of a horn blaring from the driveway makes Mary jump.

"Oh, that man," says Mary, a bit irritated. "We left you twenty-five dollars on the kitchen table with a note," she says, as she walks over to Skyler and gives him a hug and kiss on the cheek.

"I hope you have a good time. You both can use a rest."

"Yes, we all can," says Mary with a notable sigh. Turning, she heads for the door and closes it behind her.

Skyler can hear the front door close loudly as Mary hurries out to the car and gets in. Soon Jason and his wife are off for the day. As far as Skyler is concerned, not soon enough or long enough. Skyler heads to the bathroom and leaves the door open.

Deceit flies several miles from Joe's house to Skyler's house and lands on the roof. He gracefully slips through the roof and into the living room. He hears humming and goes to see where it is coming from. Realizing it is Skyler in the shower, Deceit decides to check out the house. He passes through Skyler's bedroom wall and into the hall.

Nothing unusual here. Deceit passes through another wall and finds the guest bedroom. It is large, clean, neat, and orderly.

"All that seems to be missing is a chocolate on the pillow," he says sarcastically.

He flies around the room taking in all he sees. A chest of drawers and a dresser with a mirror are against the wall. Huh, nice bedroom, thinks Deceit, as he moves silently passed a mirror. He catches a glimpse of himself and stops short, then heads back to the mirror.

"Hmm, you are a handsome devil. Fit and trim," he says aloud, as he turns and admires himself in the mirror. His red, beady eyes catch a mark on his backside.

"What the hell is that?" he says with a look of shock and disbelief. A high-pitched scream leaves his lips.

"Oh my beautiful body has been scarred for eternity," he says, whimpering as he looks at the long, lumpy scar on his right butt cheek.

"Oh, are they going to pay for disfiguring my beautiful body? If they think they can get away with this, they have something else coming to them. I'll hunt down those two fallen warrior angels and do away with them for doing this to me!"

Deceit lets out a long, wailing sound as he remembers the painful incident that caused his scar.

"Drama queen," says Backbiter softly, as he watches Deceit from behind the corner of the dresser.

"Wait a minute. This can work for me and not against me. Yes, yes," Deceit says with a slight hiss, his eyes narrowing.

"This can be a sign to everyone just how brave I am in battle."

Taking one more look at his backside, Deceit kisses his long, black, boney, slightly burnt finger and touches it to his right butt cheek which he has pointing out toward the mirror. He gives his little butt a shake, and, with a smile, he goes into the wall and into the master bedroom. A bed sits up against the opposite wall. The blue bedspread is neatly placed on top of the queen-size bed. Four pillows are propped against the headboard. A small lamp sits on each of the nightstands placed at the head of either side of the bed. The two windows are closed and locked. *Nice, as far as guest rooms are concerned.*

Deceit makes his way to another room. This room is more decorated and warmer than the guestroom. The dark green carpet is thick and plush which sets off the sea foam green walls and white trim. All the furniture is white in color with gold hardware. The locked French doors lead out to the backyard. Dark green drapes are gracefully pulled back and held in place by gold-colored hooks. Covering the windows are white, sheer curtains that set off the rest of the room. There are several nice paintings hanging on the walls.

On top of a corner shelf are some framed photographs and a photo album. The photos look like they were taken back in the early nineties.

Deceit recognizes Jason, Mary, and Skyler as a child. But he does not recognize the woman standing alone with a big smile on her face and her hands on her large belly. He gets closer in order to read the inscription on the photograph. It reads, "To my son Skyler. This is to show you I love you and named you before you were born. Love you always, Mommy."

Deceit's beady, dark red eyes soften a little upon reading the inscription. He has often wondered what happened to his own mother. That is, if he ever had one. He knows that the warrior and other fallen angels along with his mighty lord, Satan, were not born of a woman, but were created by the Most High God. He also knows that Amon was once a high-ranking angel prior to being cast out of heaven along with his lord and master, Satan.

Deceit studies the face of Skyler's mom. He notices Skyler resembles his mother more than his father. Ingrid Riggs, Skyler's biological mother, had long, silky, blonde hair and clear, large, expressive, blue eyes. She was tall and beautiful. Deceit takes his time in looking at each individual photograph. They tell a story of Jason Riggs and Skyler's mother Ingrid.

Deceit easily pieces together how Jason Riggs loved and lost his one true love which he tried to replace, but never could. He notices that there are no more photos of Ingrid after Skyler's birth.

Deceit closely searches the faces of Jason Riggs with his infant son, Skyler. Jason's eyes look hollow and sad. This is the face of a man who had lost all but his infant son for whom he seems to hold no love.

He looks through the photo album and pauses to reflect on this newfound information while stroking his pointy chin. His eyes glow as he realizes he can use this information to his advantage.

"Yes," Deceit says aloud, "I will have to go and think over my plan. With this new information, I can redo my strategy and proceed from there."

Within seconds, Deceit is gone up through the roof and out of sight. After rethinking his plan, Deceit sits up and says, "Yes, that should work. Now, to find out were Damian Tingly is and have a little chat with him."

Backbiter comes out from beneath the bed where he was hiding and also heads up like a shot into the heavens to report back to Amon.

8

"I 'll just have a diet Coke," says Christine, as she settles into the last booth of the Coffee Cart.

"Me too and some fries," says Brittney.

"And you, miss?" the waitress asks Courtney.

"I'll have a regular Coke and a burger with curly fries."

"Put them all on the same ticket, please," says Skyler to the chubby cheeked, middle-aged waitress. Smiling, she turns and leaves saying under her breath, "Oh, to be young again."

"So," says Brittney, "what do you want to know?"

Taken aback by her directness, Skyler shifts uncomfortably in his seat. He lowers his head and thinks what would be the proper questions to ask.

"Um, I want to know if there is any way you can make someone, who has been gone for a long time, come back and talk to you."

"You mean talk to the dead?"

"Yes."

"Sure there are ways, but it'll cost you," Brittney says with a mischievous smile. She winks at Courtney as if to say, *We've got a live one here.* They continue to talk as they sip on their frequently refilled drinks.

After a couple of hours, Skyler leans back in the booth and lets out a long sigh. Rubbing his face with both hands, he says, "Well, I think we have a deal. When do you want the money?"

"Tomorrow, Saturday. We meet here again at the same time. Make sure you bring cash. Small denominations. Got it?"

"Got it," replies Skyler, as he stands and up stretches his legs. He picks up the check and heads toward the cashier.

"Remember, here tomorrow, same time."

"Right," replies Skyler, as he pays the tab.

"He's really cute," says Courtney with a smile.

The other girls look at her with a smirk, as they gather their purses and head out as well.

Skyler mulls over what he and the girls have discussed. Getting into his car, he checks his watch. Eight fifteen sharp.

"Have one hour and forty-five minutes before I have to be home," he says out loud.

Wasting no time, he heads home. Arriving early, he goes inside.

"Hey, Skyler," says his father with unusual cheeriness, "you're home early."

"I'm tired. I'm going to my room."

He walks over to his dad and kisses him gently on top of his head, then walks over to Mary, his stepmother, and does the same.

"Good night," his parents say almost in unison.

Skyler makes an effort to keep his actions as normal as possible. Reaching his room, he opens the door quickly and closes it quietly behind him. Kicking off his shoes, he flops on his back onto bed and puts his hands behind his head and crosses his ankles. He falls asleep thinking of his conversation with the Daughters of Amon and dreams of his mother, Ingrid.

Backbiter bows deeply before Amon.

"My lord," he says with confidence, "I have found out Deceit's plans to corrupt the young Skyler Riggs. He has managed to sway him into seeking information from the young women who call themselves the Daughters of Amon. They have managed to extract money from him in exchange for allowing him to speak to his deceased mother."

Amon strokes his chin carefully accessing what he had just heard.

"So, these so-called Daughters of Amon are going to attempt to call up the spirit of Ingrid Riggs?"

"Yes, your lordship," replies Backbiter with a prideful look.

"When is this to take place?"

Backbiter shifts his feet uncomfortably.

"That is to be decided tomorrow, your lordship," Backbiter answers with a slight shaking in his voice.

"Very well, return to your assignment and get as much detail of his plan as you can," says Amon, as he waves Backbiter away. Without hesitation, Backbiter turns and heads out the double doors of Amon's office.

Amon rings a bell which brings in a beautiful fallen angel. He walks over to Amon's desk. Enepsigos is known for his ability to transform himself into the form of a human female.

"Enepsigos," says Amon, "go to the house of Skyler Riggs and look for a picture of Ingrid Riggs. You are to meet with the so-called Daughters of Amon at a time and place I will inform you of when you return from this assignment."

"Yes, your lordship," replies Enepsigos, as he leaves Amon's office.

"This should be interesting," says Amon softly to himself, as he reclines back in his chair.

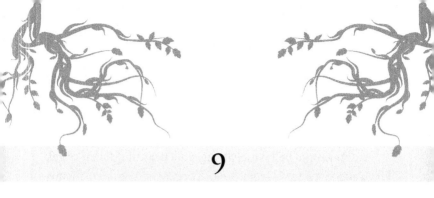

9

"Rise up, oh mighty one," said Mr. Tingly to the leading man, Peter Warren. "Rise up and address your adoring crowd."

Peter steps forward and lifts up his hands and looks at the audience. His eyes are ablaze with an unnatural light and are the color of red wine.

"My people," says Peter with a voice too deep to be his own, "look at me!"

A hush comes over the auditorium. Peter says something to the audience only a few understand and respond to at first.

Joe and Ann feel a fright come over them. They look nervously around as the crowd begins to chant softly at the first mention the name Eras. Then their voices begin to rise in volume.

The ones which are not affected are already trying to make their way out of the hall. But the harder they try to leave, the more the others prevent them from leaving.

Peter smiles and fixes his gaze upon a young woman at the front of the stage. The throngs of people have pushed both Ann and Joe up to the front of the stage.

Peter moves deliberately toward Ann. She desperately wants to turn away, but for reasons beyond her understanding she cannot. Her body shakes partially with fear, partially with a strange feeling of excitement.

Peter leans toward her and stares into her eyes. He reaches out to touch her face. Ann tries to back away, but the crowd keeps her pressed against the stage. Peter reaches out again to her, touching her face. His hand is oddly cold to the touch. Ann's eyes are locked in an unbreakable, intense stare. His hand caresses her face, when suddenly, he grabs her by the back of the neck and pulls her harshly to him. Ann lets out terrified scream.

Joe succeeds in freeing himself from the front of the stage and grabs Ann's arm. He forces his way through the crowd toward the back of the hall with Ann in tow.

Angelo makes his way through the pushing, crying, and punching crowd, heading toward Joe and Ann. Relief sweeps over Joe as he hands Ann off to Angelo. Taking Ann by the hand, Angelo easily pushes his way through the crowd. They reach the back doors and out they go. Angelo gives the very frightened and tearful Ann his cell phone and instructs her to call nine-one-one.

He turns and reenters Brinkman Hall as the crowd begins to sway back and forth chanting, "Eras, Eras." Peter seems to have hypnotized most of the remaining audience.

"What the hell kind of play is this?" asks Joe.

Upon seeing Angelo, he yells above the crowd, "Hey, Angelo, what you say we get outta here?"

"You wanna go now? It's just starting to get good," Angelo shouts over the crowd.

"What?" Joe yells back. "You like this sort of stuff?"

"Yeah! I was made for it!" replies Angelo with a gleam in his eye.

"Come on, big boy!" Angelo shouts to Peter, as Peter tears off his shirt and shouts obscenities.

"You're crazy," shouts Joe. "I'm outta here."

Just as Joe turns to make his way out between the pushing and shoving audience, he hears a chilling cry. Peter flings himself off the stage and lands on top of Joe. They fall on to the crowd which is now a mass of screaming, yelling, and punching group of college kids. It resembles more a mash pit instead of a college drama.

Peter Warner lives with his parents whose neighbors are Jason and Mary Riggs. His parents moved here a few years ago from Washington DC.

He, like his neighbor Skyler Riggs, is an only child. But unlike the Riggses, his family is very well to do. Used to the better things in life and having more freedom from his parents, Peter feels free to seek after things that his Christian parents, had they known, would not approve of. Two of these things are seeking after the occult and the other is illegal drugs. Since he attends the class Damian Tingly teaches on world religions, and studies drama, he is thrilled to be the lead in one of Tingly's plays.

"What are you doing, man? Are you crazy?" cries out Joe to Peter who is clawing, hissing, and punching Joe without mercy.

Damian Tingly smiles sinisterly from behind the stage curtain. Mass hysteria is now in full swing. Some girls are screaming and crying hysterically trying desperately to get out, while others are following after Peter's lead. They jump on the bewildered, the defenseless, and the grandparents and parents of those who are in the play.

Scratching, punching, pulling hair, and letting out screeching sounds heighten the fear and panic of the others trying to fight their way out of the madness.

"Angelo, Angelo, help me man!" yells Joe, as he pulls himself up by holding on to others.

"Adria, I need your help. They are becoming too many for me alone," yells Angelo from up on stage.

The other actors have pounced on Angelo, and he is on one knee trying to fight off the multitude of dark, transparent spirits and not too few fallen angels which no one seems to see, but Angelo. Shirts, shoes, and even hair flies in all directions.

"Angelo, help me, man!" a desperate Joe cries out between a barrages of punches.

"Over there, Adria. Help Joe Austin," shouts Angelo, pointing to Joe.

A bright flash of light temporarily blinds Joe as he manages to get to his feet. The sound of Peter growling and shouting obscenities is heard above the melee.

Suddenly, Peter is lifted off his feet and tossed on the stage by Adria, a tall, handsome, long-haired angel. He lands across the stage with a loud thud.

Damian Tingly rushes toward Peter. Upon reaching him, Tingly roughly grabs him by the face and forces his eyes open. His eyes are blue again. Damian Tingly then quickly gets to his feet and runs to the back of the stage and heads to the nearest exit.

The sound of sirens eases some of the tension of those still trapped inside. A large portion of people have made it outside safely. Some of them run toward the handful of security guards who are trying to restore some sort of order, while the remaining few guards inside fight to rescue the ones they can.

Angelo calls out again to Adria, a warrior angel of the Most High God, whose name in Hebrew means noble and powerful. Together, they fight off foes, seen and unseen. Bodies fly through the air as Adria and Angelo clear the stage. Joe stares in amazement as Angelo jumps from off the stage and onto a small group of young men who are hell-bent on pummeling to death a security guard who is curled up in a ball on the floor.

Angelo pulls each one by the back of the arms and tosses them several feet away. Soon the attackers are left strewn on chairs and the floor; a couple are on stage which is ten feet away. Angelo quickly picks up the unconscious security guard and, in a blink of an eye, carries him out the front doors and hands him off to the paramedics which keep arriving.

The riot police arrive, and they disembark quickly and rush in to the hall where they stop short and stare in disbelief.

The place is littered with both men and women. Some lay like limp rag dolls across the back of seats, while others lay groaning on the floor and stage. A few are hanging on top of the back scenery, while others are trying to wiggle themselves free from the stage floor. Two or three are hanging from the catwalk.

"Good luck in writing this one up," says Officer Steve Logan who smiles at Sergeant Greer as he makes his way over to Joe who by the way, has not moved an inch since seeing Angelo in action.

"Sir, sir, are you all right?" says Officer Logan, as he puts his arm around Joe and gently guides him outside.

"I need a medic here, this man is in shock."

A female medic rushes over to Joe and quickly and expertly starts to administer first aid.

Ambulances come and go quickly with their charges to the nearest emergency room. Joe is being strapped in for his ride to the hospital. Order now being restored; the police take statements from those left outside and still able to speak. Ann is one of them.

"This is Myra Smith of KNCS Channel Eight signing off. We will bring you more information as soon as we know more."

Miss Smith and her camera crew pack it up for the night, being that the police are still very tight-lipped at this point. Miss Smith, even though she is new to news reporting, has learned early on that when something of this caliber hits you'd best go home and get rested for the eventual fight with the editor in chief as to why she hasn't gotten more information from the police.

"Thank god, Price is on vacation until tomorrow," she says to her cameraman, as they drive back to the station.

10

"Hi, Joe," says Ann, as she timidly walks toward Joe's hospital bed.

"Hi, yourself," replies Joe with a grimace.

"I talked to the doctor, and he says you're going to be okay."

Tears begin to well up as she takes a closer look at Joe's face. *You have to be strong. Don't you dare cry.*

Joe closes his right eye only. His left eye is swollen shut. He tries to move to a more comfortable position, but a sharp, stabbing pain stops him short. He sighs heavily. Ann walks over to Joe and lightly touches his left hand.

"Joe, if there is anything I can do for you, just let me know," she says softly, as she bends down and kisses Joe's forehead tenderly. Not one for hospitals, she leans over and whispers into Joe's ear.

"I'll let you sleep now," she says softly. "I'll be back again tonight. Know the church is praying for you."

Getting no response, she decides to let him rest and slips out of the room and back to the elevators.

The medication starts to take effect. A nurse slips quietly in and checks Joe's IV and bandages. She finishes taking Joe's vital signs and records them in his chart. As quietly as she came in is how quietly she slips out of his room.

Ann pushes the ground floor button on the elevator and walks past Angelo. He smiles at her and continues on to Joe's room. Joe is unaware that anyone is in the room with him. He is sleeping deeply and peacefully.

Angelo silently walks next to Joe's bed and smiles at him. He is pleased at what he has seen today. He sits on the chair that is at the corner of the room, and there will stay till morning.

As promised, Ann returns in the evening. She is carrying a small bouquet of flowers in a white ceramic cup. A beautiful get-well card is clipped on to a plastic card holder. Ever so quietly, Ann places the cup on the nightstand.

It's a good thing it's small enough to fit next to several other bouquets of flowers. They are from his many friends at school and a few professors who have come to visit him.

"Do you mind cutting your visit short? I don't mean to be rude, but now that my mind is clear I have a lot to think about."

"No, I understand," she says a little hurt. "I'll see you tomorrow then."

She straightens up and walks out. A couple of Joe's friends walk past her. She looks straight ahead. Upon reaching the elevator, she turns and sees the others walk into Joe's room. Just as the doors to the elevators open, she can hear Joe greeting his new guests. Ann steps into the elevator and pushes the main lobby button several times. The doors close quietly.

Upon reaching the main lobby Ann walks out the elevator with her head down, bumping into Peter Warren who is holding a large, beautiful, clear, glass cut vase with the most beautiful array of flowers Ann has ever seen.

Peter looks like death warmed over. His clear, blue eyes are bloodshot, with dark circles under his eyes. He is a deathly pale. His upper lip is swollen and he has a large white bandage on the back of his head.

Even with facial injuries, Ann recognizes him. Her eyes are full of fear. She backs up into the elevator, Peter following her in. He pushes the third floor elevator button, and the doors close behind him.

"I was hoping to run into you again," Peter says with a shaky voice. "I don't know who you are, but I do remember you from the play. I want to apologize for terrorizing you, and I want you to know I am so very sorry for my actions."

Ann is silent, partly from fear and partly from pity. All she can do is stare at him as the elevator doors open to the third floor, and Peter steps out. She pushes the elevator button again to the main lobby of the hospital.

Peter walks toward Joe's room with a heavy heart. The young nurse who is leaving the room stops him at the doorway.

"I'm sorry," she says softly, "visiting hours just ended. You'll have to come back tomorrow. I can take these and place them in his room for you if you like."

"Ah, yes please. Thank you," replies Peter with some relief.

"Sir, are you feeling okay? Did you want some water?" asks the nurse.

"No, no thank you," replies Peter, "I'm okay."

With eyes cast down and arms limp at the sides, Peter turns and makes his way back to the elevators. Once inside and alone he places both his hands on his face and begins to weep.

Ann slowly makes her way back to her car. She pulls out her keys as she gets closer to her car and accidently presses her car alarm button. The blaring of the car alarm startles her back from her thoughts. One poor gentleman, who just happens to be walking past Ann's car when the alarm goes off, tosses his cup of coffee up in the air. It lands on the hood of the car next to Ann's.

"Oh, I'm so sorry," says Ann with a giggle. "I pressed the alarm button by mistake."

"Huh," is all the reply the older man gives her, looking sternly at her.

Ann gets into her car and begins to laugh until her laughter turns into tears. With her emotions spent, she dries her eyes and puts on her seatbelt. Checking her rearview mirror, she starts her car and slowly and carefully backs out of the parking spot. She makes her way out of the enclosed parking structure and heads for home.

11

Brittney, Courtney, and Christine arrive early for their appointment with Skyler. They have already ordered their dinner and are sipping their drinks.

"Do you think he'll come?" asks Courtney, a little unsure.

"Yup, he'll be here," Brittney says with her usual confidence.

"Let's hope he brings the money. I need to pay for a couple of new school books," says Christine, as she wipes her lips with a napkin.

"I don't like the way this new lipstick feels," she says, as she wipes the remaining lipstick from her lips.

"It feels like I have wax on. I'll have to pick up a new one, more expensive, right after we split the money and head out."

"Quiet, here he comes," says Brittney sharply. They are all smiles as Skyler approaches their table.

"Hello, I hope I'm not late," he says, looking at each girl as he sits down next to Britney.

"No, you're right on time. We just got here a little early and ordered dinner. Are you going to join us?" she smiles sweetly at Skyler.

"No, thanks. I just want to get down to business and be on my way," Skyler replies.

"You're not having second thoughts are you?" Courtney asks, a little concerned.

"No, I just want to get on with this if you don't mind," Skyler replies firmly.

"Okay, as you wish," says Brittney. "Do you have the money?" she asks a little nervously.

Skyler leans to his left side and pulls out his wallet from his right jean pocket. Carefully, he pulls out a small stack of two-hundred dollars from his wallet and holds them firmly in his hand, replacing his wallet.

"This is a lot of money," he says, looking sternly at Brittney. "Are you sure I can talk with my real mom?"

Brittney blushes slightly, as she answers.

"Yes, of course. Don't worry, we wouldn't lie to you."

Christine and Courtney give each other a quick, "Oh man, he bought it" look.

Skyler looks straight into Brittney's eyes and says, "Before I hand this money over to you, tell me who is going to call my mother's spirit back from the dead You?"

Brittney looks over at Christine and says, "Oh, we will, and we'll bring one more person we know who has done séances before."

"You mean you've never done this before?" asks Skyler, a bit agitated.

"Oh yes, yes, of course we have, haven't we, girls?"

"Oh yes, we've done hundreds of them," says Christine, as if it were a matter of fact.

"Hundreds?" asks Skyler, knowing Christine had to be exaggerating.

Brittney kicks Christine under the table and gives her a look of caution.

"Oh, did I say hundreds? I meant to say lots, maybe ten or twenty," says Christine, as her eyes widen, trying to look innocent and believable.

"Well, to tell you the truth," says Brittney, "we've sat in on a few séances, but like I said, we know someone who really does these things. She goes by the name of Chulda. I'll call her right now, and we can set up an appointment."

Brittney reaches in her purse and looks around for her cell phone. Upon finding it, she pulls it out.

"You're not going to call her right now, are you?" asks Christine with a worried look.

"Yes, I am, Chris. What better time to call than the present?"

She flips open her phone and looks through her phone contacts.

"Found it," she says cheerfully, as she makes the call. The phone rings. Brittney keeps her eye on Skyler, looking for any sign of him wanting to back out.

"Hello?" says a young female voice over the phone.

"Hello, my name is Brittney. I spoke to you a few days ago in regards—" Before she can finish her sentence, the voice on the other end cuts her off.

"Yes, I remember you. When do you want to meet?"

"Ahhh, one moment please, let me ask," says Brittney, as she covers the phone with her free hand.

"When and where do you want to meet?" she asks the others.

"Anywhere, right now, if she can," says Skyler assertively.

"Now and wherever you want to meet," says Brittney, as she listens on the phone to the directions Chulda gives her.

"Okay, guys, we're to meet Chulda as soon as we get to her house."

"Shall we all go together or separately?"

"I'll take my own car, just give me the address," says Skyler.

"Just follow us, you'll never find it on your own. By the way, I still need the money," says Brittney, as she puts her hand out. Skyler folds the bills and slaps them into her hand.

"What kind of car do you drive?" he asks.

"A red bug. You can't miss it. It's parked right out front. See it?"

Skyler looks through the window.

"Okay, let's do this," he says.

Skyler heads out the door first and out to his car. Brittney pockets one hundred dollars and hands over the remaining one hundred dollars to Christine.

"Chris, pay with this."

"Hey, where's the rest of the money?" she asks.

"I did all the work, and I'm the one taking all the risk. You two are just along for the ride."

"Can't argue with that," says Christine, as she looks at Courtney shrugging her shoulders. Christine pays the bill, and she splits the remainder with Courtney.

"Shotgun," says Courtney, as she hurries to Brittney's car and gets on the front passenger side.

Skyler is waiting anxiously in his car ready to follow the girls. Christine gets into the backseat and Brittney sits behind the wheel, not moving.

"Come on, Brittney, let's go," says Courtney impatiently. "I want to get an appointment to get my nails done tomorrow."

Brittney starts the car and off they go with Skyler following close behind. They drive twenty minutes outside of town. The view of meadows with wild flowers now in full bloom along with the scent of the trees and grass is intoxicating. It feels more like a ride on a lazy Saturday evening than a ride to misadventure.

Soon after, they turn left into a stone-walled entrance to an old estate. The driveway curves gently and is lined with lush, rose bushes, and other sorts of greenery. The manicured lawn stretches in all directions. In the distance, behind the magnificent, imposing mansion, is a thickly wooded area. The drive ends in a circular driveway in front of the house.

The white, tall, gleaming pillars remind Skyler of the old, southern houses when he once visited South Carolina with his parents when he was only ten years old.

The only thing missing is the hanging moss on the trees and roof.

Skyler parks his car behind Brittney's. They walk up the white, wide steps to the front porch. Curiosity gets the better of them, and they walk over to the graceful, arched front windows and peer in.

The silk sheers obscure the view inside. Skyler gives the front of the house a quick once over and approaches the girls.

"So this is it?" he asks, seemingly unimpressed.

Startled, Brittney jerks her head toward Skyler, momentarily confused.

"This is the address she gave me. So it has to be it."

"Okay then, let's go. I want to get this done and over with quickly," replies Skyler.

The four walk up to the double hand-carved doors. Brittney gingerly presses the doorbell and steps back, as if afraid of who or what will open the door. The faint sound of footsteps echoing through hallway can be heard through the closed doors. Courtney and Christine step closer together, while Brittney puts on a brave face.

Skyler shifts a little and straightens up, bracing himself for what will happen next. They all watch nervously as the doorknob turns slowly.

The doors open to reveal a man in a butler's black uniform. He is slightly shorter than Skyler. His thin, gray hair is cut short except for the few strands that are combed back in a vain attempt to cover his rather balding head. His steel, blue-gray eyes look intently underneath unruly eyebrows. He scans the young, nervous faces before him.

"May I say who is calling?" he says with a deep voice.

"Yes, I'm Brittney Muller, and my friends are Christine and Courtney. This is Skyler Riggs. I spoke with Chulda earlier and made an appointment to see her tonight."

The butler frowns and says, "Right this way, please."

He turns smartly on his heels and walks across the glowing, marble floor of the entryway and into a large sitting room.

A beautiful, large, crystal chandelier hangs down gracefully from the high ceiling, giving off a bright cheery light. The heavy, deep blue curtains are closed. The room is tastefully decorated with artwork, and several busts sit on top of what appears to be early eighteenth century French furniture. There are several large porcelain vases with flowing arrays of flowers. They can't help but take in a lungful of the sweet scents given off by them.

"Hello, I'm Chulda."

They all jump, startled by her greeting since they neither saw nor heard her walk in.

"Oh," says Brittney with a quiver in her voice. "Hello, I'm Brittney. I spoke with you on the phone. These are my friends, Courtney and Christine. And this is Skyler, the gentlemen I told you who wants to have a séance."

"Welcome to my humble home," says Chulda with a smile. "Please take a seat at the table."

As they settle down on surprisingly comfortable, antique-looking chairs, Chulda sits and places her elbows on the round table and reaches for Skyler's and Christine's hands.

"Close the door and turn off the lights."

Not knowing who she is talking to, they look around nervously. With a soft, collective, sigh of relief, they see the butler close the door and turn off the lights. He then steps to one side of the door and stands with his white-gloved hands clasped in front of him.

"Skyler, I want you to think of your mother. You know what she looks like by the picture you have on your nightstand. The one where she has her hands on her belly."

Skyler's eyes open in amazement and fear. The girls tighten their grip on one another's hands as they keep their eyes tightly closed. Skyler's heart beats faster as a chilly breeze gently caresses his cheek.

"Come, oh great one. Come to us, powerful and great spirit, Enepsigos. Come and bring the departed spirit of Ingrid Riggs to us."

A beautiful, tall, male fallen angel begins to form from the cold, thick fog that is forming as a loose cone emanating from the floor. The scent of lilacs begins to fill the air.

"Welcome, Enepsigos. Thank you for coming. Did you bring Ingrid Riggs with you?"

"Yes, I did. Just as you requested."

The fog greatly increases in thickness, then dissipates, leaving behind a beautiful, blonde-haired, blue-eyed, tall woman.

"Ingrid Riggs, welcome. Your son is here eagerly waiting to converse with you. You may now speak to your son, Skyler."

There is complete silence in the room. The only sound that can be heard is the shallow breathing from all present, including Chulda.

"Skyler, turn to your left and open your eyes."

Skyler slowly turns his head to the left and opens his eyes. Brittney tries to pull her hand away, but Skyler has too strong of a grip for her to be able to do so. The scent of lilacs fills the air.

"Mother?" he says softly. "Mom, I'm Skyler, your son."

Skyler takes in every inch of the lovely, long-haired blonde apparition standing beside him.

"Hello, my son. I have waited a very long time to speak with you. You have grown into a handsome young man."

"Mom, I wish I could have met you in life. I miss you. There is so much I want to talk to you about."

Ingrid Riggs smiles gently at Skyler, then turning slowly, she looks into Chulda's eyes. Chulda nods and says softly, "Skyler needs your help with his father, Jason Riggs. Will you help him?"

"Yes," says Ingrid with a kind, soft, airy voice. "Take careful note of what I require of you to do."

Chulda lights a candle that is being held in a single, silver candleholder which is placed next to her. She picks up the matchbook that lays next to the candlestick and strikes a match. The scent of it mingles with the scent of lilacs. Ingrid Riggs proceeds to tell Chulda what she requires Skyler Riggs do. Chulda writes down everything Ingrid Riggs says.

"My son, I will be available to visit with you anytime you desire to see me. But since this is our first meeting, I cannot stay long. Take the instructions Chulda has written and follow them to the letter. Then and only then will you be able to see me again. Do this in the privacy of your own room. Then, my son, we will converse more freely and longer."

As soon as Ingrid stops speaking, the thick fog begins to dissipate.

"Thank you, Ingrid, and thank you, Enepsigos."

With that, Skyler's mother disappears as mist in the morning sun. The room is dark again.

Chulda says, "You may now turn on the lights."

Skyler's face shows a mix of emotions he is feeling as he sits quietly, going over in his mind what has just transpired. Brittney pulls her hand way from both Skyler and Christine. She does not miss a moment in getting up and saying her farewells. Courtney remains seated for a few moments, while she regains strength enough to stand. Then she is up and out of Chulda's house even before Brittney and Christine.

Chulda smiles as she sees her guests rushing out the front door. Skyler rises last from his seat and extends his hand to Chulda.

"Thank you. I am ever in your debt," he says sincerely, not knowing Chulda will be calling on him to repay that debt soon.

"You're welcome."

She smiles a wide smile. Her metal braces sparkle in the light of the chandelier.

12

Joe lies comfortably in his hospital bed. The medication for his severely bruised ribs have given him a feeling of tranquility, he has not felt in a long time. The doctor and nurse come and go as if in slow motion.

Joe hears the murmur of the voices of his friends who have been coming and going at a steady pace. He acknowledges them as politely as possible since his mind is trying to focus on something else. Something he had not thought of for a very long time.

"I hate to be rude, but I need to rest now. Thanks a lot for coming," says Joe as kindly as he can say it.

His friends agree and leave him, closing the door silently behind them.

Now that he is alone and able to concentrate, he tries to recall the name of his former spirit guide from his days when he openly attended self-hypnosis and new age classes.

He begins to recall, only a scant five years earlier, Abby had moved into town. She would have Joe over for dinner once or twice a week. Joe's parents were happy that they got along so well. She was bright, charismatic, and a licensed practical nurse by profession, but in her private life, she was a certified, card-carrying, practicing witch who would introduce him bit by bit to the deeper things of the occult. It was obvious to his friends and family and especially to Abby, his much older, first cousin, that he was quite sensitive to the spiritual realm. Joe soon realized what her true motives were and tried quite unsuccessfully to distance himself from her. Unfortunately, the harder he tried, the more entangled he became.

Soon she was inviting him to classes in the occult. Something he had tried to avoid, but she was quite persuasive. The first of several classes he would attend were held in a rough neighborhood and would take place at night. His apprehension grew the closer they got to the meeting place. Joe decided he was not going to attend this class or any other class she tried to get him to attend. He even told her so.

Since she would not stop the car or turn it around so he could get out Joe opened the car door and leaned out. With a vise-like grip, she grabbed his left arm and pulled him back into the car. Her reaction was not one he was expecting her to have. She was laughing.

"We're here. Let me park the car, and we'll go in together."

Not knowing where he was, Joe felt it would be in his best interest to go in with her. Besides, the thought of staying alone in the car was not an option.

As they walked closer to the side door, a heavyset man was welcoming all that came in through this side door.

"He reads auroras. Let's see what he has to say to you."

Joe did not wait around to hear what he had to say and walked right past him as quickly as possible. The first room they entered was a small kitchen. There were a couple of small tables against the wall laden with paper plates, forks, knives, spoons, napkins, and Styrofoam cups on them. On the stove were a few pots. One was for hot tea and the other was for coffee. The third was a large pot filled with beef stew. The aroma of stew slowly simmering in the pot, and the scent of freshly brewing coffee filled the air and his nostrils. In a strange way, it was quite comforting.

A steady stream of people kept coming in. His cousin pulled him over to meet a petite, short-haired, blonde woman who appeared to be about forty years of age.

"Hello, Pastor Watley. I'd like you to meet my cousin, Joe. He's here for the very first time."

"Welcome, Joe. It's good to see young people taking an interest in what we do. Come, let me show you the rest of the building while our guests settle in."

Pastor Watley led Joe and Abby back outside and to the front of the small church building. She unlocked the front door, and they walked in.

"This is our little church. We don't meet up here, but we do leave the light on until we leave for the evening."

The church looked like any other church except it was rather small. It looked to hold about sixty people. The wooden pews were neatly lined up, and the only thing at the altar was a small, plain, white pulpit which included a small microphone attached to it.

"The reason we don't meet up here is because if the police find out what we are doing, they'll close us down."

Joe was to taken aback by what she said to ask any questions. He was also too afraid to find out what all they did do. Soon they walked back to the church basement.

The room where they would meet was dimly lit, large, and void of anything except for the thirty or so folding chairs set up in a circle and one small, square table set at the head of the circle. The atmosphere in the room made the hair on the back of his neck stand on end. They carefully made their way to their chairs and sat down next to each other.

His cousin talked to others sitting next to her whom she seemed to know quite well. He wondered where in the world Abby had learned about this place. Apparently, she had been coming here for quite some time. What they were talking about he didn't know, nor did he care to. He was busy trying to make himself at ease and was also scoping the place out.

All in all, nothing unusual stood out except for the six candles that were lined up on the table where Pastor Wately was standing behind.

"Everyone, please be quiet. We are about to start."

A hush came over the room. Pastor Watley turned her head to the left and said, "You can turn off the lights now."

Sitting in complete darkness, the silence was eerie. Only the sound of a match being struck against the side of a matchbox, along with a couple of coughs and throat clearing, could be heard. One by one the candles were lit. First the red one, then the yellow, then the green, then the white, then the blue, then finally, the black one.

Joe's eyes had become accustomed to the darkness, but now with the light of the candles, he could make out some of the faces in the circle. As the pastor started the prayer, Joe scanned the room. The faces were mainly of middle-aged women. There were about ten men in the group as well as a couple of eighty (or so)-year-old women.

His attention was drawn back to the pastor as she gave instructions on how to "go deeper into your subconscious mind and relax." Joe followed her instructions and soon he was fully relaxed and feeling as if he was among friends. The soothing sound of Pastor Watley's voice giving them instructions allowed him to see his spirit guide.

His happened to be a man with flowing white robes, blond hair, and blue eyes. For a man, he was very beautiful and very graceful. Everyone was invited to welcome their own spirit guide and allow them to enter into one's body through the opening of the spirit guide's choice. Joe felt an increasing pressure on the back of his neck. At first, he resisted, but as the pastor's voice assured them it was okay to allow the spirit guide in Joe relaxed again and felt a presence enter into the back of his neck, infilling him and taking him over.

Some people began to chant softly; others shifted in their seats as if trying to accommodate their new guest. Joe sat quietly listening for further instructions. They came in the soft, assuring voice of the pastor as before. Next, they were supposed to allow their spirit guide to take them back in time to revisit a previous life. Joe saw what appeared to be a movie rewinding.

In his mind's eye, he could see scenes from the present day going back very quickly until it finally stopped around the 1330s. Joe saw a young man about twenty-two years of age being held securely by two large bald men.

A beautiful young woman stood several feet away from him. She was about twenty-five years old. Her black, straight hair came down evenly just below the collarbone, and she was wearing an amethyst and pearl-beaded headdress. Around her long, graceful neck was a large, flat, plain gold metal necklace. Her sheer, cream-colored dress with its wide shoulder straps lay snuggly over her shoulders. Pleated with tiny pleats and gathered at the waist with a thin, gold cord, her silk dress was sheer enough to see her undergarments. It clung gently to her and flowed down her long legs and ended at the top of her feet. Her sandals were but a few straps of leather attached to a thin, leather sole, accented with gold, amethyst, and pearl beads. In her hands was a medium, finely and tightly weaved basket with a lid. Taking a few steps forward, she held out the basket to the young man who was struggling in vain to free himself.

"Will you tell me the name of the traitor to my queen?" she asked in an authoritative voice.

"I don't know. I am innocent. I know nothing of the plot to murder Her Highness, the Queen," replied the young man, with fear in his eyes.

"Very well then, let this be by your choice," she said calmly.

The two men dragged him up to the woman. Calmly and carefully, she removed the lid from the basket. Slowly, she reached in. A smile began to form on the face of the young, lovely woman, as she pulled out a small but deadly asp.

"This is your last chance. Will you tell me who is behind this?"

"I do not know," the young man said, his voice shaking and his knees giving way.

Without hesitation, the young woman reached out with the asp to his outstretched forearm. With lightning speed, the snake struck out, sinking his fangs deeply into the young man's arm. Just as quickly, it withdrew its head and curled itself around the woman's wrist. With a nod of her head, she signaled the men to drag the dying man into another room.

"Now, thank your spirit guide and allow him or her to leave," said Pastor Watley in soft, gentle tones.

A feeling of relief came over Joe as the spirit guide left him through the back of his neck the same way it had entered. He opened his eyes and looked around at the others who were stirring, as if they had been asleep in their chairs and had been awakened by the lights which had come on again.

"Okay, everyone, let's take a deep breath. We are now back to the present and fully awake," said the pastor, as she cupped her hand around each candle and blew them out one by one. Soft whispering could be heard across the room. Joe's cousin was still sitting with her eyes closed as she let out a few deep breaths.

"Okay, everyone. Tell us what you saw and what the name of your spirit guide is. We'll start from here," as she points to the first person on her right. They gave the names of their guides and told what they saw. Now it was Joe's turn to name his guide.

"The name of my spirit guide is Enepsigos."

"Joe, Joe."

Ann's soft voice cuts through his thoughts. Opening his eyes, he sees Ann leaning toward his ear.

"How are you doing?" she asks.

"Feeling much better, thanks."

"I spoke to the doctor just before I came in. He said you can go home next week."

Joe smiles, not paying much attention her. His mind is on other things which he knows he should not even remotely be thinking about.

"Joe, did you hear me? You're well enough to go home next week."

Ann looks at him with a puzzled look.

13

As Enepsigos walks up to Amon's office, the majestic double doors open of their own accord, and Enepsigos walks up to his desk. Bowing his head slightly, he looks straight into Amon's eyes.

This would normally not occur—that is, looking into your superior's eyes and not acknowledging them with the proper respect—but in this case it is Ingrid Riggs who stands before Amon.

Amon looks up from his desk and looks with amusement at Ingrid. Leaning back in his chair, Amon strokes his chin as he slowly takes in Ingrid's form from head to toe. His eyes twinkle with delight.

Ingrid daintily lifts her hands and twirls slowly, her filmy, silvery, white gown swirling gracefully around her.

Amon throws back his head in laughter. His rich, baritone voice resonates throughout the high-ceilinged office. Ingrid also tosses her head back in laughter.

"I must say, you are very convincing. Even I, had I been created human, would have been fooled as well. I take it your Skyler Riggs and the others were taken in?"

"Yes, they all were. Even Chulda believes she called Ingrid Riggs back from the dead," says Enepsigos with a smirk.

"The fools," says Amon. "They are so easily deceived."

"Yes, many are, except for most of those who belong to the Most High God," says Enepsigos with some concern.

"Yes, those that delve deeper into His word and test the spirits are not so easily fooled. Those are the ones we have to keep our eyes on," replies Amon, as his frown deepens.

Enepsigos is now back to his original, angelic, male form. He pulls up a chair and sits down and begins to tell Amon all that transpired at the séance. Together, they make plans for Skyler Riggs and Chulda.

Enepsigos stands up with manly grace and bows his head. He walks out the door of Amon's office.

Pacing just to the right of Amon's office door is Backbiter. Enepsigos glances at him and continues down the arched hallway and around the corner.

Backbiter stares after Enepsigos. As he thinks of the beauty of the fallen angel, Enepsigos; he is brought back to the present by Amon, who is clearing his throat loudly. Backbiter walks calmly toward Amon who is seated at his desk. He bows deeply before Amon, and he too clears his throat.

"Commander, I have come back from following Deceit. The appointment between the Daughters of Amon and Skyler Riggs was very successful."

Amon relaxes in his chair as Backbiter describes in detail what transpired before, during, and after the séance. Amon smiles as Backbiter's account and Enepsigos's versions are exactly the same, except that Backbiter's version is much more detailed.

Amon stands and walks to the front of his desk and stands next to Backbiter and looks down at him for what seems to be an eternity to Backbiter.

Finally, Amon speaks and says robustly, "Good work, Backbiter. You have served me well today. I would tell you to take refreshment and enjoy yourself for the remainder of the day, but since you hunger and thirst but cannot eat nor drink, I will let you have the remainder of the day off. Go and enjoy yourself as much as is possible."

With that said, Amon waves Backbiter away. He turns and walks out the doors feeling pride swell in his chest. As he walks out of the building, he is up and out into the atmosphere in no time flat.

Deceit returns to the large cottonwood tree in Joe's backyard. He has been contemplating the events of the last two weeks. Before he visits Damian Tingly, Deceit wisely assesses the incident at Brinkman Hall. He sensed something evil was about to occur, but he was not privy to the plan, nor who it was that planned it.

"There seems to be a second powerful being bringing much hurt and chaos to the life of Skyler Riggs and Joe Austin. I wonder who is causing all this commotion. Granted, it has worked well in my favor, but I don't want to get caught up in any fallen angel's affairs. That would not go well for me," says Deceit thoughtfully.

With so much going on. I believe the best cause of action will be for me to snoop around and see what or who is behind all this.

Deceit flies up out of the tree and flies toward Brinkman Hall.

14

"Hello?"

"Hello, honey. It's mom."

"Hi, Mom," says Skyler, a little hesitant.

"How are you doing?"

"Good."

"You don't sound too well, are you sure you're okay?" asks Mary, with motherly concern.

Skyler hears the concern in Mary's voice and says cheerfully, "Yes, Mom. I'm good. I was just thinking of something. Not important. How's your day going?"

"Okay, well, actually, your father and I are doing very well. I think this little trip has done both us a world of good."

"That's great, Mom. Really. You guys going to stay the whole weekend?" asks Skyler, with hope in his voice.

"Well, honey, that's what I was calling you about. Your dad decided a few months ago to take a couple of weeks' vacation. He even got tickets for a cruise. He surprised me when we got here. He packed our bags and hid them in the trunk. He still has three more weeks of vacation time coming to him. Sooo…"

"You'll be gone two weeks?" asks Skyler, not even trying to cover up his excitement.

Mary laughs lightheartedly and replies, "Gee, you don't have to sound so happy."

"What about the meeting with the therapist?"

"Oh, honey, don't worry about that, your father has taken care of it. The therapist actually agrees this would do us all some good."

"Sorry, Mom. I just wanted to make sure you and Dad didn't miss your first appointment. Don't worry about me, I'll be fine," Skyler replies, sounding as cheerful as he can at this moment.

"Sweetheart, don't worry about that. We've taken care of everything. Your dad and I left you one hundred and fifty dollars. I put it in the left top shelf over the frigid."

"Tell Dad thanks and you too, Mom. I really appreciate this."

"Hello, son? This is dad. I heard what you said. Be careful and don't spend the money all in one place."

"I won't, Dad."

"Remember, call me if you need anything. And remember the house rules. No parties, no staying out late…"

"I know, Dad. Don't worry. Have a good time and don't worry," Skyler says, hoping his dad will hang up soon.

"Okay, Skyler. You're grown up enough now to take responsibility for yourself. We'll see you in a couple of weeks."

Jason Riggs hands the cell phone over to Mary.

"Bye, honey. Be good now," says Mary, eager to start her and Jason's first real vacation in years.

"Okay, bye, Mom. Have a good time. Don't worry about me, I'll be fine," replies Skyler, happy to end the conversation.

Skyler leans back in to his car seat and closes his eyes. He puts his cell phone on the passenger seat and places his hands on the wheel and grips it tightly. A long sigh of relief escapes his lips. Calm comes over him like a warm shower gently pouring over him. His parent's trip could not have come at a better time.

The money he gave Brittney was from his secret savings account he had opened over three years ago, with the very nice gifts of cash his family and friends gave him when he graduated from high school.

He remains in his car for a while as his mind goes over all the last few days' events.

15

"Thank you for taking such good care of me," Joe says to the doctor and nurse who were assigned to him during his hospital stay.

"Here's my card. Call my office on Wednesday and make an appointment for a follow-up," says the doctor smiling warmly at Joe.

"Will do, Doc. Again, thanks for taking such good care of me."

The doctor turns and leaves, disappearing into another room. Joe is happy to leave this place and all its memories. He searches for his cell phone as he makes his way to the elevator. The doors open; Ann stands before him. If she would have dawdled in her car any longer, she would have missed him.

"Hey," she says, perplexed to see Joe at the elevator. "I spoke with the doctor and he said you would be dismissed later today. I wanted to come early and help you with all your flowers."

"No need, I told the nurse to give them to the geriatric patients and the stuffed animals to the kids. I know they'll be appreciated."

"Oh," says Ann, a little disappointed. She had her eye on the crystal vase with the beautiful flowers in it Peter had brought Joe.

"I was just about to call a cab," he said, as they walked out to the hospital lobby.

"This is your lucky day. I'll take you home. Did you want to stop and get something to eat on the way home?" Ann says, hoping he'll say yes. She had skipped breakfast, and she was a bit hungry. Joe thinks it over.

"Well, I don't have anything at home to eat. I'm sure most of the stuff in the fridge is spoiled by now. Why don't we stop at the grocery store and pick up a few groceries? That way, I'll have something to eat tomorrow."

"Okay. Wait here and I'll go get the car," she says, taking her keys out of her purse.

"No, I want to get used to doing things on my own as soon as possible. That's if you don't mind. The sooner I can fend for myself, the better."

"Nope, I don't mind."

They take their time walking to the parking structure. Joe groans as they climb up the short amount of stairs to the second level. He is beginning to regret his decision at not letting Ann pick him up in front of the hospital.

"You parked a ways away," says Joe, winded from his walk to Ann's car.

"Well, I did suggest I'd pick you up at the front door," she replies curtly.

Joe sees, by the expression on Ann's face, he has hit a nerve. They get to Ann's car and Joe decides the less he says, the better off he will be.

Oh, this is going to be a long ride home. As if Ann could hear his thoughts, she turns and gives him a "don't you dare go there" look. Joe sits quietly for the duration of the ride to the supermarket.

Ann makes several rounds in the parking lot looking for a spot close to the front doors. Her efforts pay off. A green SUV backs out as she makes her turn around the long line of parked cars. She whips into the parking space and slams on the brakes. They both go forward and are held back tightly by their safety belts.

Remind me never to make her angry again. The pain makes Joe nauseous. They unbuckle themselves and head toward the front doors. Joe pulls out a cart and clutches the handle tightly as a sharp pain goes through him. He stops at the first display of food and pretends to see if he wants anything from there. As he stands looking, the pain begins to subside. Not wanting to tip his hand, Joe pushes his cart slowly away without picking up any items. Soon they come to the produce section.

Joe picks up some salad fixings and a few pieces of fruit. They go down the aisle slowly. Joe reaches in the dairy case and carefully picks up a quart of milk instead of his regular gallon. The pain in his ribs is now just a dull ache. They turn the corner to go to another aisle. Joe picks up a few more items. Their last stop is to pick up the prescription for pain the doctor has called in for Joe.

Soon they are walking out to the checkout stands. Joe quickly scans the rows of cashiers hoping not to run into Sara. To his relief, she is nowhere in sight. With his groceries bagged and paid for, Ann and Joe make their way out of the supermarket and out to her car.

He only bought two bags worth of groceries and has placed them in the trunk of Ann's car.

Soon they arrive at his house. Not soon enough for Joe. He decides he will tell Ann not to walk him to the front door. All he wants to do now is get in and lie down. The ride home has been a silent one, for which he is grateful. Speaking makes his ribs hurt, and he has nothing to say to Ann at this point.

Ann parks besides Joe's car. It was towed and left in the driveway after the incident at Brinkman Hall.

She pops the trunk for Joe. He carefully gets out of her car saying to her, "Thanks, I can take it from here."

Ann sits quietly with the car running as Joe closes the passenger door and picks up his grocery bags from the trunk. Slowly, he pushes the trunk firmly shut. The sound of it engaging brings a sigh of relief to Joe. He makes his way toward the driveway and up to the front door.

The sound of squealing tires can be heard down the street as Ann heads for the nearest fast-food restaurant.

"Temper, temper," he says, as he places the key in the front door and let's himself in. Joe is glad to be home again.

He carries his groceries to the kitchen and puts away the few items needing refrigeration. Much to his surprise, the refrigerator is clean and fully stocked. He then puts away the dry goods.

"Rover, Snowball. Where could they be?"

He goes looking for them. Walking to the bathroom, he finds a large white piece of paper taped to the mirror. It reads as follows:

> Joe,
>
> Hope you don't mind, but I took the liberty of cleaning out your fridge and restocking it. While I was here, a couple of your friends from school came over and made you a few meals and put them in the freezer for you. Tony Watkins said he'd take Rover and Snowball to his place till you get settled in and feeling up to care of them. Well, buddy, you're all set. Let me know if there is anything else I can do for you.
>
> Signed,
> Angelo de Fuego

A feeling of love and gratitude fills Joe's heart. Looking up, he says softly, "Thank you, Lord. You're always there for me."

He goes back to the kitchen and opens the freezer. As he reads the labels on the plastic containers, one of them stands out. Vegetable lasagna.

Wow, is God good. One of my favorites.

He pulls out the container and puts it into the microwave, heating it up. As the microwave hums, he pulls out salad fixings and a Coke. After a couple of minutes he hears the beep go off.

He sets the table, taking in a deep breath filled with the scent of fresh, hot, gooey, cheese sauce and vegetables, making his mouth water. He places his piping hot food on the table and returns for his drink.

Opening the kitchen cabinet, much to his surprise, he finds a loaf of French bread and takes it out.

What's missing? Oh yes, the salad dressing. He settles down for his first home-cooked meal in two weeks. After giving grace and thanks to God for keeping him and Ann safe, he digs into his food with gusto.

After his meal, Joe makes his way to his bedroom. Feeling full and very sleepy, he decides to take a shower then go to bed. The warm water hits his head and runs down his bruised and sore body. He stays under the water for a long time. His muscles now more relaxed and his mind at peace, Joe turns off the water and towels off. He then slips into his favorite pajamas and turns out the light in the bathroom.

Turning down his bed, he lies down and, in his mind, goes through if he has already locked all the windows and doors. Remembering his buddies from school had been there prior to his returning home, and he rests assured all is secured. He knows he locked the front door when he arrived home, he relaxes between the cool, clean sheets. Gently covering himself, he closes his eyes and is soon fast asleep.

His sleep is deep and uninterrupted. Unknown to him, Deceit has come calling. He takes his time in searching Joe's house from top to bottom.

He can feel the presence of something evil. His search has not yet revealed the source of evil that beckons to him.

Deceit decides to stand still and wait for the spiritual being to call to him again. His efforts are soon rewarded. A low pitch sound can be heard coming from outside the house. To Deceit, it sounds like a low hum. He flies out through the wall and doors of the house and out to the shed in the backyard. The closer he gets, the louder and clearer the humming becomes.

Deceit pokes his head through the wall of the shed. His ears scan the shed from side to side, trying to locate the exact location of the humming. The box at the top of the stack is the one he is looking for. A sinister smile forms on his black face. He pulls out the box and opens the game that calls out to him.

He converses with Ouija for a while, responding to the strange hum emanating from the game. When their sinister conversation ends, Deceit walks out of the shed and flies back into Joe's bedroom, gently landing on top of his chest and sits down. He strokes Joe's forehead and speaks a curse over him. Several evil spirits appear at Deceit's call. They attach themselves firmly to Joe as Deceit gives them instructions, then he takes flight toward the end of town according to the information given to him by Ouija.

The sky is partially cloudy, but with a full moon Deceit can see clearly into the back woods. The low sound of drums can be heard. Human forms can be seen dancing around what appears to be an orange, yellowish, red light.

Deceit flies closer to the action alighting on a nearby tree. He sees six people chanting and dancing naked around the light. He has seen this before during the time of the druids. But the dancers, he does not recognize. There are three women and three men. They seem oblivious to his presence. Deceit soon realizes why. He sees hundreds of evil spirits, imps, and demons coming from within the light.

Carefully, he moves in a little closer surveying what is before him. The smell of sulfur is strong. As he moves slowly closer he realizes the campfire is not really a fire at all. The light and smoke coming out from the open earth makes it appear as fire. Deceit realizes it is an open portal or gateway to and from hell itself.

The dancers are an elite group of elders from the dark side. He has seen this happen through the centuries where a human gatekeeper is assigned to the opening and closing of a portal to hell. Deceit watches with great interest as a large figure forms in the middle of the light.

"Oh mighty one, we have called upon you to grant us your great wisdom," Chulda says with much respect and not a little fear.

"You have summoned me and I have heard. What is it you desire to know?" asks Gusion.

"What to do next now that we have seduced Skyler Riggs into seeking your wisdom through us. He has told us he is in our debt, and he is willing to work for us to bring forth Enepsigos.

Skyler Riggs has been led into thinking his deceased mother, Ingrid Riggs, was speaking to him. We have done what you have told us to do. Skyler Riggs was very impressed with the information you gave us about him. He believes it is by our own power and wisdom that we brought his mother back from the dead to speak with him."

"You have done well. This is what I want you to do next," says Gusion, the fallen angel who's ability is to discern the past, present, and future.

They all remain perfectly still, and each dancer makes mental notes of what Gusion is telling Chulda. A few minutes later, Chulda bows deeply and Gusion seemly disappears back into the fiery-looking pit, but in reality, he heads skyward.

She remains with her forehead touching the ground for a few moments and then she gets up and puts on her robe. The others follow suit. They all walk back to the house in silence and make their way to the sitting room. There, they all take their place at the table. Chulda discusses with each of them what their part in this assignment is, and each one has been assigned imps, demons, and fallen angels to complete their task.

With that settled, they change into their clothes and hand their robes to the man servant standing at the door. They all head for their own homes. It is three o'clock in the morning. Fatigued, Chulda goes up the stairs to the second floor and walks back to the master bedroom where tonight she will sleep soundly.

Deceit pokes his head in from the corner of the sitting room. He alights on top of the table and thinks on the events he has been witness to this evening.

"What good luck to have stumbled upon this information. First, the board game who called to me and told me where to go into the woods and now this. I owe you big, Ouija," says Deceit.

I must go and search out this gateway again. I can certainly learn more to aid me in my quest, thinks Deceit, as he flies through the ceiling past the second floor and out the roof. He heads back into the woods behind the mansion and sniffs out the gateway to hell. As he draws closer, he can still see some smoke from the fading light from where the gateway was opened. Sniffing around until the repugnant order of sulfur is strongest, he makes note of where the gateway is and heads into the night.

16

Joe sleeps through the night and well into the morning, unaware of what has its sharp claws firmly attached to him. He lies in bed resting comfortably and slowly opens his eyes. He feels an odd sensation of a familiar presence surrounding him, but can't quite pinpoint why it is. The presence is oddly comforting, so he does not give it another thought.

Stretching slowly, his muscles relax. Careful not to overdo, he stands to his feet moving carefully over to his back window. He pulls open the window, marveling at the beauty of the midday sun as it shines on the leaves of the trees. He opens the window completely.

"Finally, a week all to myself at home without any place to go. Oh, that's right," he says with a sigh, "got to make a follow-up appointment with the doc."

Not one to procrastinate, Joe dutifully looks into his wallet and pulls out the doctor's card.

"Dr. Morgan's office," says a pleasant young voice over the phone.

"Hello, my name is Joe Austin, and I need to make a follow-up appointment with Dr. Morgan, please. I just got released from the hospital."

"Yes, Mr. Austin. How about Wednesday at 1:00 p.m.?" asks the voice pleasantly.

"That would be fine," replies Joe, as he notes it on his bedside calendar.

"Anything I need to bring with me?" he asks.

"No, we have your records here from the hospital."

"We'll see you at 1:00 p.m. on Wednesday."

"Thank you," replies Joe, as he hangs up.

That being done, he heads to the bathroom and closes the door. An hour later he emerges clean, shaven, and in his old Levi's and an even older shirt.

"Rover, Snowflake," he calls out, wondering where they went off to. Then he remembers Tony has had them since he went into the hospital. "I hope they don't cause him any problems," he thinks aloud.

Joe decides to pour himself a bowl of cereal and a glass of grape juice. His jaw is still a little sore, and he figures the cereal will be soggy enough to eat if he waits long enough. He walks to the back porch and places his food on the table. Pulling out a chair, he sits down slowly. While he waits for his cereal to soften, he pulls out his cell phone and calls Angelo de Fuego first. The call goes straight to voice mail.

"Hey, Angelo, I wanted to thank you for all your help during the ruckus at Brinkman Hall and also for the food. Thanks, buddy. You're a real friend and I appreciate it."

He hangs up and calls Tony Watkins. Tony picks up on the third ring.

"Hey, Tony, this is Joe."

"Hey, Joe, how you feeling? Anything I can do for you?" asks Tony, genuinely wanting to know.

"No, thanks. I'm doing pretty well for my first day at home you know? How's Rover and Snowflake? They aren't giving you any problems are they?" Joe asks, a bit concerned.

"No, they're doing fine. They're both pretty mellow. I know they miss you. But I think its best they stay with me till the end of the week. That's if you don't mind, of course."

"Nooo. I'm feeling pretty good, but I think its best you keep them till next week. Thanks a million, you're a good friend. I know you're in class, so I'll let you go. Thanks again." Joe hangs up promptly.

"Oh man, I forgot to tell him to thank the others for me. I think I'll just text him," Joe says aloud.

Then he proceeds to do just that and asks for the names of the people who have helped. He leans back on the chair, closes his eyes, and starts to hum a very familiar sound.

"Ohm, ohm, ohm," he hums as he drifts back into the past. The dark forces attached to him, egg him on, with very little resistance. Joe has already taken his pain medication, and he is an easy target for the familiar spirits. His mind and heart are becoming more accustomed to them and to what they are revealing to him.

At one time, he was so comfortable with their presence; he would call on them fairly regularly for guidance. That is until he got born again. But like any bad habit, if you don't denounce and lose all contact with the old, it will latch itself back onto you as a tick on a dog's back. You may want to scratch it and try to rub it away, but without proper help the fleas remain and evidently take hold and repopulate.

17

Mr. Tingly stands behind his desk looking out the window across the campus. Some of the flowers are in bloom and the trees are losing their blossoms and sprouting shiny, new leaves. The grass has grown to the point where it looks like a lush, thick, green carpet in need of a good mowing. Spring is in the air at last and none too soon for him.

Since moving to get away from the frigid cold winter of the Canadian Rockies, Mr. Tingly has thoroughly enjoyed the four seasons here. It is much to his liking in most ways. The college where he works as a professor is medium in size. He can move about freely without everyone knowing his business, not to mention his affiliations.

Yet it is small enough to keep a good ear and eye out for who is into the occult and new age movement. His cover is well hidden, even though he teaches a bit too much on ancient and present occult religions. His excuse to those who ask him why he does not teach on Christianity as much as the occult ones is, he has so often stated, "To understand Christianity today, one must fully study the religions of the past and present who oppose it."

His answer has worked very well, most of the time, but there are those pesky born-again, fundamentalist Christians who are not so easily appeased. Much to his concern, the few Christians he has had dealings with have proven quite a challenge. Even though they are in the majority, most prefer to complain about the state they find the world in instead of standing up for what they know to be right and to fight for it.

"Ohhh, if they only knew the power they have and authority they possess, I'd either be forced out of town or would join them gladly. They do make a very convincing argument," Mr. Tingly says out loud.

A shiver runs up his spine at the thought of how close one particular student came to convincing him to turn from his evil ways and turn to the one true God.

Joe Austin was one of his students just a few years back before he entered college. Even though he was a new Christian, Joe would attend seminars on the occult during the summer. When asked why he was attending the classes in the occult, Joe replied, "I figure I need to know my enemy and his ways well so I can fight them."

Mr. Tingly found this to be true of most of these young Christian students.

Don't they know that they are playing with fire? It's as if they were young children taught to hide under a bed or in a closet when fire breaks out instead of running out the house at the first notice of smoke or fire.

I best keep an eye out on young Joe Austin. That kid is a born leader. Question is, how do I win him back? He'll have to be seduced back into the occult carefully. After the incident at Brinkman Hall, I thought for sure he would be tempted to fight unholy fire with unholy fire. Too bad, Peter Warren decided to quit my classes. Oh well, he served his purpose.

He hears a knock on the door of his office, which breaks his train of thought. He turns and walks over to open the door. Being somewhat of a cautious man, he asks, "Who is it?"

"Just me, Chulda. May I come in?"

Without saying a word he opens the door and is greeted with a big smile.

"Hello, Chulda, please do come in," says Mr. Tingly pleasantly.

A small framed, young woman with her thick, dark, shoulder-length hair pulled back into a pony tail walks in past Tingly. He turns and closes the door behind him and walks up to her and nods his head slightly. Chulda nods her head as well and says as she motions with her hand to a couple of chairs in front of Mr. Tingly's desk, "Shall we sit?"

Deceit finds this very strange indeed.

"She looks very familiar. Very much like the young woman in the woods behind the mansion. But of course with her clothes on, she does look like the cashier at the grocery store where Joe Austin shops for groceries. Even though she's wearing a cashier's smock with the supermarket's name embroidered on it and a name tag clipped to her collar with the name Sara printed in bold, black letters. Who pays attention to a face when there is so much more to look at," says Deceit, licking his lips.

"So, she's Chulda, the human gatekeeper, masquerading as a cashier at the local supermarket," says Deceit loudly.

Deceit steps back deeper into the shelves lined with books in Mr. Tingly's office. Completely hidden from view, Deceit waits silently for the two to speak.

She's the gatekeeper. She's not only able to open and close portals at will, but she can summon some of the most powerful fallen angels and demons I've heard of. The thought of this makes Deceit giddy with delight.

So she's the one responsible for the possession of Peter Warren at Brinkman Hall. I wonder what she's up to now. Deceit focuses in on the conversation as they discuss Skyler Riggs.

"So that's why I was assigned to Joe Austin and Skyler Riggs. The two are planning to set Joe up to fall and use him to lead other Christians in Tingly's classes to follow suit. This will strengthen the powers and principalities that are currently a stronghold over this state," Deceit softly mumbles.

"Oh!" he says aloud, as he falls backwards with unrestrained joy. Falling head over heels through the wall and into the office of Janice Simmons, he lands on his back on top of Professor Janice Simmons's desk.

She has just finished her classes for the day and is now sitting back in her well-worn, swivel chair. Her eyes are closed, and she is snoring loudly.

Deceit sits up and looks over at her. Her mouth hangs open as drool travels down the side of her chin and makes its way slowly down her neck and onto her blouse.

Deceit then turns over on all fours and crawls around the desk looking for what he suspects has caused her to fall into such deep sleep. He pokes his head over the edge of the desk and sees an empty bottle of vodka lying on the floor next to her.

"Huh," says Deceit out loud. "If I had to teach on women's issues, I'd drink too."

Deceit pushes off gently from the desk and flies back into the common wall of Simmons's and Tingly's offices. He stops short of the book spines and cocks his head to better hear the conversation between Tingly and Chulda.

"Well, I guess that does it," says Chulda with a sigh. "I've got to get back to work. I work late today."

"By all means, please don't let me keep you," Mr. Tingly replies with a smile. Chulda picks up her purse and heads for the door and waits for Tingly to open it for her.

"It sounds like a very good plan," he says, as he opens the door.

With a smile, he waves good-bye to Chulda as she walks down the hall and out of the building. Mr. Tingly leans up against the door frame momentarily, and with a quick shake of his head, he smiles and turns off the light, closing the door to his office behind him and locking it. He whistles as he makes his way out of the building.

"What the hell?" says Deceit, surprised at how short the meeting was between Chulda and Tingly.

"Damn it, I missed every important thing they said."

He turns angrily and goes back through the wall and into Janice Simmons's office. Flying over to her, he sticks his fingers into her head and whispers into her ear.

"I expect to hear some good news about you tomorrow," he says, as he violently kicks her in the head. Janice Simmons shakes her head violently as her troubled dream continues. Then Deceit flies through her office door and out the building.

Backbiter stares at her for a moment, shaking his head slowly and says, "What a waste."

He also flies out of the building, following the light puffs of smoke Deceit has left in his wake.

"Lucky for me, Deceit's wounds on his backside are not completely healed, and kicking the woman in the head has reopened them again. Without the puffs of smoke to follow, I would have had to return to your favorite hiding place and wait for you to return. Well, at least I heard everything Chulda and Tingly said. I must admit, it is a good plan," says Backbiter, as he follows Deceit back to Joe's house.

Joe is sitting on his bed in the lotus position softly chanting his old mantra. Deceit flies in through the open window and lands gently on the floor in front of Joe. Backbiter follows Deceit at a safe distance and slips into Joe's bedroom wall and into the headboard. Backbiter watches as Deceit sniffs around the room. He smells the faint odor of sulfur, but he cannot see the demons that he has assigned to Joe. Unbeknownst to Deceit, they have just left and are headed into town. Deceit returns to Joe after searching the entire house for the others. Anger begins to rise in him.

"Where are those fools? I told them to stay close to Joe Austin and make sure he returns to his old cultish ways," Deceit says aloud, his eyes bright with anger.

"You can't trust anyone nowadays. Why I remember back in the day, the only one I couldn't corrupt was Noah and his family. A lousy six people was all that was left of the humans on earth. The rest of the world had turned to their many false gods, perverse, lustful, wicked, and exceedingly violent ways. One could count on all the powers of darkness back then. Not like today. Good help is truly hard to find, as the humans are so fond of saying," says Deceit in disgust.

"Shoot, come to think of it, it's kind of funny. We can all fill the rest of eternity with speaking clichés to each other. We'll have one hell of a good ole time doing it too. I know where I'm going, and if I have anything to do about it, Tingly and all the rest of these sorry, pathetic humans I've had the pleasure of helping to kill, steal from, and destroy will be joining me," says Deceit.

"Oh brother, we've got a regular comedian here," says Backbiter, as he realizes that he too has picked up human speech patterns, as well as Deceit.

Realizing he has picked up more clichés from the humans than he thought, Deceit reprimands himself.

Backbiter lets out a howl of laughter. Deceit hears it and stands quietly, his ears focusing on where the laughter is coming from. Backbiter stops laughing and sinks deeper into the wall. Deceit sniffs the air again, while Backbiter quickly backs out of the wall and shoots skyward.

Deceit loses the faint smell of sulfur. He growls slightly hoping to flush out any imps that might be hanging around. Since he neither sees nor smells anyone, Deceit returns to Joe's bedroom, but he too has gone.

"Now where did he go?" says Deceit with growing frustration, letting out a string of profanities.

"Well, I guess I'll see how Skyler Riggs is doing. Surely, he should be home by now, being its six thirty-five in the evening."

Deceit flies over Skyler's house and circles around it. He doesn't see any lights burning and notes all the curtains are closed. With trepidation, he flies into the house and searches for Skyler or whomever may be home, spirit or human. Nothing or no one can be found.

"Oh, this can't be good," he says, as he continues to search the last room of Skyler's house. He even checks the cabinets in the kitchen, hoping to find the evil spirits he has assigned to Joe. They might be there.

Deceit sticks his nose in the air and sniffs again. He notes a different scent emanating from Skyler's bedroom. It smells like lilacs. The scent is rather pleasant. He struggles to remember where he first smelled this scent, then it hits him.

"Ingrid Riggs or shall I say, Enepsigos!" he shouts. "That's who was here. But why did he come here? I didn't hear anyone saying there would be another séance. Especially here in Skyler's own house. That would certainly not be a wise thing for him to do. If Jason and Mary Riggs would catch him having a séance, Skyler would surely pay dearly for it. Something I know he doesn't want."

Deceit scratches his head and wonders what is going on. Fear begins to slowly come over him like a cold, body trying to give him a bear hug. His legs begin to shake and is momentarily stuck to the floor. With great effort, he fights the effects of the spirit of fear and heads up through the ceiling, zigzagging his way up into the atmosphere. He flies east as fast as he can, hoping to lose fear.

He finds an active satellite and hides behind it, vigilantly keeping a look out for anyone else that might be following him. All night long, he sees demons, imps, and angels—both good and evil—fly back and forth from heaven to earth. His heart pounds furiously at the thought he is having. To his surprise, he begins to regret that he had ever left the original assignment from the moment he was created to follow after Satan.

Cowering behind the satellite for the third time in his existence, Deceit begins to cry. With much wailing and gnashing of teeth, Deceit implores the angel Gabriel to give the Most High God a message from him.

"Please, in His great mercy, if He can find it in His heart to forgive me and let me return to my former state, I will serve him faithfully for all the rest of eternity."

As before, Gabriel answers him with a resounding no. Deceit curls up on the satellite and cries till there is no more strength left in him. There he stays until morning. Knowing there is no hope from escaping his final fate, he resolves to take down as many humans as he can. First from God's protection, then into hell and finally, into the Lake of fire— evil's final stop for all eternity. He stands up on the satellite and strengthens himself with the thought that he can at least take a few more thousand souls into hell with him before the final and terrible day of the Lord. Deceit heads for town formulating a plan as he goes.

Backbiter follows Deceit at a safe distance. He too has been having regrets, but none like last night when he saw and heard Deceit cry out to the Most High God for mercy and receiving none. He too resolves to cause as much havoc and misery to the humans as he possibly can. All of the forces of evil know, without doubt, where their final destination will be.

Rarely do Deceit and Backbiter see any of Satan's followers imploring the Lord to forgive them and take them back to when they were created, but none have been forgiven, even though they carefully seek it. After all, they all were made with a will of their own and did chose to follow after Lucifer. But they did follow after their own desires and left their first station only to have millions of years to live in regret. Havoc, hunger, and thirst plague them, never finding satisfaction even though they seek it always.

Backbiter decides to make Deceit pay for what he has gone through this night. It had been a millennium since he had felt such sadness and remorse. But because he followed orders and spied on Deceit he is suffering much now.

"He'll pay for making me feel this way again. I swear it by my lord, Satan," Backbiter says vengefully. "He will pay heavily."

18

He follows Deceit back into town and back to Joe Austin's house again. Joe has been pacing for half an hour in front of Mr. Tingly's house. His stomach feels like a tennis ball being batted back and forth. He rubs his sweaty hands on his jeans.

"Come on, Joe, make up your mind. Either you do this or you don't. It's up to you," says Joe angrily, as he continues to pace. A young boy walking his dog passes by Joe, looking up at him with caution and concern.

"Hi, kid," says Joe, sounding more like a predator than a friend. The young boy's frown deepens as he says to his dog, "Come on, Spike. Let's go home."

The young boy senses evil surrounding Joe and carefully turns back to look and see if he is following him. Spike's fur stands on end as he turns back occasionally to growl at Joe.

"Come on, boy, let's keep going," says the young boy, as they walk to the end of the block and turns right at the corner.

Like a ton of bricks hitting him, Joe realizes that this little boy and his dog sense the evil near him. Joe slowly starts to walk to his car as nausea begins to increase as he thinks of what he was just about to do.

Headlights catch his attention. He sees Mr. Tingly's car coming down the street. As if he were a man being chased by rabid dogs, Joe runs across the street to his car. With shaking hands, he unlocks the driver's car door and quickly slips into the driver's seat. He begins to panic as Mr. Tingly's car approaches at a slow pace. Joe speeds away.

By now, Mr. Tingly's car is turning into the driveway of his house. The garage door opens, and Tingly drives in unaware Joe is the one in the car that sped by him a moment ago.

He says out loud, "Kids, they ought to not be allowed to get a driver's permit or license until they turn twenty-one."

Mr. Tingly's mind was on the conversation he and Chulda have just had a scant half hour ago. He shuts off his car and opens the door exiting with his briefcase in hand.

Unbeknownst to Joe, Tingly does not know what kind of car he drives. Besides, Tingly now has bigger things to concern himself with. He thinks about his conversation with Chulda and says, "How extraordinary, the plan is brilliant."

Joe heads back home, driving recklessly. Something he does not normally do.

"Joe, get a hold of yourself before you kill yourself or someone else," he says angrily.

Taking a deep breath, he pulls over to the side of the street. With his hand firmly gripping the steering wheel, Joe hangs his head, partially in regret of how he was just driving and partially at the realization of just how far he has fallen back into his old ways. His spirit feels the conviction of what he was just about to do. Repenting, he searches his heart for the reason he has returned into his old way of thinking. After much reflection, he realizes his need to truly delve deeper into his motives and his heart.

Taking a hold of himself, he turns the car around and carefully drives away and heads for his place of solitude. It is a small lake thirty miles from town.

Deceit has had no luck in locating Joe. Backbiter has returned to keep an eye on Deceit. The day is almost spent, as well as Joe's and Backbiter's emotions. Backbiter has had a full day of frustration and disappointment. He knows he has failed off and on in his service to Lucifer. He has seldom, in the millions of years of his existence, felt the way he has. Since watching Deceit and his pathetic display of raw emotions, Backbiter has never felt so angered and tortured as he is now.

Joe is also feeing badly at this time. He arrives at the lake he remembers fondly. As a young child, his father would take him up here during the summer for a day of fishing and boating. Just the boys' day out, no girls allowed.

Here is where Joe gave himself over completely to the Lord. This has been his favorite place to be alone and reflect on all his problems. Joy, sorrow, and just everyday life. It is late in the afternoon when he arrives. He parks his car in the usual spot. Being that school will soon be out for the summer and it is only Tuesday, there are but a few people here. Joe sits in his car looking out over the expanse of the shimmering lake that is before him.

His thoughts are clouded with a sense of foreboding that he is unable to shake. The evil spirits assigned to him by Deceit have all but gone their separate ways, all except for one.

He is the smallest, yet the craftiest of them all. His name is Denial. It does not take much to blind a human into thinking that they are right and everyone else is wrong. Denial comes masquerading as many things such as pride, false humility, self-righteousness and his favorite, hard heartedness.

With these things going for Denial, he can come and mislead even the most righteous of Christians, thereby making it easy to mislead and beguile anyone whose heart has been hardened by pride, hurt, and lust, just to name a few. Joe has proven to be like any other human he has ever encountered.

Given the right circumstances, the mightiest of them all will succumb to Denial. For example, King David, who the Most High God called "a man after my own heart."

Now if there were anyone you would think would be free of denial, it would be him. But alas, we know from Scripture he falls and falls hard. One wonders if King David can fall, what chance does the rest of humanity have? That is the beauty of this.

Deceit and Denial have worked together for a millennium. That is why Denial has stuck close to Joe Austin. Denial knows just what type of demon Deceit is and what power he has been endowed with. Unfortunately for Deceit, Denial has a stake in this assignment as well.

Nothing is what it appears to be in the service of Satan. True, they do follow after their new master, but unlike the Most High God, there are always hidden agendas on the dark side. But alas, we digress.

Joe gets out of the car and walks to the edge of the lake. He stands there admiring the handiwork of the Lord. The sun is reflecting off the clear, cool surface of the water, while a clean, crisp breeze caresses Joe's face. The water ripples slightly as the breeze flows gently across it, causing the water to sparkle as if there were a million faceted diamonds showing off the brilliant colors of the rainbow.

Joe sits down and takes off his shoes and socks, putting his feet into the water. His first reaction is to pull his feet out quickly being the water is very cold to the touch, but like with anything else, Joe gets used to it and eventually begins to enjoy it.

His feet rub against the sand and the smooth stones as the water ripples up against the cuffs of his pants. Slightly irritated, Joe folds his pants up to his knees, his thoughts drifts back again into the deep recesses of his heart.

The sunset is magnificent. The colors of chrisom, yellow, and orange make a wonderful backdrop to the pine trees that line the shore. Joe has not been at peace like this in many months. He knows there is something he still needs to rid himself of, but he is not quite ready to do so.

Excuse after excuse rears its ugly head as Joe reflects on his actions of the past few months. His mind will not admit to the fact that this really makes no sense as to why he keeps going back to his old ways. Could it be that he is in denial and that he is using the death of his parents as an excuse to revisit his old ways?

"Come on, Joe, you know that your parents weren't meant to die in a crash that night. They were supposed to be alive and well to see you get married and have children and then to die of old age," Denial says gently to Joe.

"No, that can't be. Only the Lord can allow death to come when and where He deems it necessary. But maybe you're right, they shouldn't have died. They were much too young and full of life," replies Joe, not realizing he is speaking with Denial and not having a conversation with himself.

"Yes, they were. That is why you have to seek the spirits of truth. They will enlighten you as to what you need to do now. Being that your parents left this world prematurely, they have left a lot of work undone. Therefore, it is up to you to seek the spirits and find out what they were meant to do and you must do it for them," says Denial in a most convincing way.

"Yeah, that's right. They did leave a lot left undone. Dad did always say that at the end of your life, you should have completed your task for the Lord. So I do need to find out what they were supposed to finish and do it for them."

Joe stands up quickly, picking up his shoes and socks. He walks back to his car and unlocks the driver's side door and gets in. Taking his shoes and socks, he shakes them out and puts them on. After, he unrolls his wet and cold cuffed pants. Starting up his car, Joe backs up and heads for home, leaving Denial to keep up with him.

19

Mr. Tingly walks toward his office building only to meet with a couple of police cars and the coroner's van. Confused as to what is going on, he stops to talk with a police officer who is just finishing taking statements from several students and faculty members. Before he can speak with the officer, Mr. Tingly is distracted by the coroner's assistants who are pushing a gurney to the coroner's van.

The body of the former Janice Simmons lies hidden inside the black body bag which lies strapped down on the gurney.

They open the back door of the van and not so gently push the gurney in the open doors. The assistant jumps in the back with the body, and the coroner and his other assistant go up to the front and drive away. Several of the students and a couple of the faculty members are weeping openly. Mr. Tingly turns back to the officer.

"Excuse me, sir, what's just happened here?" asks Tingly, thinking it may have been a shooting since there have been so many of late throughout the country.

"When the janitor came in last night to clean the offices, he found the body of Janice Simmons dead at her desk."

Taken aback, Mr. Tingly does not respond for a few moments. "Was it foul play or natural causes?" he asks, trying to grasp the news.

"Well, as of right now, we don't know for sure, but the coroner's office will advise us as to the cause of death as soon as the autopsy is done."

"Oh," is all a bewildered Mr. Tingly can get out. He stands there trying to figure out what could have been the cause of her death.

She seemed to be relatively healthy. But I did smell alcohol on her breath from time to time. Maybe she passed out and hit her head on something and died, thinks Tingly as he makes his way to his office.

He stops a few feet away from his office where the police are finishing their examination of Janice Simmons's office.

They place yellow police tape in front of the door and nod politely to Mr. Tingly as he stares in unbelief at the site before him. He then continues slowly to his own office door, unlocks it and goes in. He walks over to his desk and sits down.

The message light on his phone is blinking. He stares at it for several minutes, too numb to do much of anything but sit. A loud knock on his door startles him back into reality.

It is Coach Saunders wanting to talk with him. But before Mr. Tingly can say a word, Coach Saunders is already through the door and halfway to his desk.

"Morning, Tingly. I wanted to see if you had heard about Ms. Simmons," says Coach Saunders loudly. He had known Ms. Simmons for several years and had become good friends.

Confusion and pain are written all over Coach Saunders's face. Without being asked, Coach Saunders pulls out a chair and sits himself down. Mr. Tingly, surprised at his own actions, pulls out a chair next to him and sits down.

"Do you know who found her?" asks Coach Saunders, knowing Mr. Tingly would know less than he does, but nevertheless, needing to ask anyway.

"No, no, I don't. I just got here myself a just a couple of minutes ago. I talked to the police when I got here, and they said an autopsy would have to be done in order to find out how she died," replies Mr. Tingly, unaware that he did not answer the question.

"Who found the body?" asks Coach again, seeming to need an answer.

"Oh, sorry. It was Charlie, the janitor. He was cleaning up last night, and when he came in to clean Janice's office, he found her dead, sitting on her chair. At first, he thought she was asleep. Then when she failed to answer him, he went over to her and found she was dead. He was the one who notified the police. Poor guy, I can just imagine what he must've felt when he realized she was dead."

By this time, Coach Saunders is not listening; instead, he has his hands over his face and is sobbing. Mr. Tingly, moved by compassion at seeing this man, who to him, is the image of strength and character, Mr. Tingly pulls his chair closer to the coach and puts his arms around him, saying nothing.

"Well, this is quite a site," says Deceit sarcastically, as he sits in the middle of Mr. Tingly's desk.

"Next thing you know, you'll both be putting on dresses and prancing about like silly women seeking to find consolation in each other's arms. Booh, hoo, hoo, you big babies. Every one of you has to die sooner or later. Humans, they cry over spilt milk. But over their sins, not even one tear of regret," says Deceit, who happened to see the commotion on campus as he was making his way back to Joe's house.

"I told that stupid woman, one more drink wasn't going to hurt her, but I lied. Now look at her. A rotting bag of flesh on her premature way to hell. See you there!" says Deceit with much contempt. He then flies up and out of the building and back over to Joe's house in hopes that he is finally there.

Joe sits in front of the television as he sips his morning cup of coffee. As usual, he is listening to the morning news. He leans forward with the cup still in hand as he hears the news of the death of Janice Simmons. Joe sits quietly, not hearing anything else, only the words repeating themselves in his mind, sudden death of Janice Simmons.

Joe had met her several times and found her to be a very pleasant woman. He had heard rumors of her being an alcoholic, but he never believed them. They were just rumors. *Poor woman, she seemed to be doing so well,* thinks Joe, as he sips his coffee.

"What is this world coming to?" he says aloud.

"Yes, what is this world coming to," Deceit says mockingly. "The end!" he yells.

"Humans, you're all idiots. You can't see the forest for the trees," he says in disgust, as he flies around the room mumbling to himself.

The phone rings. Putting down his cup, he spills some of the coffee on the table. He pulls his cell phone from his shirt pocket and answers it. It is Angelo de Fuego. He is calling to advise Joe of the tragic death of Janice Simmons. They discuss what they think might have been the cause of death.

"How are you doing?" asks Angelo.

"Oh man, my mind is whirling. I've just had a lot going on. When you have time to think, your mind tends to go wild," says Joe wistfully.

"You know, I'm here if you need to talk about anything bothering you."

"I know. It's something I have to deal with on my own."

"Well, if you feel that way, okay. I still think it would be better for you if you would discuss this with me."

"Discuss what with you? How would you know I need to discuss anything with you?" asks Joe defensively.

"I'm just saying you can always talk to me. I'll let you go. If you need anything or decide you want to talk after all, give me a call. That's what I'm here for."

Angelo hangs up the phone leaving Joe to ponder, if somewhat irritably, about what Angelo has just said.

"Huh, he thinks he knows it all. Well, you don't. And don't call me, I'll call you," yells Joe into all air.

"Ohhh, trouble in paradise? Now, now, boys, there will be no fighting unless I start it," says Deceit with a smirk on his face.

Hmm, I think I'll go and look up this Angelo de Fuego character and see what I can find out. Sounds like I can use him to cause some trouble here, thinks Deceit as he heads out of Joe's house and into the atmosphere.

20

"Did you hear what happened to Ms. Simons?" asks Christine of Courtney, as they make their way to their first class.

"Yes, I did. Do you know what she died of?" asks Courtney.

"No, I heard she passed out and hit her head and died. There was a lot of blood when Charlie the janitor found her. They said he got so sick, he threw up all over the place."

"Oh, yuck! How disgusting. Who told you that?" asks Courtney, not believing anything Christine has said.

"You know, them, the ones who saw Charlie talking to the police. He found her late last night. But they just took her body out this morning.

"Thing is, she was already beginning to smell when they took her to the mortuary this morning," says Christine.

"Ye gads, Christine, you're always exaggerating. Can't you stop at least this one time? I'm sure the dean will call an assembly to let us know what happened. You know, Brittney had a class with her. I wonder how she's doing. I better call her and find out," says Courtney with genuine concern for her friend.

"See you later," she says, as she walks to her first morning class. She opens her purse and pulls out her cell phone and dials Brittney's number. Immediately, the call goes to voice mail.

"Hi, Brittney, this is Courtney. I suppose you already heard about Ms. Simmons. I just called to find out how you're doing. I know you had a class with her, and that she was one of your favorite teachers. Give me a call to let me know how you're doing and if you need anything. Love you." Courtney hangs up and walks into class.

———

A tall form stands motionless next to the refrigerator as he listens to all Tingly is saying, taking note of the when, where, why, and how the plan—Phase Three: the Downfall—will be executed. The tall form follows Tingly as he goes from room to room, thinking out loud.

He returns to his home office library and sits behind his desk to type up his notes from his meeting with Chulda. The invisible form moves quickly behind him and peers over his shoulder. Tingly opens a new document on his home computer and titles it, Phase Three: the Downfall. As accurately and quickly as any professional typist, Tingly gets the plan down in neat, reasonable, and understandable form.

The being reads every word being typed and makes accurate note of every detail. Click, click, click is the only sound heard as Tingly's fingers fly across the keyboard.

Deceit is reading all that is being typed as well, but from a safe distance. He is hoping he has not been spotted by the other spirit that stands behind Tingly reading as well.

Tingly prints out the phase three plan and makes six copies, gathering them up and divides them neatly into stacks of three pages each and staples them, putting each one in a large, white envelope being careful not to fold the papers. He licks each envelope and seals them. With a sense of satisfaction and relief, Tingly places all six envelopes into his briefcase and locks it.

"I hope Tingly hurries up and gets out of here soon, I'm getting bored," says Deceit, as he goes into the bathroom unseen.

"Well, Damian, ole boy, it's time to eat dinner. Now where shall I go? I deserve a celebratory meal," he says cheerfully.

He walks over to his bathroom and checks himself out in the mirror. Tingly stands staring into the mirror thinking of what effect the phase three plan will do to the community. Deceit is floating just behind him, both staring at each other in the mirror. Deceit slowly floats down to the floor, with his stomach sinking down to his feet.

With his lips quivering, he manages to say, "I'm just a figment of your imagination."

He is too frightened to move. All he can think about is what Amon is going to do to him for allowing himself to be seen by a human, especially one like Tingly.

"Presentable," says Tingly with a smile, as he looks himself up and down in the full-length mirror that is fastened to the back of the bathroom door.

"Steak and lobster it is."

With that, he opens the bathroom door and goes out into the living room. Picking up his suit jacket and keys from the ashtray on the table top next to the front door, he heads out to the garage. As the garage door opens, it reveals a beautiful sunset.

A slight breeze lifts the scents of the evening up to his face. He fills his lungs with the cool, fragrant air and gets into his car and drives out onto the street. With a press of the garage door opener, the door closes smoothly as he drives into the evening, humming to his favorite aria.

The tall figure disappears up into the heavens in a flash of light. It goes at the speed of light. He will meet with others like himself, and together, they will report to the Lord of Hosts.

Deceit sits mumbling to himself still stunned and still unable to move. Backbiter, having had enough of this nonsense, walks over to him and slaps him hard across the face, then again on the other cheek. This time, he sends Deceit rolling halfway across the bathroom floor.

Shocked by the second hard blow to the face, Deceit shakes his head to clear it. Angry, he stands up and looks around for whomever struck him. Not seeing anyone, he stands up and flies around the house looking for Tingly and the spirit he had seen looking over Tingly's shoulder.

He figured it was him that had struck him, and he was going to return the favor. Not finding him nor Tingly, his courage begins to build.

"Why I'm going to slap that infernal demon to the other side of eternity when I find him. Why I'm going to slap him right in front of Amon and all the others to show him he can't do this to me and get away with it. I pity anyone who dares to stop me."

"Blah, blah, blah. You big wind bag. Shut up and get over it. Amon should promote me for all this nonsense I have to put up with," says Backbiter, as he sinks back into the wall.

"Well, that fool of a human must have gone to dinner. I think I'll see what Joe Austin is up to."

Deceit flies out through the roof in a flash, Backbiter following him at a discreet distance.

21

Samantha drives slowly past Skyler's house and parks in front of another house. It is 4:30 a.m. She leans over to pick up her cat, Blackheart, and leaves the car carrying him.

"Okay, baby, I'm going to leave you here. You know what to do. I'll be back for you after I pick up Mia. When you're done, come and wait for me in front of the house. Did you get that?" asks Samantha, as she places her cat down on the sidewalk and points to Skyler's house.

Blackheart meows as if it understands and walks toward Skyler's house.

Mia is waiting anxiously in front of her house for the arrival of her friend, Samantha. She wastes no time in getting in the car and asks, "Did you do it?"

"Yes, of course, I did. I'm not a novice, you know. That's why I was picked to do this, remember?"

"Okay, okay, point made. Now let's get out of here."

They head out to Chulda's house. Upon arriving, they see a couple of police cars and several uniformed officers going around the grounds, while others in plain clothes go in and out of Chulda's house. Before they can drive away, they are stopped by a uniformed policeman who stands in front of their car.

"Please turn your car off and come with me, both of you."

"What do you want from us? We haven't done anything wrong," says Samantha, as she and Mia get out of the car.

"Please, step this way," says the police officer, as he escorts the two into Chulda's house. Inside there are more officers who are packing up boxes with papers and various other things and loading evidence into a police van.

"Hello, I'm Sergeant Mike Greer. I need to ask you a few questions. Mind coming with me please," he says with authority, as he leads them into the sitting room.

An uneasy feeling comes over the two women as they follow Sergeant Greer into the sitting room and take a seat at the table.

Sergeant Greer gives them a look which makes Samantha wish she had not said anything. Sergeant Greer pulls out a chair and sits down. With his pen and notepad in hand, he takes a moment to look at the two pretty faces before him.

"Now, what's your name," he asks Mia, who by now is ready to spill all she knows.

"Mia Allred," she says, her voice tense with fear.

"How do you know Ms. Cunningham?" he asks.

Mia feels Samantha stepping on her foot. Frowning, she looks intently down at the table and takes a moment together her thoughts before she answers.

"Why did you come here?" Sergeant Greer asks impatiently.

"We had a lunch date," she answers with a smile.

Samantha lets out a heavy sigh and looks away in disgust.

"You always met at six in the morning for lunch?" asks Greer.

"Um, no, we're supposed to have lunch today, but she asked us to come early. She wanted to discuss something with us."

"Oh, is that so. When did she call you?"

"Last night about seven or eight, right?' she asks, looking at Samantha in hopes of sounding truthful.

"Yes, yes, I'd say about that time," replies Samantha.

"We needed to discuss something, so since we already made plans to meet for lunch, she thought we should come early, and we could catch up then," repeats Mia, sounding nervous.

"Look here," says Samantha, a bit too forceful for Sergeant Greer's taste.

"What do you want with us? We haven't done anything wrong. Either you tell us why all these questions or let us go."

"Okay, ladies, you can go for now. We'll be in touch with you."

They all get up. Samantha and Mia hurry out to their car. Sgt. Greer motions to Officer Steve Logan and says, "Steve, keep an eye on those two and report back to me. You know the drill."

"Sure thing, Sarge," replies Officer Logan, as he hurries to his unmarked police car and follows after the two women.

22

Skyler is soon asleep. He begins to dream, a very troubling dream where he is walking down a long winding path that is marked with signs on both sides of the path. They are very inviting indeed. As he draws closer to one of the signs, he feels a tug on his arm. A seductive female voice is telling him he should follow his heart and let go and come with her. Her voice is silky smooth and very appealing. But Skyler feels apprehensive about this. He stands peering into the darkness as the tug on his arm becomes more forceful. The seductive voice is becoming harsh and begins to sound more like a man's voice.

"Come, come, time is of the essence. Don't resist. You can't resist, you owe me. Let go and come with me," the voice says harshly, as Skyler is being pulled into the darkness.

"No," he yells out, "no, I don't want to go. Leave me alone. I don't want to have anything to do with you."

"You have no choice! You have made a pact with me, Enepsigos, remember?"

"No, I don't," replies Skyler, as he tosses in bed trying to release the strong grip on his arm.

"You made a pact with me and now you must follow through if you wish to see your mother again," says Enepsigos, not trying to disguise himself anymore.

Skyler yells at the top of his lungs the only name he can think of, "Jesus!"

As soon as he speaks the name, Enepsigos releases him, and Skyler stumbles back onto the path. His heart is beating fiercely as he heads down the path like a man who is in shock. Weaving back and forth, he makes his way further down the path. In his dream, he continues to call out the name of Jesus, which he remembers from his days as a child growing up and going to Sunday school.

His father, Jason, had taken him for the first six years of his life to church. First, to the nursery where the attendants would sing hymns to him, then as he grew, he attended children's church. During this brief time, he had learned this valuable lesson.

"Remember, Skyler," said Mrs. Brown, his Sunday school teacher, "whenever you're in trouble and need help, call on the name of the Lord Jesus and He will help you."

Skyler wakes up from his nightmare and lies on his bed, his eyes wide open, his heart pounding, the sheet tangled around his legs.

"Oh, man, what a nightmare," he says with relief, as he continues to lay sprawled in bed until his heart returns to beating normally. Five, then ten minutes pass. Skyler swings his legs over the side of his bed and sits there gathering his thoughts.

Untangling his legs from the bedsheet, he stands up and slowly heads to the bedroom window. Timidly, he pulls the curtain back and looks out. Nothing looks out of the ordinary, except a large cat walking toward the bedroom window as if he were stalking prey. Skyler opens the window and leans out.

He calls out to the furry, black cat. Skyler reaches out to pet the round, green-eyed cat, as it slowly walks toward him. Just as Skyler leans out further from the window, the cat's eyes change into red slits, as it crouches, then pounces on Skyler. With a cry of pain, he tries to pull off the cat which has hold of his outstretched arm as the vile creature sinks its claws deeply into Skyler's right arm.

Terrified and fighting for his life, Skyler screams loud enough to be heard by his next door neighbors. Being early risers, they sit outside on their back patio, sipping coffee and reading the newspaper when they hear Skyler's desperate cries for help.

Without hesitation, both husband and wife drop their coffee and come rushing through their side yard and out to the front of Skyler's house.

Mr. Warren fumbles at the locked side gate desperately trying to open it. The screams intensify and then become muffled. Mr. Warren kicks open the wooden side door. With a loud crack, it gives way, and both husband and wife run to the back of Skyler's house. Sounds of breaking glass and furniture being thrown over is heard along with Skyler's cries for help.

They make their way into Skyler's bedroom through the open window. What they see takes them back momentarily. A hairy creature the size of a child about four to five years of age, snarls and hisses as it attacks Skyler. With long hairy arms and with claws that rip right through the bloody bedspread it continues to attack Skyler. He tries in vain to protect himself from the claws that tear at him.

"In the name of Jesus, leave him now," both Mr. and Mrs. Warren yell out almost in unison, as they watch in horror. The creature lets go of Skyler and turns toward them menacingly.

Hissing as he slowly makes his way toward them, his eyes glow red with hate. Before it can leap on them, Mr. Warren yells out, "In the name of Jesus, go back to hell from where you came and never come back."

The creature lets out a howl that causes their blood to run cold. Backbiter, who has taken full possession of Blackheart, runs between Mr. and Mrs. Warren and jumps out the window; it disappears in a cloud of smelly, black smoke, but leaves behind Blackheart's dead, bloody carcass.

Skyler slumps to the floor with his blanket in shreds, shaking violently as Mrs. Warren pulls the fitted sheet off his bed and covers the badly bruised and bloody Skyler.

He stares at the open window as Mrs. Warren tries to comfort him. Mr. Warren runs out the front door and back to his house where he grabs his wallet and car keys. He leaves the front door open and runs to open his garage door. As quickly as he can, he unlocks his car, gets in, and starts the engine. Pressing the gas pedal, the engine roars, but the car goes nowhere. He shakes his head and mumbles under his breath, while he puts the car into reverse and steps on the gas, making the tires squeal as he backs out of the garage and pulls up in front of Skyler's house. He leaves the car running as he runs back into Skyler's bedroom. He carefully picks up Skyler in his arms and carries him out to his car. Mrs. Warren follows them out and closes the front door behind her. They rush to the nearest hospital.

23

Jason and Mary Riggs pull up the driveway. Mr. Riggs parks the car in the driveway and heads back to the trunk of the car. Mary emerges from the car looking tanned, relaxed, and very content. Mr. Riggs opens the trunk, while Mary Riggs opens the front door to their house.

"Skyler, honey, we're home," calls out Mary. Jason also calls out to Skyler, being glad to be home. He is loaded down with both their suitcases he and Mary had purchased while on their cruise.

Jason is actually looking forward to seeing Skyler again. As he carries the suitcases to their bedroom, he hears a scream that startles him. He drops the suitcases. Before he can take a step forward, Mary Riggs let out another ear-piercing scream.

Jason runs to Skyler's bedroom stopping short. He surveys the scene unable to grasp what is before him. Blood is splattered everywhere. Mary stands next to a torn and bloody bedspread. Upon seeing him, she runs the short distance to her husband. Jason tries to comfort his hysterical wife, putting his arms around Mary as he looks in horror and disbelief.

He says calmly and softly, "Mary, honey, come with me. Let's go to the living room."

He walks her to the living room with his arm around her and heads for the sofa. Gently but firmly, he sits her down.

"Mary," he says softly, "stay here. I'm going to call the police. Don't move from here."

Mary shakes her head in agreement. Still unable to speak, she sits rocking, her eyes unblinking, staring in front of her. Jason Riggs pulls out his cell phone from his festive island shirt he bought while on their cruise and calls the police.

"Hello, this is Jason Riggs. My wife and I have just arrived home from a cruise, and we found our son's bedroom splattered in blood and furniture thrown about. My son is nowhere to be found. My address is Forty-two Fair Oaks Lane. Have you had any report of a crime committed here?" he asks, with surprising control and calm.

"Yes, Mr. Riggs. We had a call to nine-one-one early this morning about a wild animal attack. We sent out a crew to investigate. Your son was transported to the hospital by your next-door neighbors, Mr. and Mrs. Warren. He was admitted to Saint Luke's Hospital with severe lacerations, but with no life-threatening injuries."

Joe Austin, Peter Warren, and Paul Miller sit quietly as each one thinks about what the others have shared regarding Mr. Tingly.

"More refills?" asks the waitress, looking at each face thinking they look like they could use a strong drink instead of ice tea.

"No, thank you," says Paul. "Not for me."

Both Joe and Peter request refills.

"Wow," says Peter, still trying to absorb all he has heard.

"So now that we are all on the same page," says Paul, "where do we go from here?"

"I think we need to talk to my dad and let him in on all we know. I'm sure he'll be able to help us," says Peter, not realizing the extent of involvement his parents already have in this bizarre plan.

"Yes, I think you're right," says Paul, as he leans back into the booth.

"How soon do you think it will be before we can have a meeting with your dad?" Joe hopes it will be soon.

"I really want to get this done and over with."

"I'll talk with my dad tonight, and I'll call you as soon as I know when we can all meet."

"Yes," says Joe, "the sooner the better."

24

"Hello, sweetie," says Mary, looking more rested than when she first arrived at the hospital. Her blue eyes light up as she moves closer to Skyler who is now resting comfortably in his hospital bed.

"Hi, Mom," replies Skyler, a little faintly as he is just waking up. A smile slowly forms on his young face. Then his eyes move past Mary to his father who is standing just behind Mary.

"Hello, son. How are you feeling?" asks Jason, concerned that Dr. Bloomington is still in the room with them.

"Much better, thank you," replies Skyler, grateful to see his parents home again.

"Dr. Bloomington says I'll be okay in a few weeks. There will be very little scarring," says Skyler, with hope in his voice.

Dr. Bloomington walks closer to Jason and says quietly, "Mr. Riggs, may I see you outside alone for a moment please?"

Jason Riggs turns to look at the doctor with a quizzical look, then turns around to face Mary and Skyler.

"I'm going to speak to Dr. Bloomington outside. You two relax and I'll be back soon."

Mary smiles at Jason, and Skyler nods his head in acknowledgment. Both the doctor and Jason step out the door and walk a few feet down the hall.

Dr. Bloomington looks down for a moment gathering his thoughts. He wonders how he is going to ask Jason Riggs about the faint scars on Skyler's back.

"Mr. Riggs, I don't know how to ask you this without sounding as if I am accusing you or your wife of something. So, I'll just come right to the point. Have you or your wife ever hit Skyler as a youngster or now, as recently as one month ago?"

Jason's face drains of color as he looks straight into Dr. Bloomington's eyes. Jason tries to swallow, but his mouth feels as dry as a cotton ball in the noonday sun. He opens his mouth, but nothing comes out. Jason continues to stare into the doctor's eyes like a deer stares at the oncoming lights from a speeding car.

"I see," says Dr. Bloomington. "When was the last time you struck Skyler?"

Finding his voice, Jason softly says, "A few weeks ago."

"What did you hit him with?"

"My, my belt. This one I'm wearing now," says Jason, still unable to disengage his eyes from the doctor's.

"I see. Apparently, you've been hitting him with your belt for quite some time," says the doctor, not without compassion.

He has seen on more than one occasion the current injuries inflicted by a parent on a child. Parents and caregivers who abuse their charges are usually abused as children themselves. Strong emotions stir in Dr. Bloomington. Looking down clears his throat and tries to keep his emotions in check.

He says not too gently, "I have come across this more times than I care to remember, but I have come to the conclusion over the years that sending people like you to jail for abusing children does very little to nothing in stopping the violence in the home when the abuser returns home. I am going to have to report this to the authorities. I will ask that you, your wife, and Skyler be ordered to go to counseling."

Dr. Bloomington looks down, while he gathers his thoughts and calms himself.

"You see, Mr. Riggs, your child is a gift from God. A gift that should be cherished and prized, not abused and tolerated. When you left your parent's care, you should've sought help immediately. But that didn't happen."

Dr. Bloomington draws a deep breath, and with compassion in his eyes, he explains how his own child was beaten to death by his ex-wife's boyfriend at the tender age of five.

Jason Riggs's knees give way, and he slowly slides to the floor feeling pure disgust, guilt, and remorse and glad someone had the courage to finally report him.

Dr. Bloomington looks down at Jason and says, "You should be hearing from the police in a few minutes."

Then the doctor turns and walks briskly to the front desk and calls hospital security and then the police. Armed hospital guards arrive promptly and pull Jason Riggs to his feet. They escort him to the first floor and place him into a holding room as they wait for the police to pick him up.

Dr. Bloomington returns to Skyler's room where he finds Mary sitting on the edge of the bed holding Skyler's hand. He walks over to Mary and taps her on the shoulder and says quietly, "Mrs. Riggs, Skyler needs his rest. Let's step outside please."

Mary gives Skyler a kiss on the forehead and then on the hand she is holding. Gently laying his hand back on the bed, she turns toward the door and goes out of the room as the doctor holds the door open for her.

He walks her down the hall to the elevators and says, "I need to talk to you about your husband and his relationship with your son Skyler."

Mary's bright, blue eyes quickly fill with tears as they enter the elevator, and the doctor pushes the ground floor button.

Mary drives home alone. Drained and still reeling from the day's events, she wearily walks to the front door of her house and slips her key in the front door lock. No sooner does she drop her keys and purse on the entryway table when the doorbell rings. She turns and takes the few steps to the front door. Looking through the peephole, she sees Mr. Warren and opens the door.

"Hello, Mrs. Riggs. My wife and I want to know how you and Mr. Riggs are holding up."

"I'm doing all right, thank you."

"Good, I don't know if the police told you. We were the ones that saw the attack on Skyler. We've stayed with him until you returned. Since we were told at the hospital you and Mr. Riggs had arrived, we decided to step back for a while. We just wanted you to know. I understand Skyler is doing fine."

"Yes, he is doing much better," says Mary, lowering her head. The look of stress and fatigue on her face is undeniable. Mrs. Warren steps up to Mary and places her arms around her saying, "It's going to be okay. Come on, let's go inside."

All three go in. Mary and Mrs. Warren sit on the sofa, while Mr. Warren sits on a chair across from them.

"I can't tell you enough how much I appreciate all you've done for Skyler. I'd hate to imagine what would've happened if you both hadn't been there to help him," says Mary, as tears run down her cheeks.

"We're just thankful we were at the right place at the right time and were able to help," says Mrs. Warren.

"Is Jason still at the hospital?" asks Mr. Warren.

"No, no he's not. He's not going to be home for a while, I suspect," says Mary with a sigh.

Mr. and Mrs. Warren give each other a look of concern.

"Where is he, Mary?" asks Mr. Warren to get answers but trying not to be too pushy.

"Oh, he's at the police station. They have a few questions they need him to answer," says Mary, glad to tell someone about Jason. She sits quietly and lets her mind drift to the carefree days she and Jason spent on their cruise.

"Honey," says Mrs. Warren to her husband in a soft voice as she leans towards him, "why don't we have her stay with us tonight and tomorrow when she's feeling better. We can find out exactly what's going on."

Mr. Warren stands up and walks over to Mary and leans down and says firmly, "Mrs. Riggs, Julie is going to pack an overnight bag for you. You're going to spend the night with us."

Mary looks up at Mr. Warren, nodding her head yes and offers no resistance as Mr. Warren helps her up and leads her to his house. Julie Warren remains and packs Mary an overnight bag. The smell of dried, old blood assaults her nose as she passes by Skyler's room, her stomach turning at the smell.

"I hope the police are done with that room so I can get someone to come in and clean it up and paint it," Julie says aloud, as she finishes packing Mary's things.

She walks to the front door, picking up Mary's purse and keys as she gladly leaves through the front door, closing and locking it behind her. She walks the short distance to her house, taking in a lungful of the scents of the end of the day. As the sun sets, it shows off its beautiful colors.

Being her favorite time of year, Julie and her husband usually go to the botanical gardens around this time and check out the new plants that have been brought in. But with all that is going with the Riggses and the End Times Association, she wonders if things will go back to normal anytime soon.

Julie Warren walks in the kitchen to see Mary sitting at the kitchen table sipping a cup of hot cinnamon tea, while her husband starts dinner.

Julie walks over to the guest room and unpacks Mary's overnight bag and puts her things away. She then pulls back the bedcovers and closes the blinds. As she walks to the door to leave, Julie takes a quick look around to make sure she hasn't for forgotten anything and gently closes the door behind her and heads for the kitchen.

"What a pretty picture," says Backbiter, as he leaves through the kitchen ceiling.

25

Backbiter takes his time returning to Amon's office. He has changed somewhat since taking on this assignment. Gone is the bumbling, stuttering, insecure demon of eternity past.

After his dealings with these with humans of the last days and having his emotions stretched from deep inside him, he has become more secure in his abilities and his role as Amon's spy.

He knew from the moment he made his alliance with Satan, he would eventually end up miserable, hard-hearted, and scared to death, if it were possible for him to die. Knowing he and the rest of Satan's followers, both spiritual and human, will eventually end up in the Lake of Fire, has him scared as well. Now that he has spent eons under Satan's rule, he can no longer deceive himself as to this fate. It seemed as if these times would never draw near. Yet he finds himself unusually frightened, his eyes wide open to the terrible truth of the dawning of the end of time.

What do I have to lose? I made my choice eons ago and now the time has come to pay in full. Why should I be afraid of Amon or anybody else in this world or in mine? I will go not as I came in. I will do as much harm and damage, not only to the end time humans, but to anyone else that hurts me in any way, shape or form as long as I am free. He feels rather melancholy, something he has not felt for a very long while.

"So Deceit, you better watch your step from now on. Our time is drawing near to our inevitable fate and that of the world. As you have reminded me of what I had successfully been able to conceal from myself for all this centuries, you will be at the top of my list," Backbiter says bitterly.

Backbiter lands softly near the gigantic gates of the compound and walks confidently toward Amon's office. Others who know him notice the change that has taken place. Some lesser demons turn their backs to him in fear as they whisper to one another. Even some fallen angels turn and exchange looks between themselves noting the change in Backbiter.

"I wonder what's come over him?" asks Eligor.

"Don't know. What I do know is that this is happening more often now than thousands of years ago. We all know our end is near and that nothing can change it. However, since none of us have anything to lose, Backbiter probably decided to go out in glory instead of with his tail tucked between his legs."

"How do you think Amon will react to him now?" replies Eligor.

"Who knows? But it will be fun to find out," he says with a laugh.

Backbiter walks up to Amon's office and stands a few feet away from the massive doors of his office and waits to be summoned.

A tall, beautiful woman with long, blonde hair and flowing gown walks gracefully past Backbiter and toward the doors. Backbiter looks her up and down, then uncharacteristically, he turns away, straightening his back looking forward and waits for Amon to summon him. When he does, Backbiter walks in confidently as the doors open automatically.

Amon notices the change and is taken aback slightly. Backbiter looks steadily at Amon, something he would never do. Amon leans forward and motions with a flourish to Backbiter to sit on one of the chairs in front of his desk. Backbiter comes and sits with a ram rod spine, his feet set apart and his arms resting on the arm rests.

"Welcome back, Backbiter. What news do you have for me regarding Deceit and the humans?" asks Amon with a twinkle in his eye.

"As you well know, sire, Deceit has tipped his hand and has exposed much of his plan."

"Now what makes you think I know anything of the sort?" asks Amon, amused at the news given to him by Enepsigos just moments before Backbiter entered.

"With all due respect," replies Backbiter, "I know for a fact Enepsigos has been working with the humans you have assigned Deceit to manipulate and bring down. Since you assigned me to follow and report back to you on Deceit's plan to climb up the ranks, naturally, I was privy to much of what is going on. Therefore, I am sure there is not much I can add to what has already been told you by Enepsigos."

"Oh, on the contrary, my dear friend. I am sure there is plenty that you can enlighten me with. First of all, you can tell me what caused you to change so dramatically," says Amon, his eyes narrowing as he leans over his desk at Backbiter.

"I am eager to hear all the details. Please, go right ahead and tell me everything."

For a brief moment, Backbiter returns to his old, bootlicking, weak self. Amon, on the other hand, is slightly amused by this and slowly leans back into his chair. With his elbows resting on the armrest, he laces his fingers together and with a smile, he says, "Go ahead, I'm all ears."

26

"Laura, will you come to my office please?" asks Mr. Delmore, as he looks out the window of his office.

"Yes, I'll be right up," replies Laura and hangs up her phone and walks to his office.

"Mr. Delmore wants to see me, Eleanor," Laura says to his secretary.

"Go right in."

"Mr. Delmore, Miss Parson is on her way in."

Laura goes into the corner office of the Warren Law Firm. The light from the window comes in from behind his desk. From here, one can see the entire length of the majestic mountains and the city neatly nestled partly up the mountain through the window which has been tinted to avoid the heat from morning sun from coming in.

For a seasoned attorney, one would think he would have decorated his office in a more traditional manner. Not being one for sticking to traditions, he has lined one of the office walls with awards, pictures of himself alongside of the president and other notables. On the other wall, shelves are filled from top to bottom with law books. The opposite wall has a large, beautiful, scenic painting hanging in the middle of it. Soft-cushioned, green, leather chairs sit directly in front of his desk.

He sits back in his chair momentarily, as he thinks of how he is going to deliver the news to Laura. She has been an exemplary worker. All has been going smoothly, until now.

"Miss Parson, it has come to my attention you have been neglecting your cases of late. The Ashford case for one and the Peterson case for another. These should have been closed weeks ago. They are both open and shut cases. Any good reason why they are still active?"

Laura opens the Ashford file and scans over the pages. She does the same to the Peterson file.

"I don't understand. I know I've completed these files and personally date stamped, closed and filed them myself. I made sure everyone involved got a copy, and I even got two replies stating how well I handled them in a timely matter."

"Can you produce these letters on paper? I take it you made copies and had them filed as well."

"Yes, sir, I did. If you will allow me, I'll go get copies and bring them back."

"Very well then, come back as soon as you get them."

"Thank you, sir," replies Laura, jumping to her feet and rushing out the door.

"Eleanor, will you please come in here and bring your notepad with you."

"Yes, I'll be right there."

Laura goes down the elevator to the second floor and heads for the personnel office. She hurries down to the file room and calls out to Jessie Langford, the file clerk.

"Come on back."

"Thanks, Jess," she says hurrying to the back of the file room and straight to the cabinet containing her files. She pulls the drawer open, noticing it is not locked as is required.

Odd, it should be locked. She walks over to a table and looks for the two letters she personally placed in the file. Not finding them, she goes page by page through every piece of paper twice.

"Oh no, they have to be here," she says softly, the color draining from her face.

"Jessie," she calls out, "will you come here please?"

"Coming," he says, as he walks briskly over to Laura. "What do you need?"

"Did you or anyone else go through my personnel file or the Peterson and Ashford files recently?"

"No, there's no reason to."

"Well, somebody did. I didn't even have to ask for a key to the cabinet. It was unlocked."

"No, it was locked. I gave you the key just before you went back."

"I would have remembered taking the keys from you had you given them to me."

"Well," says Jessie getting a little offended, "what do you call these?" he says, as he points to the keys hanging from the lock.

Laura stands staring in disbelief at the set of keys still attached to the lock.

"This can't be," she says softly.

"Oh, it can be and is," says Jessie. "Did you find what you were looking for?"

"No, that's the problem. I know I put two letters in here myself just a little over a week ago. I date-stamped them like everything else I get."

"I don't know what to tell you, Laura."

She walks back to Mr. Delmore's office.

"Mr. Delmore wants to see me, Eleanor."

"Go right in."

"Sir, Miss Parson is on her way in."

Laura's high heels make no sound as she makes her way across the thick, new beige rug to his desk and takes a seat on one of the two matching green, leather chairs.

She clears her throat and Mr. Delmore turns around, motioning her to sit. Slowly seating at the edge of the chair, she places both her hands together on her lap.

"Well, did you find what you were looking for?" he asks rather gently.

"No. I don't understand. I did receive two letters stating what a good job I did, but for whatever reason, they're not there."

Her pretty face is pale and her eyes are pleading for him to believe her.

He gets up and walks over to her and says, "Why don't you take a couple of days off and come back when you're feeling better. I'll call personnel myself and tell them you're taking two sick days."

Laura stands up and Mr. Delmore walks her out of his office, locking his door. Both take the elevator down. She gets off on the fourth floor and steps out while he continues down to the main floor.

Laura takes her purse from her desk and heads out, wanting to get as far away from there as possible. She sits in her car for a minute trying to decide who to call. Taking out her cell phone, she calls John Langer. It goes directly to voice mail.

"John, it's me, Laura Parson. John, I've got to see you. Please can you meet me at the park in an hour? It's vitally important you do so."

She hangs up, starts her car and heads for the park. She walks to the nearest bench and sits scanning the street for Langer's car. The smell of food cooking from a food vendor's truck makes her hungry. She must have her wits about her before she speaks with John. Some food will help. She orders a small burger and a large Coke. Taking her food, she heads for a table under a nearby tree where she eats quickly. Looking at her watch, she realizes she still has half an hour before she can meet with Langer.

Looking around the park, sadness begins to come over her as she recalls the world she had left behind just a scant few years prior. She was young, ambitious, and ready to conquer the world. Wanting to help those less fortunate than herself in any way she could, a career in law seemed to be a natural choice for her.

Her parents, being wealthy, traveled abroad often. But since she had become a Christian, their views conflicted sharply with hers. They were adamant that she was not going to receive any financial help from them until she renounced her newfound faith and returned to the way of thinking she was brought up with. Refusing to do so, they cut off all communications with her.

"Laura, until you come to your senses, don't bother to contact us," were the last words her father had spoken to her.

A few days after entering law school, she goes to dinner alone to relax. Sitting a couple of tables away from hers, she catches the eye of Damian Tingly.

He boldly comes over after dinner and asks if he can join her. In need of company and especially that of a father figure, Damian Tingly seems to be the right man for the job. She's eager to confide in him as she would of her absentee father. Damian Tingly, in some ways, reminded her of him. A good listener, articulate, and worldly, she took to him right away.

As for Damian Tingly, she was exactly what he had been looking for to become a spy for him. She was young, eager to please, and in obvious need of money. He approached her a few weeks later with his proposition telling her lies about the Warren Law Firm. Before long, she was under his spell and would do anything he asked her to do.

Now she was in trouble and needed help, but not so much from him, she thought as from Langer. She was in love with him despite his treatment of her. As for Joe, she considered him more of a social stepping stone than as a boyfriend.

Langer was confident, secure, well-educated, and older. Joe had the same attributes, except his age, which was closer to hers.

She longed to reunite with her parents especially now. But all she could think about was how to get out of the mess she is in.

John walks up behind her, placing his hand on her shoulder, startling her. He sits across from her and asks what the emergency is. She fills him in completely, leaving no detail out. John listens intently and asks only one question, "Who have you talked to about this?"

"No one, just you. I'm in trouble, and I need your help."

"Sorry, I can't help you." He stands up to leave, but Laura grabs him by the wrist holding on tightly.

"Why not? You're the only one I know who can help me, now more than ever," she says, pleading for his help.

John places his hands on the cold, concrete picnic table and leans over to her, looking her straight in the eye and says, "Laura, Tingly gave me orders and made sure in no uncertain terms, I was not to have any kind of relationship with you, only what our assignments require me to do. That's it. Sorry."

He turns and leaves Laura along with the weight of the wrong decision she has made, squarely upon her shoulders.

27

"Okay, when would be a good time to call? I need to talk to you about something," asks Joe.

"Joe, I really am busy, and I will continue to be busy for the next few days. I have a situation going on, and I need to take care of it as soon as possible. I'll call you when I get some free time and then we can talk. Got to go now, bye."

Joe is taken aback by Laura's abruptness. *What in the world is going on here?* he wonders, as he replaces his cell phone back into his pants pocket.

Nothing seems to be going right. Could it be that she has found someone else and that's why her behavior has been so strange of late? Or is it that things are getting stirred up again in the spirit?

He decides to seek the only one who can help answer these questions. He kneels down in front of the sofa and begins to earnestly pray for answers. Just then, the phone rings. Not wanting to be interrupted, he turns off his phone.

As he starts to pray again, Rover chases Snowball past him and throughout the house.

"Rover," shouts Joe, as the dog runs by hitting the end table knocking over a table lamp. Joe gets up angrily and goes after Rover who is still chasing Snowball.

"Rover, stop! Come here, come here," he says sternly, as he follows Rover into the bedroom. Grabbing Rover by the collar, Joe pulls back hard on the collar, but Rover refuses to budge. He has chased Snowball up to the top of the dresser where Snowball stands with her back arched and is hissing at Rover. Joe continues to pull Rover, trying to get him to stop barking.

As suddenly as it starts, Rover ceases to bark, turns and walks away, going back to the living room and laying down in his favorite place.

Snowball quietly sits on top of the dresser licking herself, as if to rid herself of the faint smell of sulfur she can still detect.

Joe grabs her and puts her down on the floor. She looks up at Joe with round eyes, looking as if she is trying to convey to Joe she and Rover were not at fault, but that indeed it was the fault of an unseen visitor who had decided to ride Rover like a horse. Joe stands looking at Snowball wondering out loud.

"What is going on here? First, it's Laura, now it's you two."

Joe returns to the living room and looks Rover over to make sure he doesn't have any cuts or something else that made him angry enough to chase after Snowball. Not finding anything, he decides to get answers directly from Laura.

Joe knocks on Laura's apartment door. The door opens slowly as Laura peaks from behind the door.

"Oh, it's just you," she says, as she opens the door and lets him in.

"Happy to see you too," he replies sarcastically.

"Sorry, I didn't mean it the way it sounded," says Laura with a sigh. She turns and walks toward the kitchen.

"Want something to drink?"

"No, thanks. What I do want is some answers."

Laura stops pouring wine into her glass and slowly turns to Joe.

"What question do you want answered?" she asks, as she takes a drink of wine.

"You've been acting strangely lately, and I want to know why."

Laura walks over to Joe.

"What were you doing at the park the other day?" asks Joe, looking her straight in the eye.

"Jogging, is that all right with you?"

"Look, you're free to do whatever you want. I think something is really bothering you and you aren't telling me. I want to know what the problem is so I can help, if I can."

"Listen, I don't have a problem, and if I did, you wouldn't be able to help me anyway," says Laura.

"See, this is what I'm talking about. You're not acting like yourself. Babe, what's wrong, tell me, maybe I can help," pleads Joe, grabbing her arm.

Laura jerks free of Joe's grip and looks straight up at him and says in a low-pitched voice, speaking slowly, "Listen, I don't want your help. You can't help me. What I do want is for you to leave now and never come back. Do I make myself clear?"

"Perfectly," says Joe, as he turns and walks out the door closing it slowly behind him.

Laura walks quickly to the door and grabs the knob and turns it, but does not pull the door open. Leaning into the front door, she lowers her head and closes her eyes. A tear runs down her cheek.

Joe sits in his car for a full minute before starting it. His mind is racing and his heart is beating hard. He starts the car and looks to the left before pulling into the street when a dark limousine pulls up and an older man gets out and heads for the stairs, disappearing from view.

You know, it just may be the guy Laura saw the other day. If it is, I couldn't care less, he thinks as he pulls out and heads for church.

Mr. Tingly knocks on Laura's door and waits patiently for her to answer.

"I told you I don't want to see you ever again," yells Laura through the closed door. Mr. Tingly knocks again. The door opens abruptly and there stands Laura who starts to shout, "Get lost!"

Seeing that it is Mr. Tingly, Laura apologizes profusely and invites him in. Mr. Tingly walks calmly in, looking around the small one-bedroom apartment.

"I wonder why you're not living in a, shall we say, place befitting of your status."

Laura says nothing.

"Now, what is the reason for your call?"

"I'm in trouble, and I don't understand why. Someone or something is causing a lot of trouble for me at work. I didn't know who to call for help, so I called you."

"Let's sit down and tell me what is going on," says Tingly, choosing to sit on the couch. Laura joins him and begins to cry softly. She covers her face with both hands. Being slightly moved by her tears, he leans over taking her into his arms. He holds her for a long while, thinking that she needs to get this out of her system before she can answer my questions.

Laura reaches over to her left and takes a couple of tissues from the box of Kleenex. She blows her nose and pockets the tissue and places her hands on her lap, drawing in a deep breath letting it out slowly.

"Now, child, what's the problem?' says Mr. Tingly in a fatherly tone, which surprises even him.

Laura tells him what happened at work and wonders if she is losing her grip on reality or if it is a possibility of the resurgence of spiritual activity.

Mr. Tingly sits quietly saying nothing. He is not aware of any other gatekeepers assigned to this area which may have opened and called forth dark spirits.

Laura is not aware of his position as the new gatekeeper. All she knows is that he is a professor at the university and a kind man who has helped her in her darkest moments. Tingly has kept his position a secret in order to keep his enemies and former acquaintances from recognizing him and possibly ending his plans.

Laura has become a liability. Tingly sits quietly, as he listens to her pour out her heart. *Too bad. She was a great help, at first, but now she must go.*

28

"Yes, Mr. Tingly, I understand. I will do just as you say," says Langer, as he hangs up and goes over to his wife. "Honey, I've got to meet with Tingly. He has some new information for me. I'll be back as soon as I can. Then maybe we can go have an early dinner and take in a movie."

"Sure, that'll be nice," Yvette Langer says, looking up at John with love and admiration in her eyes. He leans down and kisses her lightly on the lips.

Turning, he goes out to meet the elusive, Mr. Tingly, the new gatekeeper to the underworld.

Mr. Tingly sits in the bar and grill situated just outside of town. He has picked this place to make sure no one in his past would recognize him. Nursing his drink, he casually looks around the room.

This new island lifestyle seems to agree with him. Tanned and surprisingly fit for a man of fifty, his brown hair still free of any signs of graying is long enough to comb straight back and be tied into a short, neat pony tail at the nape of his neck. His once clean shaven face is now covered with a nice and neatly trimmed full beard. His clothes are much finer than before and stylishly casual.

"Hey, Charlie," calls out a voice from the bar, "over here."

Charlie walks over to a burly, younger man sitting at the bar. They greet each other warmly, and Charlie orders a beer and sits next to his friend. They chat for a few minutes and decide to move to a table. A young waitress comes over with a couple of menus and hands them over to them. As they decide what they want to eat, the same waitress goes over to Mr. Tingly's booth.

"Would you like another glass of wine?" she asks with a bright smile.

"Yes, please, that would be very nice."

As the waitress turns and walks over to the bar, Langer walks in. Tingly motions him over.

"Hello, Mr. Smith," says John to Damian Tingly, as he sits across from him. Just then, the waitress comes back with a fresh glass of wine.

"Hello, what would you like to drink?" she asks Langer.

"Nothing for me," he says politely. They wait to speak making sure the waitress is out of ear shot.

"Sure, you don't want anything?" asks Tingly.

"Quite sure, thank you. Now what information do you have for me?" asks Langer, placing his elbows on the table and lacing his fingers together.

"Always right to the point. I understand you had a little trouble with Miss Jones," replies Tingly.

"Yes, but nothing I can't handle."

"Good. Anything else you might want to advise me of now that I'm here?"

"No, sir. All is going according to plan."

"Good," says Tingly, as he leans slightly closer to John. "Now here is some new information I received just last night."

Tingly relays all he was told and what needs to be done in order to accomplish their new plans. The waitress, noticing how intently the two men are conversing, decides not to interrupt them.

Tingly finishes of his glass of wine and places a twenty-dollar bill on the table. They both get up and leave. The waitress looks at them until they walk out the door. She goes to clean the table and smiles as she pockets the twenty-dollar tip.

Mr. Tingly sits poolside drinking mineral water and enjoying, the sunny afternoon. He reflects on how his life has changed since he accepted the offer to leave town a scant two and a half years earlier.

Yes, life has been great. No more money worries, a wonderful place to live, and a new position as the new gatekeeper to the underworld where he can open any portal, anywhere in the world.

He had imagined after he had worked as second in command under Chulda, eventually he would move up to her level and get assigned to other duties involving keeping of the gate.

After learning of Chulda's death and the downfall of the End Times Association, Tingly thought that he would live his life out on the islands free and unencumbered by anything else other than a normal life would have to offer.

The millions given to him were, at the time, offered by the Warren Group. They had him under surveillance for quite some time. They knew his price and were willing to pay dearly for his removal as second in command to Chulda and as a tenured professor at the university. It was an offer too good to refuse.

Here I sit, enjoying the good life with the help of the Warren Group. Who would have guessed that all it took, was to give access to all the connections of the End Times Association. Being that was the only option the Warren Group had to counteract the Phase Three Plan, it's good to know your price.

Tingly gets up and takes a dip in the clear, blue water of the hotel pool.

Staying at this five-star hotel is better than renting Chulda's old mansion from month to month. Here I get pampered and there I'd have to hire a lot of help to serve me. But it is a bit grand for my taste. Hum, maybe I should rent a nice villa and hire a housekeeper that can cook. Yes, I think I'll do that tomorrow. And now I'll have an early dinner, turn in and read a good book.

29

"I really feel badly about what we are putting Laura through."

"I feel badly as well, but you know that we have no other choice. We discussed this at length. Since our eyes have been opened to the truth, we know that if we would have told Laura about our change of heart, she would have never believed us."

"I know, but we should have tried anyway."

"Well, it's too late to do it now. We have to finish what we started. Besides, she may have started off right, but somewhere along the way, she took a wrong turn and is getting awfully close to nearing the path of no return."

"I was sure when she hooked up with Joe Austin that she would see the error of her ways. But for some stupid reason she took after John Langer."

"Well, up until a few months ago, we thought he was the best man for her. So you can't really blame her for that."

"You're right. I should have called her the minute we realized what fools we have been, apologized and asked for her forgiveness."

"It's not too late. We can call her and have her meet with us. Then we can explain everything to her."

"Richard, I don't think the time is right. We started this mess she's in now, and we must be careful not to tip our hand. Tingly thinks we are still on his side. Laura believes the money Tingly has given her is from him and not from us. If we tell Laura we have been paying for most of her schooling instead of Tingly, it might turn out to be disastrous. We have to continue to keep her in the dark as well as Tingly."

"You're right, we can't stop now," says Mr. Parson to his wife.

Joe awakens tired and feeling in need of someone to confirm what he thinks happened in his dream. He hurries and gets ready for church. As he is about to leave, he remembers he has not fed Rover and Snowball. Calling out to them, he fills their bowls with food and water. They both come running. Rover slides in almost knocking over his bowl of water. Snowball hurries in and starts to eat.

"Wow, it didn't take you guys long to get here," he says, smiling as he heads out the front door. Soon he is on his way to church with Deceit hot on his tail.

"Where's the fire?" asks Deceit.

Joe arrives shortly and meets up with Claire Deaton, saying, "Yes, I do know that, and I'm willing to go through with it regardless of what happens."

"Okay, now wait here while I gather a few other prayer warriors to fight alongside of us."

Joe smiles and nods his head, watching Claire Deaton gather four others to join them in spiritual warfare.

They all do spiritual battle by praying in unity alongside the other saints as the angels of the Lord of Hosts, including Angelo de Fuego, fight the forces of darkness. They continue to pray until they feel the release to stop.

Deceit fights alongside the other demons and not too few fallen angels for hours and is exhausted, even though the fight is not yet over. He decides to leave the fight, but continues to watch from a safe distance.

The others, including the fallen angels, realize this, but it is a matter of pride for them to continue without him. Since he is the one who ordered them to fight per Amon's orders. They want to prove to Amon and their god, Satan, that they are just as brave and strong as the angels of the Lord of Hosts. Deceit decides to reenter the fight. He comes in cautiously, not realizing Backbiter is watching. Deceit leaps on the back of Angelo de Fuego. Backbiter nears the fight and carefully gets the attention of the others. He gives the sign for retreat, and immediately, the fallen warrior angels and the other demons depart in a brilliant flash of light.

The angels of the Lord of Hosts give a cheer and also depart to report to their commanding officer.

Backbiter has been keeping tabs on Deceit during this altercation and has reported to Amon just what Deceit has been up to. Amon had ordered Backbiter to stop the fighting and return to the compound. He will have them fight another day.

Deceit is not sure what has taken place, but he is positive the fray is over because he jumped back in to do battle. Left alone, he looks around and sees no one. Backbiter has hidden himself again.

"Just as I thought," says Deceit.

"They saw me coming to their aide and left because they knew my presence would win the fight."

Deceit lets out a howl of triumph as he pounds his chest. Strutting around, he cries out, "I am the greatest demon that has ever lived! Why just the sight of me can scare anyone away!"

"You've got that right," says Backbiter softly from his hiding place.

"Anyone who's ever had the displeasure of seeing you would agree, you ugly, boney, skinny-assed, fool of a lying demon," says Backbiter, as he leaves his hiding place to follow Deceit.

—⟡—

"Well, Ms. Stiles. You come highly recommended. You understand you will be my housekeeper as well as my personal assistant? Yes?"

"Yes, I understand, Mr. Tingly," says Heady Stiles, as she stands up and extends her hand to him.

"Good. Then you can start tomorrow. Here is a check for five hundred dollars. This will be your expense account to help you get whatever you need at the present time to make yourself at home here and for any moving expenses you may have at this time."

"Thank you, sir. You are quite generous. I won't be needing but half of this. So I'll be returning what is left over."

"Oh that won't be necessary. May I call you Heady?"

"Yes, most certainly, sir."

"Good. Then it's all set. I'll see you tomorrow, say about nine?"

"If it's okay with you, sir, I would like to make it around seven in the morning."

"If you like. But please, don't bother me until after eight."

"Yes, sir," she says, as she takes leave of Tingly. She closes the door softly behind her as she heads for her car. As soon as she is in, she pulls out her cell phone and calls a close friend.

"I got the job. This will certainly make things a lot easier for me. He turns out to be quite a generous man."

"Good, I'm very happy to hear that. Well, call me in a few days. We'll exchange information then."

Heady hangs up. She smiles slightly as she sits thinking about her new job.

30

Arriving at church, Joe sees Claire Deaton and says good morning to her as he gives her a warm hug.

"Good morning, Joe. It's good to see you here. How are you doing?"

"Better since I told you about the strange dream I had. Are you free for lunch after church?" asks Joe, hoping she will say yes.

"Why yes, I love to have lunch with you. What do you want to talk about?" she asks, genuinely concerned.

"About the dream I had last night."

"Sounds interesting," she says, as they make their way into church.

"A dream?" says Deceit. "It's probably the one I had something to do with the other night. Boring. I think I'll see what Laura Parson has been up to since the last time I checked on her."

He gives one last look at Joe before flying off to Laura Parson's apartment. Deceit's mind is now on Laura and what she has been up to since he last checked on her.

"These two idiots have kept me busier than when I was assigned to Nebecanezzer. He may have been the king of Babylon, but he sure was a lot less trouble than these two."

"Nebe," as Deceit has always referred to Nebecanezzer, "already had a hard heart and pride enough for the whole region. So all I had to do was deceive a few other key people under his rule and the rest followed. But these two, I need a scoreboard to keep up with them," says Deceit, as he goes in through the front door of Laura's apartment. He flies from room to room looking for her, but does not find her.

"Okay, now where in the world could that girl be?" he asks, scratching his head as he heads out in search of Laura. First, he goes to Tingly's hotel room and flies around looking into closets and anywhere he thinks he or Laura may be. He soon realizes Tingly has checked out when he sees a portly, balding, forty-something man, standing in front of the bathroom mirror, trying to suck in his bulging belly and admiring himself.

"Deceit, you are such an idiot," says Backbiter from his hiding place. "What would he be doing in a closet? He should be downstairs getting breakfast. Why don't you go look for him there? Idiot!"

"Hmm, I think I'll go look in the restaurant. He just may be getting something to eat," says Deceit, as he flies downstairs. Backbiter shakes his head as he follows Deceit at a safe distance.

He finds Laura and Tingly having breakfast together. Feeling smug at his discovery, Deceit lands on the table and sits down in the middle between Tingly and Laura.

"I'm glad you were able to meet me here this morning, Miss Parson. I take it you're feeling better today."

"Yes, I am."

They order their breakfast and sit quietly, enjoying their coffee.

"So, Mr. Tingly, what have you decided I should do?" asks Laura a bit nervously. Mr. Tingly waits before answering her question. He has thought long and hard about this and has come to a decision.

"Laura, I have decided to keep you on at the Warren Law Firm for the time being. You have been a great asset up to now, and I have spent a great deal of money on your education, not to mention your living expenses," he says convincingly. Laura blushes, feeling guilty by what she believes to be the truth.

"I have contacted a close friend of mine and he informed me of who or what has been causing you all these problems," says Tingly.

"He told me he had assigned an engineer who works for Austin Robotics to eliminate the person who is causing you these problems from his position. Jessie Langford should be gone by the end of the week. So my dear, what have you done in order to correct the problem you find yourself in?"

"I've contacted the two people who wrote me letters of appreciation and asked them to send me a copy of the original letter they sent me."

"Good, that is what I was hoping to hear. Do you know the names of the persons who sent you these letters?"

"Yes, the letter from the Peterson case is from Linda Mason, the manager of the regional office. And the other is from Mr. Ashford himself. I plan to call them tomorrow first thing," says Laura, hoping Mr. Tingly approves of what she plans to do.

"Sounds good to me. Now are you sure there is nothing else that they can call you on the carpet for?" asks Tingly, hoping to hear of none.

"No, sir, there is nothing else, to my knowledge that they have against me," says Laura confidently.

"And they call me a liar!" says Deceit. "No wonder why they appointed him to be the new gatekeeper. I should lie so good. I think I'll stick around him more often. I could take lessons from him," he says, meaning every word.

"If you would do your job as you're supposed to, you wouldn't need to take lessons from anyone, you overgrown son of a cursed frog. You mincing, fruit pie!" says Backbiter, as he listens in from under the table.

31

"Hello, Mr. and Mrs. Parson. I'm glad to see you again. Please come in and have a seat," says Mr. Delmore.

"I would like to get to the point, if you don't mind," says Mr. Parson. "This has been very hard on us, as I know it has been hard on Laura. Being a father yourself, I know you understand how we feel."

"Yes, only too well. But as we discussed this prior to our putting this plan into action, you know this was going to be a pretty rough situation for all of us, especially for Laura."

Mr. Parson takes in a deep breath and lets it out slowly, nodding his head yes.

"When we got together with Densmore and the Warrens to set up a plan to get Laura into trouble with the firm so as to get Damian Tingly back into town and deal with him as swiftly as possible, we knew it would take a lot of faith in God and a lot of prayer to carry this off. So now that we've come this far, I can't quit now."

Since the Parsons have given their hearts and lives to the Lord, they had kept close tabs on Laura, but had decided not to let her know of their change of heart and mind.

They figured since Laura had become entangled with Damian Tingly, letting her in on their plans to rid the city of the End Days Association would put her in grave danger and making her choose between God and Tingly. Now, together with the Warren Law Firm and others in the church, they have devised a plan to get Tingly back into town and do away with him and with the black forces reemerging in their city.

This kind of plan takes a lot of money and secrecy to pull off. They realized almost too late, the root of the problem has not been cut out and dealt with. That remaining root is Damian Tingly.

So the Warrens and the Parsons have gotten together and hatched another plan to uproot once and for all the covens, cults, and the powerful gatekeeper. One good thing about this is that they know what kind of man Tingly is and what his connections are at present; thanks to the unwitting help from Laura and the help of her parents, the Parsons. This time, they will not leave anything to chance nor will they spare anyone, even their own daughter to accomplish this. From their experience, the Parsons know only too well what the forces of darkness and of self-deceit can do to a person, not to mention a country. They are determined they are going to save Laura and this city from the clutches of Satan if that is the last thing that they do.

"Okay, now that we have everything in order, let's pray again to make sure this is what the Lord would have us do," says Mr. Warren, as he leads them in prayer.

———⁂———

The pivotal battle is over. Allocen and Gusion have been sent packing. The cry of victory coming from the angels of the Lord of Hosts can be heard for miles. They rejoice for the victory over the enemy and as they worship and give praise to God. Their gowns are made as new, and their swords shine with the power it had before, during, and after the battle.

Michael the Archangel is flanked by the twenty warrior angels summoned to help do battle by Angelo de Fuego. They dance before the Lord, giving him praise for their victory over the formidable forces of Satan. Michael the Archangel raises his sword high and kneels before the Lord of Hosts. All the other angels do the same. Then Michael sheaths his magnificent sword as the others follow suit. He and the other warrior angels return to heaven to give a report on the battle and to receive any other orders the Lord of Hosts may have for them.

Deceit has witnessed the crushing defeat of his comrades and as usual takes off in search of a place for him to lick his wounds and come up with something to tell Amon.

Backbiter has also been a witness to the battle and has decided he should stay out of the fray.

"I was sent here to spy on Deceit and report my findings to Amon, not engage in battle," he says, as he flies back to the compound to make his report.

Deceit contemplates what he should do.

"Should I wait to tell Amon my story or shall I report to him on how I fought bravely to win honor and glory for him," says Deceit, still literally licking his wounds.

Then it hits him, "I shall go and tell Amon just how hard I fought and as proof, I will show him my many wounds, superficial as they are. Even though the others report things differently, I will have these wounds to prove to him, I too fought and fought bravely," says Deceit, as he leaves the comfort of the tree he has been hiding in.

"Yes, I will tell him how I thwarted and led the others in glorious battle, but due to my grievous wounds, as you can plainly see, I was unable to continue doing battle, which is why we lost this battle. I will tell him how the pathetic human, Damian Tingly, has escaped while I did battle," says Deceit, as he makes his way to headquarters.

32

Mr. Tingly turns around and sees Mr. and Mrs. Lee Warren walking toward him. They stop briefly at his table and exchange pleasantries. Mr. Tingly has heard that Mr. Warren, Peter's father, is a well-connected attorney who moved into town a few years ago from Washington DC, where he was a prosecuting attorney for a prominent law firm for the last fifteen years. As for Mrs. Warren, she is still very active in Christian causes.

Mr. Tingly smiles politely and rubs his right temple as if he is relieving an itch, but in reality he is wiping away a drop of sweat. He shakes hands with Mr. Warren.

It may or may not be an imagination, thinks Mr. Tingly, *but Warren seems to have squeezed my hand a bit too tightly.*

The look in Mr. Warren's eyes seems to penetrate Tingly's façade of the meek and mild college professor and into the recesses of his dark soul.

Mrs. Warren offers him only her fingers which he holds firmly in his grasp. A quick look from her steely, gray eyes and Tingly releases her hand as if it were a red-hot poker. The Warrens leave to meet their party several tables away.

No doubt, more of the same kind, but if our plan goes as it should, you and your ever loving friends will soon fall from grace and we will take over, thinks Tingly as he relaxes with that thought in mind.

"Here you are, sir. Is there anything else that I can get for you?" asks the waiter with practiced professionalism.

"No, thank you. This looks like all I'll need for now," says Mr. Tingly, taking in his dinner with all his senses.

"Enjoy your meal, Mr. Tingly."

Without further delay, he places his bib around his neck and cracks open the lobster which is set before him.

"Yes, this is very serious business," says Mr. Warren, lifting his cut crystal, wine glass taking a drink of the dark, rich liquid inside.

"When did you first find out about the project?" asks Mr. Warren to the current CEO of Jenkins Enterprises International.

"I first heard about the takeover last year. I was at a corporate function, and I just happened to overhear Pierce and Radcliff discussing the merger. Unfortunately, they noticed they were being overheard, so they took off to another room, and I wasn't able to hear any more," he replies with a bit of concern.

"I heard about it six months ago. I had a few people gathering information for me ever since. Tricky business this. One of my people has had to go to obtain the information I received late last night. I took the liberty of having it transferred over to a USB stick. You and I are the only ones privy to this information. I don't want this to fall into the hands of the others, friends or foe. As for the rest of you, we will discuss the project at our next meeting. There we can speak freely without the worry of being overhead," says Mr. Warren as a matter of fact.

Mr. Tingly wipes his mouth and takes another drink of the delicious, red wine, which he is quite fond of and smiles at the ever attentive waiter who quickly and quietly removes his dinner plate and silverware.

Mr. Tingly leans back in his chair as he waits for his favorite dessert. The waiter makes a show of lighting the Cherries Jubilee on a cart beside Mr. Tingly. With a smile on his face, he thanks the waiter and takes his first bite of his dessert. Closing his eyes, he savors the delicious morsels now sliding down this throat.

"Mmm, this is so good," he says not so softly.

Mr. Warren and his party make their way past Tingly who is finishing up the last of his dessert. Mr. and Mrs. Warren give Mr. Tingly a look of disdain. Blissfully, Tingly is unaware of them as they file past him.

"Is there anything more I can get for you, Mr. Tingly?"

"Oh no, thank you, my dear man. There is nothing more I desire. You have been a picture of efficiency and grace this night, and I thank you immensely," says Mr. Tingly, as he presses a twenty-dollar tip into the ever so professional waiter's palm.

The waiter pulls out the chair for Mr. Tingly as he gets up to leave. Leaving the restaurant with a bound in his step, he smiles and nods his head to all he passes.

He is glad he parked his own car at a distance from the restaurant, thus allowing him to walk off part of his very rich meal. Reaching his car, he unlocks it and slides on in.

Backbiter has been watching Mr. Tingly since he left home. Seeing the smug, satisfied look on his face gives Backbiter more fuel for the odious hate he has for Deceit. Mr. Tingly drives away unaware of Backbiter who is riding shotgun.

"This gluttoness, fool of a human will pay, as well as Deceit for this torture. I know the plan Chulda and this one have put in place. Since Deceit has no idea what is going on, I will use this to my advantage, and it will be I who will be promoted and not that black-faced, low ranking idiot of a demon," says Backbiter. "I must control my emotions and think clearly."

Backbiter departs Tingly's car and flies up to the heavens to report back to Amon.

33

Joe begins to pace as he ponders his conversation with Angelo. Frustration and a sense of hopelessness slowly begin to take over.

"What's happening to me? What did I do to cause all these stupid things to happen?" Joe says, as he pulls at his hair. He looks up with tears beginning to fill up in his eyes. "I want to know why." He is still looking up as if he sees the invisible being he is calling out to. His heart begins to pound harder, and the veins in his neck protrude with every beat of his heart. He continues to walk around the living room floor, tearing at his clothes and throwing whatever he can get his hands on.

With his emotions spent and his strength all but gone, Joe lowers himself to the floor and leans against the sofa. He cries uncontrollably.

Outside the sun is beginning to set over the horizon. Shadows are cast across the grass and the back of his house.

A light cool breeze begins to stir, rustling the leaves on the trees and lifting the sweet scents of the flowers into the air and in through the open windows of his house.

As Joe leans against the couch, the sweet fragrance reaches him. He takes in a deep lungful. It reminds him of the times he has spent meditating on God's word and communing with Him. The sweet presence of the Holy Spirit can be felt.

At these times, a gentle, soft voice can be heard, speaking words of comfort and peace to him. He breathes in deeply, desiring to fill his entire being with this new fresh hope and comfort.

Deep within his heart, a fire starts to stir. Joe pushes himself away from the sofa, and kneeling, he raises his hands in true worship and praise. Lost in his adoration to the Most High God, he is unaware of the dark forces surrounding him.

Shadows jump and scream with pain and frustration as they try and get through the glorious white light that surrounds Joe.

With a sudden burst of energy, Joe jumps to his feet and begins to quote Scripture. Every word that flows out of his mouth causes the dark forces to retreat further until the demons can stand no more.

Joe calls upon the angelic forces of the Lord of Hosts and an angel of light comes from the east and chases after the demonic beings as they try to get away. Some have escaped and call in for reinforcements. The clash of swords brings flashes of fire and light to fill the room and they are seen by all who are within a mile's distance from the warring factors of good versus evil.

The harder Joe prays and rebukes the forces of darkness, the harder the angels of light fight. As quickly as the fight starts, it ends. Soon, all is quiet. Joe opens his eyes and sees he is standing alone in the middle of his living room.

The only light he sees is coming in from the full moon. His curtains are wide open as are his windows. Joe turns on the lights and closes and locks the windows and curtains. He looks at his watch, and to his surprise, he sees it is nine o'clock in the evening.

He heads toward the kitchen and makes himself a light meal. Then he heads for the bedroom. As he gets into bed, he thank the Lord for this evening and is asleep within a couple of minutes. Tonight his sleep will be peaceful and deep. When he awakes without getting out of bed, he raises his hands with a grateful heart and asks the Lord for strength, joy, and wisdom for this new day. Then he gets up and proceeds to the bathroom.

—⊷⊶—

"Hi, how do you like your work as a housekeeper?"

"Well, it's not too bad, at least for the time being."

"Can you meet me for lunch today?"

"Well, let me ask Tingly if he needs me to do anything for him. I'll call you back in ten."

She walks out to the dining room where Tingly is finishing up his second cup of coffee and asks, "Sir, will there be anything you need me to do before I leave for lunch?"

Tingly turns to look at her and says, "No, I can't think of a thing. Go and have a good lunch. As a matter of fact, why don't you take the remainder of the day off? I need to make a few calls. I'll see you tomorrow. Enjoy your day."

"Thank you, sir," she says, as she heads out the door quickly before Tingly can change his mind.

"Hi, this is Heady. I can meet you in about half an hour. I'm looking forward to seeing you."

Arriving at her destination, she parks as far away from the door of the diner as possible. She looks around the parking lot to see if she recognizes any car, then she quickly makes for the door of the diner. Once inside, she lets out a sigh of relief as she walks toward the last booth and takes a seat.

"Hello, would you like something to drink?"

"Yes, some ice tea. I'm expecting someone to join me shortly."

"I'll be back with another menu and water," says the waitress.

Taking a long drink of water, she looks nervously toward the door and then at her watch. *Okay, what's taking you so long? Your fifteen minutes late.* As if her thoughts were being heard, in comes her lunch date.

"Hi, Heady. So sorry I'm late. Gotta phone call that I had to take. Have you ordered yet?"

"No, I was waiting for you. So, tell me what's new?"

"Well, here's the latest. I spoke earlier with—"

"Sorry, I didn't mean to interrupt. Are you ready to order?"

"No problem. Yes. Heady?"

"I would like a club sandwich, on sour dough bread and potato salad."

"And you, sir?"

"Hamburger with all the fixings, fries, and coffee. No cream."

"Would you like a refill on your tea, ma'am?"

Nodding her head yes, she looks at her companion.

"Now you were saying?"

Her lunch date informs her of all he has learned as she listens intently.

"That was quite an earful. Anything else I should look out for?"

"No, not really. Honey, I hate to have to leave, but duty calls. If you need to talk before we meet again, try and call me around nine or so. I'll be home by then and we can talk freely."

Heady smiles as her companion picks up the check and leaves a generous tip. She finishes her tea at leisure. Letting out a long sigh, she walks to her car. Once inside, she sits for a moment trying to decide if she should go to Chulda's former house. She decides against it at the present time and heads toward town. Halfway there, she changes her mind and makes a quick turn.

She arrives and quickly makes her way into the house. She closes the door behind her and walks to the sitting room and through the French doors. The air is stale and dust can be seen floating across the rays of sunlight filtering in through the slightly open drapes. Slowly, she walks to the south wall and stands in front of a beautiful original oil painting. She remembers how she loved that painting as a child. She shakes her head and focuses on the task at hand.

She reaches up and removes the painting carefully. With deft fingers, she dials the combination of the wall safe, but hesitates before opening the door. She reaches in and picks up the only item in the safe and places it in a bag. She folds the top several times as if to keep anything from escaping. Closing the safe door, she replaces the painting and turns to leave. She takes a few steps before standing a moment to look around the room. A sense of dread comes over her. She hurries out to her car. Feeling better knowing the bag is safely in the trunk of her car, she decides to treat herself to a manicure and pedicure and just maybe have her hair done.

"I may be working as housekeeper, but I don't have to look like one."

34

"Hello, I'm Daniel Green and this is Nathan Fine. We have a meeting with Damian Tingly."

"Yes, please do come in. I'll let Mr. Tingly know."

They follow Heady into the living room of Tingly's newly rented villa. Both look around the tastefully furnished room.

"Wow, what a view," says Daniel, as he looks at the view through the French doors. The sun filters through the white, sheer curtains leading to a large red, brick patio. Nathan walks around the room slowly taking in the rich, leather sofas and wooden furniture. Just then, Tingly walks in smiling from ear to ear.

"Gentlemen, good to see you. Would you care for a drink?"

"Yes, I'd like a beer in a glass."

"I'll have ice tea, light on the ice," says Nathan.

"Heady. Oh you're fast. Just like a cat too. I didn't hear you coming. You seem to know what I want before I can call out your name. Gentlemen, your drinks. And wine for me. Thank you, Heady. That's all for now."

She leaves the room and heads for the kitchen. Since she has already prepared lunch all she has to do now is set the table, leaving plenty of time to eavesdrop.

"Well, now that we have wet our whistles we can get down to business. Daniel, what news do you have?" asks Tingly, taking a drink of his wine.

He tells all he knows to Tingly who is getting more excited by the minute. Nathan Fine adds the icing to the cake.

"Gentleman, if everything goes as planned we should have 51 percent of Austin Robotics. That company is relatively new, but from all indications it should prove to be highly successful. This will aid in the financing of the End Times Association and help expedite our plan—Phase Three: the Downfall. Let us toast, to the End Times Association and to our soon-to-be Austin Robotics."

Damian Tingly, Daniel Green, and Nathan Fine lift their glasses to toast their success. Just then, Heady comes in and announces lunch is served.

"Heady, you are a treasure."

All three enter the dining room where everything is served and ready to eat. Heady excuses herself and goes into the kitchen. The three gentlemen eat their fill and leave her to clean up as quickly as possible, while Tingly goes into his office and pulls out the file on the phase three plan.

Remembering he had left some important paperwork in his briefcase, he calls out to Heady.

"Heady, will you please get me the Williams file from my briefcase. You'll find it in my bedroom closet."

"Certainly, sir," she replies, as she heads for Tingly's bedroom.

Finding it on the floor next to his suitcase, she picks up the briefcase, places it on the bed, and opens it. She keeps a look out for Tingly while looking for the file which she finds right away. There are eight loose papers which Heady quickly scans. She finds nothing worth noting until she comes to the last page. Reading it as quickly as possible, she makes mental notes of the important items. Replacing the loose paper back into the briefcase, she picks up the file and hurries to Tingly's office.

"Thank you, Heady. You have spoiled me already. What would I do without you?"

Yes. What would you do indeed? She goes to her room and closes the door behind her. Pulling out her purse, she takes out a small notebook writing all the important information she found in Tingly's papers before she forgets and replaces her notebook back into her purse. She pulls out her cell phone and makes a call.

"Hello?" answers the male voice at the other end of the line.

"Hi, this is Heady. Can we meet again for dinner tonight at the usual place and at seven?"

"Sure. I'll meet you there."

"Can't talk, huh?"

"That's right."

"Okay, I'll see you then at seven," says Heady and hangs up.

The morning goes quickly, but not for Heady. This time, her dinner date is early and she is late. Walking briskly, she goes in to the restaurant and heads toward the back booth.

"Heady, good to see you. How time flies, yes?"

"It seems to be crawling for me. It feels like five months instead of five weeks since I saw you last. But do I have some good information for you?" She spills all she has recently found out.

"Heady, I must say this is very good information you've just given me. So, Damian Tingly took the bait. I didn't think he would. Good work."

They order their food and continue to share bits and pieces of information pertinent to the plan they are working on.

Feeling in a talkative mood she tells John Pollard, the attorney for the Austin Robotics Company, about what she has found.

"John, I went to Chulda's house after the last time we met."

"Heady, I could kiss you. What else did you find out?"

"Well, Tingly is the new gatekeeper. He was the second in command to Chulda. I knew she was in a coven from a young age and wanting to go as high as she could, but I was somewhat taken back to find out she had gone through with her threats."

"You mean to tell me you knew Chulda? I had no idea."

"John, there is so much more to me than meets the eye. Why, I have more education than that fool of a boss of mine. I could be the dean of that stupid college he used to teach at, or should I say, was working at as a professor."

I have my PhD in economics and a master's in business administration. Tingly thinks he can talk about mergers, takeovers, and business dealings while I'm in earshot and I won't know what he's talking about. He thinks he's so smart. Why I could show him a thing or two," she says, her voice rising in volume.

"Heady, keep your voice down. I don't want anyone else to know our business."

"Well, here I have all this education and experience and I'm working as a housekeeper."

Heady takes a long drink of her tea and leans back, her emotions quieting down. John Pollard looks around nervously, hoping no one heard what she had said.

"Honey, it won't be long before you can tell Tingly to take a hike, and you can go anywhere in the world you want with no worries about anything. Especially about money. Now, tell me, how do you know Chulda and how did you get in to her house?"

Heady takes another drink of tea and motions the waitress over.

"Sorry, I had a big table to take care of," says the waitress, as she refills the drinks. Would you like anything else?"

"Yes. I'd like a bourbon on the rocks," says Heady calmly.

"And you, sir? Anything else I can get you?"

"Yes, a beer in a glass, please."

"You got it."

Heady waits till the waitress brings their drinks and leaves.

"Well, to answer your question, I grew up in Chulda's former house. When our parents died, Chulda, I should say Sara, inherited pretty much everything our parents had. You see, she was my older sister."

John does not respond. He leans back into the booth and looks with amazement at Heady.

"You better take a drink or two of your beer and make yourself comfortable. This may take a little time," she says, as she takes a long drink of bourbon.

"Sara was two years older than me. She was into the occult at an early age. At the age of fourteen she joined a coven. The things I saw would curl your hair. I wanted to tell our parents what she was doing, but they were both too interested in making money and climbing the social ladder to care or bother much with us.

"Our dad was a doctor turned real estate developer, and mom was deeply involved in charity projects to have any time for us.

"By the time Sara was seventeen, she had advanced in the coven and was second in command to the original gatekeeper of the portal to hell. She and the others had opened the portal two years earlier in the backwoods behind our house.

"When I told Sara I was going to the police to tell them about what they were doing, she threatened to conjure up a demon by the name of Backbiter and kill me too. I knew she would do it because I had seen it happen before. I didn't dare cross her in any way.

"One night, while she was out back in the woods with the coven, I saw her cavorting with the evil spirits and fallen angels the gatekeeper prior to her had brought up. They were making plans to kill our parents and make it look like an accident.

"I ran back to the house as fast as I could to tell our parents. Sara walked in to the house just as I was telling them. When they saw her, they were furious.

"Father grabbed her by the shoulders and started shaking her and yelling. All Mother could do was cry and ask why she was doing this. That's when Sara called out to Backbiter. She told it to kill our parents. It did. Sara and the others covered it up with the help of the police chief who was an active member of the coven at the time. He has long since been dead from supposed natural causes."

Heady is as pale as a ghost. John sits stunned at what he has just heard. Finding his voice, he says, "Heady, are you all right? Let me order you another drink."

He motions the waitress over and orders a bourbon for her and another beer for himself. The waitress returns with their drinks and quickly leaves to wait on the other patrons.

"Yes, I'm fine, thanks. Listen, I decided to go to Chulda's place. I took something from the safe. I knew she had kept important things there, so I decided I'd check it out. Maybe there could be something we could use. I took some paperwork from the wall safe.

"There were a lot of things in there, but I only took out some paperwork. I knew Chulda had taken great pains to keep secrets, and the wall safe was a good place to start. I read it all twice to make sure I was reading it correctly. I begin to make mental comparisons with the information I found in Tingly's file. And lo and behold, Tingly, Roger Green, and Nathan Fine are planning on the takeover of Austin Robotics. From what I have seen and heard, they are well on the way to doing just that. They believe they can do it too.

"John, this seems to be getting out of control. First, Chulda dying, then Tingly and the other two conspiring.

"I don't like this one bit. I wonder who Tingly has involved in the spirit world to help him. And the other two; I don't know who they are exactly. But I can find out."

Heady stares straight ahead, her mind replaying the night her parents were murdered in front of her while the others stood by doing nothing. The look on Sara's face has haunted her since it happened and probably will to the end of her life.

Heady downs her drink quickly and orders another, a double this time. They sit, saying nothing. Heady is somewhat relieved to have someone she knows and trusts, aware of the horrors she lived through.

John calls the office and lets his employer know he will be an hour late. He tells them his car battery has died, and he will be in as soon as possible.

They finish their lunch in silence, neither one sure of what the other is thinking, nor what effect the information Heady has told him about her family may have in their relationship.

35

"That was quite a fight we had last night," says Deceit, as he looks around at his defeated comrades.

"Yes, that was quite a fight we had," says Denial, looking worse for wear.

"Did you see the way I fought off the two angels of the Lord of Hosts when they came after me with their swords?" Deceit asks with a gleam in his eye.

"What are you talking about? If Belial had not been summoned to help, we would not be here right now," yells Denial, as he flings his hands in the air and walks up to Deceit, putting his face two inches from his.

"You took off the minute your fingers got burned when you touched the holy fire that surrounded Joe Austin. We did all the fighting. I all but got my ears cut off and you have the audacity to say we fought well? Huh!" says Belial, as he and two other fallen angels watch Deceit and Denial closely.

"Weren't you assigned to the human, Joe Austin, to bring him down and thereby lead others to their downfall?" says Belial, one of the fallen angels.

Deceit says nothing, for he is frozen with fear.

"Well? Aren't you going to answer him?" says the other fallen angel, looking sternly at Deceit.

"Yes, I am assigned to him. I have caused the human, Joe Austin, to fall a little more every day. I almost had him had he not cried out to the Most High God," says Deceit in unusual bravery.

"He is a man of courage. He has fortitude beyond his years. This type takes time to manipulate and deceive. His family bloodline is one of strength and virtue."

"Well, you should know," says Belial less harshly than before.

Deceit is taken by surprise at this and decides not to say anything else.

"Let us go and report back to Amon," says Belial to his fellow fallen angels. And in a flash they are gone, leaving Deceit alone to think over the events that of the evening.

"Whew, that was a close call," says Deceit, his heart beating rapidly. "Yes, yes indeed. This human needs to be taken more seriously. I made a tiny mistake with him early on, but now I will correct it, yes, yes indeed," says Deceit, as he flies up in to the air.

Joe is dressed and ready for the day. He has spent an hour reading the word and praying for strength and insight. He decides to visit Angelo de Fuego and apologize in person. He calls Angelo's number, but gets his voice mail.

"Hey, Angelo, I need to talk to you. Can we get together sometime today? It won't take long. Give me a call as to when and where we can meet. Thanks, hope to hear from you soon."

Disappointed, Joe hangs up and decides to call Peter Warren. But first he must find out his number. He takes a sheet of paper and writes down Angelo's name first, then Peter Warren's and he notes the time he called. As for the others, he writes down the name when he calls, determined to make things right between himself and those he has wronged.

"Hello, is this Peter Warren?"

"Yes, this is Peter."

"Hi, Peter, this is Joe Austin. We sort of met at Brinkman Hall. I'd like to get together with you and have a little chat. There's something I need to talk you about."

Peter's face drains of color. He was expecting to hear from Joe's attorney, not from Joe himself.

"Sure, where and when do you want to meet?" says Peter, with a slight shaking in his voice.

"How about today, say in half an hour?"

"Sure, that'll be okay. Will the Coffee Cart be okay?" asks Peter, with impending dread.

"Coffee Cart in half an hour. See you then," says Joe confidently.

Peter closes his book and places it into his backpack. A wave of nausea rises to his throat. Slowly, Peter pushes back his chair, and picking up his backpack, he stands momentarily looking around the library in search of someone he knows to ask them to accompany him to meet with Joe. Not seeing anyone, Peter walks out of the library and out to his car. He opens the trunk and drops his backpack into it. Taking a deep breath, he opens the driver's door and gets in.

Come on, Pete, face up to it, be a man. It's a wonder you haven't heard from him or his attorney before now. Not to mention the police. Well, I'm glad it's finally coming to a head. *It's been torture waiting and not being able to contact him or talk to anyone else about this, only my attorneys*, thinks Peter as he starts his car and makes his way to the Coffee Cart.

Joe pulls up to the parking lot and parks his car. He gets out quickly and makes his way inside the café. He advises the waitress he is expecting Peter to join him.

"Would you like anything to drink while you wait?" asks the waitress politely.

"Oh, ah, just water please. Well, a cup of coffee too," he says, not wanting to appear to Peter as if this were somewhat of a showdown.

Peter arrives a few minutes later, and he too quickly exits from his car and makes his way in to the café. The waitress leads him to the back booth where Joe waits for him, calmly sipping his coffee. As Peter draws near, Joe looks up smiling at Peter who also orders coffee before sitting down.

"Hello," says Peter nervously, as he extends his hand to Joe. "I'm Peter Warren."

"Joe Austin. Nice to meet you," says Joe calmly and sincerely. "Don't be afraid. I don't want to cause you any trouble."

The waitress brings a piping hot cup of coffee and places it before Peter.

"Anything else I can get you two?"

"More cream please," says Joe.

"Sure, hon," says the waitress with a smile.

To Peter's surprise, Joe blushes and takes a drink of water.

"I'll get to the point," Joe says, looking down at this cup.

"I want to ask you to forgive me for holding a grudge against you. I'm sorry. Will you forgive me?" says Joe softly, but honestly.

Peter sits speechless for a moment, looking with disbelief at Joe as he tries to absorb what Joe has just asked him.

"You want me to forgive you?" asks Peter, his hands starting to shake, his eyes getting misty.

"Yes, I do. I'm a Christian, and I've backslid in my faith. When the incident at Brinkman Hall happened, well, a lot of stuff I had thought I had overcome came to the surface. Since I've been home recuperating, I had a lot of time to think about my life up to now. I've been deceiving myself for a long time. Since my parents were killed in an auto accident, I've been dealing with forgiveness and I fell back into my old ways.

I use to be heavily involved with the occult and instead of denouncing it completely, I kept one board game that I knew full well was an open door to the occult. But I deceived myself into thinking no harm could come by keeping it to remind myself of those days gone by. To remember all the trouble and heartache it caused me so I wouldn't be tempted to return to it. But I found out the hard way, it was an open door to let the devil back in and try to bring me down again."

Peter sits back in the booth reliving the night at Brinkman Hall and his classes with Mr. Tingly. Peter begins to connect the two. He realizes Mr. Tingly is part of the problem. That he was a pawn in Tingly's plan to infiltrate and tear down the morals of this city.

"Sorry, I was just thinking. Yes, of course I forgive you," says Peter gratefully.

"Now it's my turn to ask you to forgive me for what I did to you. I can't tell you how sorry I am. It's as if something had gotten into me and I wasn't able to control what I was doing. I went to the hospital to visit you and apologize, but I wasn't able to see you. I did meet the girl you were with and apologized to her. I've been going over what happened in my mind ever since and I just now am putting two and two together," says Peter relieved to get it off his chest.

"First, yes I forgive you. Now what do you mean?" asks Joe wondering what he was talking about.

"You're in Mr. Tingly's classes, aren't you?"

"Yes," replies Joe.

"Do you remember how he was always talking about how Christians can be influenced to do things by the devil if they allow themselves to be?"

"Yes, go on."

"That night at Brinkman Hall, before I got on stage I was a bit nervous, so I took a couple of hits of cocaine just before I went on. I only do it when I'm under a lot of pressure. I had made up my mind that there was nothing wrong with it, but after doing it I knew I had made a big mistake. It was as if I were being overtaken by something or someone else.

"That night I felt it again, except this time it felt really strong. It felt like something really powerful had possessed me. Something or someone else was controlling me. I couldn't stop, even though I wanted to. During the fight with you, I felt someone pull me off you and fling me on stage. When I landed, I felt it leave.

"I remember hearing Mr. Tingly at the start of the play say, 'Rise up, oh mighty one. Rise up and address your adoring crowd.' That was just before I felt that thing came into me. I also remember Tingly pulling my eyelids open and looking into my eyes. But he didn't help me. He just left me there."

"So, you think Mr. Tingly is in on all this mess?" replies Joe, concerned to hear what Peter is saying.

"Yes, I'm sure of it."

"Listen," says Joe, "we have to get together again soon and have a good long talk."

"Sure, give me a call, and then we can figure this thing out together."

Joe gives Peter his number, and Peter punches it into his cell phone.

"Do you want me to warm that coffee up for either of you?" asks the waitress.

"No, I'm good," replies Joe. "May I have the check please?"

Peter protests, but Joe says, "You can leave the tip." They shake hands and leave the café.

36

The meeting with Tingly and the rest of the coven is coming to an end.

"Skyler Riggs is primed and ready for us to make our next move," says Chulda to Mr. Tingly. "We can go ahead with our plan to execute Phase Three: the Downfall."

Mr. Tingly smiles from ear to ear. *Finally, I will get what I have been waiting for such a long time. Authority and power far greater than Chulda could ever dream of.*

"Damian, Damian," she says, as she tries to get Damian Tingly's attention.

"Oh, sorry. My mind drifted for a moment. You were saying?" replies Tingly with a faraway look in his eyes.

"I was saying, we can put our plan into motion," she answers with growing concern.

"Fine, let's do it," says Tingly.

Chulda looks at him, her eyes narrowing, wondering if Tingly has plans of his own. *There is something wrong here, but*

I can't quite pinpoint it. Damian is acting weird, even for him. I'll just have to keep a closer watch on him.

Mr. Tingly realizes Chulda is beginning to get suspicious. *Tingly ole boy, you better watch yourself a bit more closely. You've come too far to screw this up now. Just smile and keep pretending all is as it should be.* Tingly bids farewell to Chulda.

"Okay then, we'll meet again same time, same day next week. Everyone has their assignments. Don't trust anyone. Keep your mouths shut and your eyes sharp. I have a feeling there is a traitor within our ranks. I don't know who it is, but I have my suspicions. Okay, everyone, see you all next week. And may Amon guide your very steps," says Chulda, as she cast a warning look at them all.

One by one, they file out of Chulda's house and each one to his and her own car. Tingly is the first to leave and heads straight to his office. As he passes the office of the late Janice Simmons, a shiver runs up this spine.

He places his key into his office door and turns it slowly, as if anticipating trouble on the other side. Feeling for the light switch, an uneasy sensation comes over him. He scans the room and quickly walks over to his desk.

Unlocking the left hand bottom drawer of his desk, he pulls out a white, sealed, large envelope and places it on his desk and closes and relocks the drawer.

He remains standing, looking down at the envelope, unsure of what he should do. *If I open it, there will be no turning back.*

If I don't and leave it sealed, everything will remain as it is and I can continue with Phase Three: the Downfall as planned.

Slowly, he pulls out his chair and sits down. He places both hands on top of the envelope and takes a deep breath.

"Damian ole boy, nothing ventured, nothing gained."

Carefully, he takes the envelope and opens it. Peering into it, his eyes light up as he pulls out a small piece of paper. Holding it by his thumb and pointer finger, he stares at it for a full minute. His heart leaps as he counts the zeros behind the number six. Six zeros makes it six million dollars. Tingly leans back in his chair as he imagines what he can do with this amount of money.

I can retire to the Cayman Islands and easily buy my own private island where I can live out my days in peace. No more putting up with this nonsense. Who needs power and authority when I can live away from all this madness?

A cold breeze passes across his face. Looking around, he checks to see if his window is open or if he left the air conditioner on. Everything looks to be in order. Quickly, Tingly folds the cashier's check in two and puts it in his left jacket front pocket.

He has decided to turn in his letter of resignation to the college tonight. Opening the locked drawer again, he pulls out the letter and quickly signs it and places it in preaddressed, stamped envelope and seals it placing it into his right jacket pocket.

Hastily, he picks up an empty box from his closet and begins to fill it with items he may need in his new life and those which mean something to him. Just as he is about to place the last remaining memento into his box, he hears a thump. Holding the item tightly in has hand, he listens for where the noise is coming from.

Thump, thump, thump is all he hears. Too afraid to speak, he drops the item into the box and grabs it with both hands and heads for the door. He turns and takes one last look around his office and opens the door.

Tingly feels a cold breeze which seems to have increased in strength as it swirls around him. He opens his mouth to scream, but nothing comes out. Again and again, the cold air encircles him.

Mr. Tingly slams shut the door and hurries down the dark hallway with his box still in hand. He reaches the exit door and pushes hard against the bar on the door, but it will not budge. He turns his back to it and tries to open it, pushing with all his strength, but it will not open. On the verge of panicking, he steps away from the door and starts to make his way down another dark hallway still holding tightly to his box.

His eyes search the darkened hallway for another door which may lead to the parking lot. Upon turning the corner, he abruptly comes to a halt. A dark figure is coming toward him, not making a sound.

Tingly can feel his heart beating rapidly as he stands motionless and powerless to move. His eyes strain to see into the darkness. The dark figure is now within arm's reach. It stands silently before him, neither one making a move nor a sound. Suddenly, the figure lifts up his left arm and places it firmly on Tingly's right shoulder.

Overcome with fear, Tingly sinks slowly to the ground. The dark figure leans over him, touching him with an ice cold hand. In the swirling darkness, Tingly hears his name being repeated over and over as the cold hand taps his face. Complete darkness engulfs him as he willingly embraces it.

A flash of light crosses his face as he is roughly shaken. Mr. Tingly comes to and opens his eyes to see the form that is bent over him.

"Please don't hurt me," he manages to whisper.

"Mr. Tingly, are you all right?" asks Charlie, the night janitor. He places his flashlight back onto his utility belt and lifts Mr. Tingly's head repeats the question.

"Who are you? Have you come to hurt me?" he asks, trying to focus on the face before him.

"No, Mr. Tingly, it's me, Charlie, the night janitor. I saw you coming, and I thought I'd come and open the door for you. I just started my shift and I locked the door after me as usual. I just finished working on the ice maker in the teacher's lounge. I didn't realize anyone was here so late at night," replies Charlie with great concern. "Here, let me take the box so I can help you up."

Mr. Tingly releases his tight grip on the box and takes Charlie's arm as he is helped up. He stands wiping the cold sweat from his brow and steadies himself, taking in a deep breath.

"Let me walk you out to your car. Here, I'll take that," says Charlie, as he takes the box again from Mr. Tingly. Together they make their way back down the dark hallway and out the building and to the parking lot.

"Are you sure you're okay? I can drive you home in my car and you can pick up your car tomorrow," says Charlie, as Mr. Tingly opens the trunk of his car and places the box in it.

"Thank you. I'm okay. I'm just getting over a bad cold which left me a bit weak, that's all. Really, I'm fine. Thank you," he tells Charlie, as he gets in his car and starts the engine.

"You know, Mr. Tingly, you need to rest. Tomorrow is Saturday. Maybe you should stay home and take it easy."

"Yes, I will, Charlie. Thank you very much," he says, as he slips on his seatbelt and closes the door. He smiles and waves good-bye to Charlie as he drives away.

"I think the death of Janice hit him harder than he thought," says Charlie softly, as he makes his way back to the building.

Mr. Tingly arrives home safely, if somewhat worse for wear. He heads into his house and to the kitchen. Opening the door to the wine cooler, he pulls out a bottle of wine, not caring which one it is. He quickly opens it and drinks directly out of the bottle. Being a wine connoisseur, this is completely out of character for him. He continues to drink until he feels the warm, calming effect of the wine.

He heads for the bedroom and begins to pack a suitcase with only what he will need for a few days. Feeling a little warm, he goes into the bathroom and splashes cold water on his face, then he gathers up his toiletries and hastily packs them as well. Then he heads into his office and unlocks the center drawer from his desk and pulls out three sealed, preaddressed, stamped envelopes. One is addressed to Chulda, the other to Mr. Padiff, and the third to Mr. Pierce. Leaving them on top of his desk, he goes around his house checking to see if there is anything else he might need or want to take with him.

Not finding any, he takes the few belongings he has decided to take and packs them. He takes them out to his car and places the items in the trunk. Returning to his house, he checks each room and turns off the lights one final time.

Satisfied, he locks the door and heads back into the garage and gets into his car. Without delay, he opens the garage door and backs out into the street. Pausing for a moment, he takes one last look at the house he has called home.

The garage door closes. A faint smile begins to form as he heads for the airport. The sound of jumbo jets taking off and landing gives him a feeling of euphoria. He heads for the short-term parking and quickly unloads his suitcases as he motions to the driver of a small electric tram. The ride to the airport terminal is short. He tips the driver generously and smiles at the sky cab which helps him with his luggage.

Without skipping a beat, he makes a beeline to the Golden Skies Airline ticket counter and buys a one-way ticket to Florida. He does not have to wait long before he is on board and headed down the runway.

Damian, you've made the right decision. It will be smooth sailing from now on, he thinks as the seatbelt sign goes off. An attractive, young woman comes down the aisle with a menu in hand.

"Would you like a cocktail before we serve dinner?" she asks, smiling.

"Yes, please. I would like a bottle of your finest champagne," replies Mr. Tingly, as he adjusts himself in his seat.

"Certainly, sir," she says with a smile, as she turns and walks past the unseen passenger sitting right across the aisle from Mr. Tingly. The unseen passenger smiles as he too makes himself comfortable.

37

"Hello?"

"Hello, Skyler. This is Chulda, we met a few days ago," she says, as she walks to the window of the supermarket break room.

"Yes, I remember. How can I help you?"

"Funny you should ask," says Chulda, as she looks out the window.

"I would like to have another séance tomorrow night. Would you be available?"

"Saturday? Sure, I can make it. Where do you want to have it? Your place?" replies Skyler, his hands starting to perspire.

"Yes, do you remember how to get here?"

"Yes, I do. What time do you want me to be there?"

"It will be fine at 7:00 p.m."

"I'll be there. Seven sharp," says Skyler, his eyes showing concern.

"Have a pleasant evening. I'll see you tomorrow at my place," replies Chulda with a smile, as she places the phone back on its stand.

"Oh, yes, let the fun begin," she says, with a sinister smile on her face.

Skyler pulls up to the front of the Chulda's house and quickly gets out. He is five minutes early, but he wonders if he is late since there are other cars parked along the driveway which he does not recognize. He rings the doorbell. Almost immediately, the door is opened.

"Come in. Follow me please," says the butler, as he leads Skyler back to the sitting room where they had previously met.

Skyler walks in and stops short. He looks nervously at the faces before him. Chulda walks over to Skyler and puts her arm through his and draws him close to her. Skyler stiffens slightly as Chulda gently pulls him toward the round table.

"I'd like you to meet Max, Julie, Paul, Samantha, Travis, and Mia. Everybody, this is Skyler Riggs."

Everyone at the table smiles and greets him. Skyler does not recognize anyone, except Paul. Paul lowers his head slightly and turns to Samantha. Leaning toward her, he whispers something into her ear. Samantha laughs coyly and smiles at Paul.

Skyler's level of discomfort rises. He does not know who these people are and why they would be interested in his deceased mother. Reluctantly, he takes his seat and turns to Chulda in hopes of getting some answers to the questions he very much wants to ask. But before he can, Chulda turns to the butler and asks him to turn off the lights.

The séance progresses as before, except that this time there is a plan that Ingrid Riggs reveals to them. At first, Ingrid Riggs states she will be contacting Jason Riggs when he is alone at home and will try to convince him to ease up on Skyler. She will tell Jason that Skyler was in no way responsible for her death at Skyler's birth.

Then there is a long pause. When Ingrid begins to speak again, the subject is no longer about her and Skyler's father, Jason, but about a plan called Phase Three: the Downfall.

Sitting quietly, Skyler listens intently to what is being discussed. Nothing seems to make sense to him. The questions the others are asking and the answers they are given, the others sitting at the table, know exactly what is going on and what part of the plan they are to execute. They speak as if in code, making it harder for Skyler to understand what they are talking about.

Soon, the séance is over, and Chulda thanks all her guests, both human, as well as spiritual.

They mingle briefly and say their good-byes to Chulda. Paul passes by Skyler; their eyes meeting momentarily. Skyler seems to thinks he has seen Paul before, but can't place him. Paul hopes no one notices his uneasiness, and he is soon on his way to the other end of town.

Skyler politely waits for the last guest to leave, thinking this will be a good time to speak candidly with Chulda.

Hastily, Chulda bids Skyler good night and all but pushes him out the door. She picks up the phone and makes a call.

"Hello? Damian, this is Chulda. You missed the séance this evening. Is everything okay? We've put Phase Three: the Downfall into motion tonight. You know what to do now. Give me a call when you've done your part. Remember, it has to be done tonight."

Chulda is unaware of Mr. Tingly's change of plans and the fact that Tingly will never get the voice mail she has left him. Being that he is the second in command, his part in this plan is crucial to its success. But she will soon find out Damian Tingly has betrayed them all. There will be hell to pay when Amon finds out about Chulda's failure to complete the most important and final part of the plan known as Phase Three: the Downfall.

Chulda paces as she waits for a call from Damian Tingly. A call she will never receive. Soon she is on the phone again, contacting anyone she thinks might know where Damian is. No one has seen or heard from him since Friday evening.

Panicking, she rushes out to her car and makes her way to Tingly's house. Just a couple of miles from his home, Chulda is stopped by the police for speeding.

"Do you know how fast you were going?" asks the officer, as he leans down to look at the driver.

Seeing who it is, he backs away saying, "Oh, I'm sorry, I didn't recognize your car."

Chulda gives him a look that could kill. She starts her car again and she speeds away, leaving the officer staring at her taillights as dust settles all around him. She arrives at Tingly's house.

No lights are on. He better be here or he better have a hell of a good reason for missing the meeting tonight, thinks Chulda as she hurries out to the front door.

She rings the door bell and peeks in the window. The house is too dark for her to see inside. So she pulls out her key ring and finds the key to Tingly's front door.

"Damien, are you here?" she calls out, as she feels for the light switch. The lights go on, and she quickly goes room to room turning on lights as she goes, calling out to Tingly.

"What have you done?" she says loudly, as she rushes out the front door leaving all the lights on in the house and the door wide open.

She reaches her car and pulls out her cell phone and frantically makes one last call. No one has any idea where Mr. Tingly can be found. She dares not call upon the dark forces to help her locate him. There will be plenty of explaining to do when she eventually has to call on them to explain what went wrong.

She climbs into her car and beats the steering wheel with her free hand. There is no answer. Fear overtakes her like a cat leaping onto a mouse.

She starts her car and backs out, narrowly missing the mailbox. Frantic, she steps on the gas pedal and speeds back to her house. Chulda decides to make one more attempt to contact Mr. Tingly.

Grabbing her cell phone, she takes her eyes off the road long enough to dial. She looks up just in time to see the lights have turned red and a trailer rig going right in front of her. Upon impact, her Mercedes explodes into flames as the big rig slides along the street for several feet.

The driver of the big rig jumps out of the cab, barely missing being hit by oncoming traffic. Debris scatters across the intersection. Several unfortunate souls witness the tragic event and immediately call nine-one-one on their cell phones.

Within minutes of the crash, the police and fire trucks are out in full force. They quickly put out the fire and help the driver of the truck.

He is bruised and badly scraped from the tumble he took as he jumped from the cab. The ambulance arrives and wastes no time in taking the cab driver, who is in shock, to the nearest hospital.

As the crash scene is being investigated and the eye witnesses are being questioned, Chulda's charred body is carefully removed from the still smoldering car and transported by the coroner's office to the mortuary where they will try and identify her body.

38

The sound of Amon's voice is heard throughout the first entire hallway and out into the courtyard as he learns of the news of Tingly's betrayal. Backbiter cowers in a corner, as Deceit tries to hide behind the massive doors of Amon's office. Amon rages on as he calls in all who were closely involved in the plan, Phase Three: the Downfall.

"This was a simple and precise plan," he shouts, making everyone present shake with fear.

"I handpicked each and every one of you. Yet you all have failed me and why? Because of a small church group of prayer warriors led by a woman. You had been warned not to be misled or to go by their looks. She may be an old, widowed grandmother in the natural, but in the spirit, she is a powerful prayer warrior," says Amon loudly, as he paces the length of his office.

The silence that follows seems to go on forever. Backbiter and Deceit have both gone to the nearest exit. They stand, shaking, holding onto each other in fear of what Amon will do to them.

Amon, being a marquis and leader over six legions of fallen angles, has been made to look the fool.

"This is unacceptable. Someone besides Chulda will pay for this," he says in an eerily calm voice.

"Leave, all of you, except Deceit, Backbiter, and Enepsigos. You will remain here with me. We have much to discuss. The rest of you, go back to your assigned posts and this time watch out for the prayer warriors."

Twenty-five fallen angels and several demons and imps leave immediately and return to their assigned posts. No one speaks a word to the other.

Deceit and Backbiter both walk together toward Amon's desk, as Enepsigos takes a seat at the far side of Amon's massive desk. They stop in front of his desk and pray they will not be sent prematurely to hell for failing so miserably.

Amon walks around them, giving them a look that almost makes their hearts fail. He stands in front of them both. With lightning quick movement, he slaps each one at the same time with the back of his hands. Both go flying, one to the left and one to the right. Each one lands sprawled against the cold, gleaming walls of Amon's office.

Amon walks back to his desk and sits down, leaning back against his chair. Both Deceit and Backbiter stumble to their feet and make their way back to the front of Amon's desk. They stand fearfully waiting for what will come next.

Amon looks at each of them with fire in his eyes and takes a long, deep breath before he speaks again. Enepsigos sits quietly at the right end of Amon's desk, not daring to move or speak. He has never seen Amon as angry as he is now. Amon motions to Deceit and Backbiter to sit. They share one chair, while Enepsigos sits in the other. Amon leans forward placing his arms on his desk and says to Deceit in a low deliberate tone, "Now tell me, where you went wrong."

Meanwhile, Skyler sits in a booth by himself at the Coffee Cart. He has written down the main points of what was said at the séance that apply to him and what he can remember of the plan known as Phase Three: the Downfall.

His part is easy; he just has to call on Enepsigos at the altar, which he has made inside his room. It is a simple one made up of three candles, a mirror, and a script which he is to read word for word in order for Enepsigos to come and bring up his beloved mother, Ingrid Riggs. Then he will send her into his father's room while he is asleep and Ingrid Riggs will do the rest. It seems simple enough.

Soon his parents will be home, and he will be able to do to put this matter to rest. Skyler closes the door to his closet and goes to bed. Soon after, he falls into a deep and strange sleep.

39

Joe enters the small church located in a strip mall not far from Brinkman Hall. This is where his parents used to attend services every Wednesday and Sunday.

It has been too long since I've been here, thinks Joe. Being Saturday, the church is almost empty. Mr. and Mrs. Warren, another two people he does not recognize, and of course, the Widow, Claire Deaton, as she is known. You can bet she will be here for every service, day or night, usually sits at the very back and always wears the prayer shawl she was given years ago on her first trip to Israel by Rabbi Goldstein.

Her small frame is hidden by the shawl as she makes intercession for Joe, Skyler and his parents, and others she has on her prayer list. Some angels of the Most High God are walking around, making sure no evil spirits come near her.

Many others are seen standing close by her awaiting orders which she will pray as the Lord leads her.

The appearance of the angels varies. Some are in full armor with their swords sheathed until they are sent out. Others, glorious in their white robes, walk through the walls making their way to the homes of the friends and neighbors of Widow Deaton.

Still others are sent across town to the Warren household and to various parts of town, including Jason and Mary Riggs's home. What they find in Skyler's room will be reported back to the Lord of Host where they will be dispatched with new orders.

One special angel stands vigilantly watching Widow Deaton's house while she is away. And, of course, her constant companions who never leave her side.

A lone elderly man walks over to Joe. He leans down and says softly, "Your prayers are being heard. He wants you to know you are not alone. He has forgiven you. He has His angels out in force to help you through this. But He would like for you not to dwell on the past, but to know you must continue going forward. Stand strong and resist the devil. Remember, He has put His angels in charge over you."

Joe looks down for a second, then he looks up again to thank the old gentleman who has spoken those words of encouragement, but he is nowhere to be seen. Angelo de Fuego smiles as he makes his way out of the church doors and down the quiet streets.

Funny, I didn't even hear the doors open or close, Joe thinks as he makes his way out to the aisle. He pauses for a moment beside Widow Deaton. Feeling his presence, she finishes her prayer and slowly stands to her feet. Joe smiles at her and offers her his arm, which she gratefully takes. They walk out into the warm summer night. Without a word being said, they walk together to Mrs. Deaton's car. Joe waits until she drives away. He reflects on knowing such a strong and gentle woman of God.

I should take a page from her book. She's gone through a lot more in her lifetime than I have, yet she has never strayed, but kept the faith always on Him.

A soft, light rain begins to fall, cleansing the air and his thoughts as well. With his spirit stirring within him, he heads for his car and then for home. He finds a note sticking out from between the door and door frame.

It reads, "Meet me in front of the gas station at the south end of town at ten thirty tonight. Signed Paul." Joe wonders which Paul this may be.

I know two Pauls. Watkins, who is in Tingly's class and Miller who is an up-and-coming executive for Jenkins Enterprises International. More than likely, it's Paul Watkins from school, probably has questions about class.

Without giving it a second thought, Joe gets back into his car and heads south for the gas station. Arriving at exactly 10:30 p.m., he scans the station hoping to see Paul Watkins. Instead, he sees Paul Miller walking over to his car. Paul leans down to speak to Joe.

"Sorry for all the cloak-and-dagger business, but it is necessary," Paul says with a concerned look.

"What's this about?" asks Joe.

"Do you mind if I join you? I don't want to stand here. Someone might recognize me," replies Paul, as he looks around.

"Sorry, get in."

He walks in front of Joe's car and gets in the front passenger side. Both turn to face each other, wondering if this meeting was a good idea.

"What's this about, Mr. Miller?"

With a heavy sign, Paul Miller looks down momentarily. He looks straight into Joe's eyes.

"Have you ever heard of the End Times Association?" asks Paul.

"The End Times Association? No, can't say that I have."

"This group is a very powerful group of people with connections that spread throughout the community. Fifteen people in all. They've been around at least three years. That's how long I've been deep undercover with them. They've set into motion a plan called Phase Three: the Downfall."

"What has this got to do with me?"

"You're well thought of and have a lot of influence over this town."

Joe lets out a laugh. "Yeah, right," he says sarcastically. Paul leans toward Joe and with a no-nonsense look on his face.

"Your parents were very active in the church and community before their untimely death. They left a legacy which includes you, like it or not."

Joe leans against the car door as Paul continues to explain what the Phase Three: the Downfall is and how it involves Joe.

"So, my parents knew about this Phase Three: the Downfall, all along? Why didn't they say anything to me?" asks Joe, not trying to cover up the hurt in his voice.

"They were afraid for your safety. They tried to keep you protected and they had, up until the night they died," replies Paul gently.

"Joe, you were heavily involved in the occult. Your parents were fighting against the dark forces while you were opening the door to them. It made their jobs that much harder. This is why I have come to talk to you. We've been watching you very closely all this time."

"Who's been watching me?" ask Joe defensively.

"There is a group of us from the church who meet in different locations and times to update each other on what we've learned and how to counteract the moves of the End Times Association."

"Is that why I was attacked at Brinkman Hall?"

"Now you're getting it," says Paul. "There are those who want to take your life and remove others they think might hinder their plan. These are determined people who will not stop until they accomplish their task. I'm sure you've heard about Janice Simmons and what happened to her."

"Yes, I did, but what has that to do with me? Didn't she die of alcohol-related problems?"

"Yes, she did. Joe, listen carefully. She was doing some digging around and found out some key information that would have greatly hindered their plan had she continued to live. These are very powerful people who are deep into the occult. They are very dangerous people. Now do you understand?"

"Only too well," says Joe, sadness covering his face like a veil.

"Joe, I am working with a coven led by a young woman who goes by the name of Chulda. She is the head of a small elite coven, and Damian Tingly is her second in command. Her real name is Sara Cunningham."

"What? Sara, the cashier at the supermarket?" asks Joe in disbelief.

"Yes, she's the gatekeeper here on earth to the underworld."

Paul goes on to explain everything he knows about the group known as the End Times Association and his role in it. He explains his connection to Peter Warren's family. Joe's mind begins to reel as he connects the events of Brinkman Hall, his encounter with demons and Mr. Tingly.

So that's why the dreams and the demonic activity I've sensed have been so strong of late. What a fool I've been. Just because I can't understand why things are happening as they are doesn't mean I have no part in them. And here I thought I was just playing around with things that I thought I could control. But instead, I opened the door for demonic activity in my life and in the lives of others. I never thought it would affect anyone else.

"How could I have been so blind and stupid?" Joe says loudly, regretting all the red flags that he'd seen and ignored.

"What can I do to help?" he asks, determined to undo, if possible, all the trouble he had unknowingly unleashed.

"I'm going to meet tomorrow morning with the head of our group. We have a counterplan to prevent any further actions of the End Times Association. Here's what we need for you to do."

Paul explains to Joe his part in this. Both agree that the other is on the level and will do their part.

"Don't let anything or anyone keep you from doing your part. Okay?"

"Don't worry. Now that I know what I've done to help bring this mess about, you can bet I'll do my part to help undo it," says Joe with determination.

"Good. I'll call you tomorrow and keep you informed of what is going on."

Paul gets out of the car and hurries back to his own car and drives away.

Joe sits for a while thinking of what he and Paul have discussed, then starts his car and heads for home. Feeling uneasy, Joe hurries inside and quickly locks the doors and windows and heads for his bedroom. Laying on his back, he places his hands over his face. His mind reeling with all he has heard this evening. Abruptly, he gets up and begins to pray. His angelic force stands guard all night, while the Lord of Hosts speaks softly to Joe to follow.

40

Samantha drives Mia to her house and parks in the driveway. "Now what do you plan to do?" asks Mia, a bit angrily.

"Give me a minute, will you? I'm trying to think," says Samantha, ready to belt Mia if she opens her mouth one more time.

"I'll call Mr. Tingly. He should know what to do," says Samantha, with hope flooding through her. She takes her cell phone out of her purse and looks up Mr. Tingly's phone number to call him.

"Come on, come on," says Samantha, as the phone continues to ring in her ear. She turns to Mia and says, "Looks like we're on our own. He's not answering."

"I'll call Chulda. She'll know what to do," offers Mia.

"With cops all over the place? Please, she's probably behind bars by now. There's no way I'm calling her now."

"Well, what are we going to do? Think, maybe we should call Paul Miller. He likes you, you know," says Mia, as she smiles at Samantha.

"Yeah, I think maybe you're right. Maybe he can help us." Samantha eagerly dials his number.

"Oh, geez," she says, frustrated. "It went straight to voice mail. Doesn't anyone answer their stupid phone anymore?"

Just after she leaves a voice message, Samantha's phone rings. She answers on the first ring.

"Hello?"

"Sam? This is Paul Miller returning your call. What's the matter? You said it's an emergency."

"Yes, the cops have caught on to us. We went to Chulda's house and there were cops all over the place. Our plan is falling apart. What are we going to do?" she asks, restraining herself from panicking.

"Okay, now," asks Paul in a calm manner. "What did you do?"

"We, Mia and I, went to Skyler's house around five this morning, and we took Blackheart with us. I called on Enepsigos to go and speak to Skyler. Then I called the demon, Backbiter, to possess Blackheart and kill Skyler if Enepsigos failed to complete his part of the End Times plans."

"Well, did you hear from Skyler?" asks Paul nervously.

"No, we didn't. Enepsigos failed us. He never showed up. But I do know Backbiter will do his part."

That's what I'm afraid of, thinks Paul.

"Listen, you have to stop Backbiter. Whatever you do, don't let him kill or hurt Skyler. If he does, then we're all in for murder."

"How are the cops going to be able to pin it on us? We're not the ones committing the murder. All they know is we know Chulda, nothing more."

"Just go back go Skyler's house, pick up Blackheart and cast out Backbiter. Then go home and stay there till I call you. Understood?"

"Yes, loud and clear. I have Mia with me. Do you want me to take her with me?"

"Yes, both of you stay together. Regardless of what happens, stay together. Don't go anywhere after you get Blackheart and go home."

"Okay, we're on our way."

Samantha hangs up and tells Mia the plan as they head back to Skyler's house with Officer Steve Logan on their tail. Samantha pulls up to the front of Skyler's house and gets out. Mia follows her to the backyard via the side gate. They look at each other in disbelief and make their way through the door careful to avoid snagging their clothes on the jagged pieces of broken wood.

"Here, Blackheart," calls out Samantha softly, for fear of calling attention to themselves.

"Here, kitty, kitty," yells Mia, as they search for Samantha's cat.

"Not so loud," says Samantha, as they continue searching through the bushes and behind the patio furniture.

Samantha lets out a stifled scream as she nears Skyler's bedroom window.

Laying on its side is the broken and bloody body of Blackheart. Samantha kneels down next to him and begins to weep softly. Mia walks closer to her and sees the body as well. She gags on the putrid smell emanating from it.

"Oh," says Mia, as she puts her hand over her nose and mouth.

"Man, it stinks! Come on, he's dead. Let's get out of here," says Mia, as she pulls Samantha to her feet.

"Damn that demon," Samantha says angrily. "Damn you to hell, Backbiter. You didn't have to kill him. All you had to do was leave," she shouts, as she shakes her fists skyward.

She continues to curse and belittle Backbiter as Mia puts her arm around Samantha and pulls her back to the side of the house. Without warning, Backbiter appears in front of them. His eyes shine brightly, barring its pointed, sharp teeth as it blocks their exit.

"You were saying?" asks Backbiter, as he raises his arms and attacks both women.

Officer Logan hears a blood curdling scream and rushes to side door of Skyler's house. He snags his pants on the broken wooden side door as he trips and falls over the bloody dead bodies of Mia and Samantha. He has seen many terrible things in his eight years as a police officer, but nothing that comes close to what lays in front of him now. Composing himself, he calls Sergeant Greer and then calls the coroner's office.

"Okay, Steve, go out front and wait for the coroner to come. I'll be there shortly. Hang in there," says Sergeant Greer, as if speaking to one of his own sons.

Sergeant Greer walks over to a uniformed officer and lets him know he will need all but a few forensic people to finish up the search at Sara Cunningham's house and to head out to Skyler Riggs's house on the double.

"Damn, this is getting stranger as the day goes by," he says to a young cop who will accompany him to the scene of the crime. When they arrive, they are met by a very pale-looking officer, Steve Logan, who informs the Sergeant to his findings. Soon a crowd of police, forensic, and coroner's cars are blocking the quiet, tree-lined street.

41

Peter walks into class and takes his regular seat. Only a few people are present and a couple of them are chatting quietly near the front door. Peter looks at his watch.

Huh, I wonder where Mr. Tingly is. He's usually here by now.

There are a couple of students remaining.

"Do you know if there will be class today?" he asks, not caring who answers.

One girl turns and says, "I don't know. We've been here twenty minutes and no one has shown up or come to inform us of anything."

"I think I'll leave as well," he says, as he picks up his books and heads for the door.

Just then a student aide from the dean's office arrives, almost bumping into Peter. She has a sheet of paper and tape in her hand.

"Oh sorry," he says to Peter, as she steps into Mr. Tingly's room looking to see how many students are there.

"Good, not too many people here. Excuse me please," she says loudly. "This class has been suspended until further notice. You will be notified by e-mail or by phone as to when classes will be resumed. Thank you."

She turns and tapes the sheet of paper to the door and hurries back to her office. Those remaining stand up and leave. Peter pulls out his cell phone and dials Joe's number.

"Hello?" answers Joe.

"Hi, Joe, this is Peter Warren. Are you free right now? I need to speak to you about something," he says rather nervously.

Joe looks at this watch and replies, "Sure, where do you want to meet?"

"How about the Coffee Cart?"

"Okay, I'll see you there in a few," says Joe, wondering what news Peter could be so important that he needs to speak to him right away.

"Paging Dr. Edelstein. Dr. Edelstein, please pick up line eight. Dr. Edelstein, pick up line eight."

The sound of a phone being placed back on its base is heard over the loudspeaker. Jason Riggs finished the last of his coffee and hurries back upstairs to the second door. As the elevator doors open, he sees Dr. Edelstein walk into the room where his wife is resting.

Jason peeks into the room not sure of what to expect. There he sees Mary sitting on the bed with her legs dangling over the side of the bed with Dr. Edelstein standing next to her. Jason knocks on the door and walks in. Dr. Edelstein turns, smiling at him.

"Skyler is out of surgery and resting comfortably in the recovery room. I spoke with Dr. Bloomington about Skyler. He says he looked worse than he really was. Nothing life threatening. He does have a few deep lacerations to his left arm and chest.

"They should heal quite nicely in a few weeks. The scarring should be minimal. You can see Skyler now. Dr. Bloomington will be waiting to speak with you both," he says with a warm smile.

Mrs. Riggs hops off the bed and thanks the doctor for his kindness. She gives him a quick hug and goes to stand near Jason.

"Thank you very much," says Jason, as he pumps the doctor's hand in his excitement. The doctor smiles and bids them good-bye as Jason and Mary head to the elevators.

Dr. Bloomington checks Skyler's chart and gives verbal orders to the attending nurse. Just then, Jason and Mary Riggs walk into the recovery room.

Dr. Edelstein introduces himself. The worried look on Mary and Jason Riggs soon disappears as the doctor explains what he did during surgery and the extent of Skyler's wounds. Both Jason and Mary hug each other in relief and thank the doctor for his part.

"Now you can stay here for only a couple of minutes. Skyler needs his rest. He should be moved into his room in an hour or so. Then you can stay until visiting hours are over," he says, assuring them.

Too soon, Mr. and Mrs. Riggs are being told to leave and wait outside. With his arm protectively around Mary, Jason leads her to a chair in the recovery waiting room where they take a seat and wait patiently for further instructions.

Peter Warren arrives a couple of minutes before Joe. He waits for him before he is seated. Joe walks in and stands next to Peter.

"Sorry to have kept you waiting," says Joe.

"No problem," replies Peter.

The waitress says, "Follow me, please."

They are seated in a booth and order ice teas. As soon as the waitress leaves, Peter leans over the table to speak confidently to Joe. They talk for an hour as Joe has filled Peter in on all he knows.

"Sorry to call you on such a short notice, but I need to talk to you about Mr. Tingly," says Peter, a bit nervously.

"Sure, no problem," replies Joe.

"Peter, I think it's time you meet Paul Miller. Let me call him and set up a meeting with him for tonight. I'll come by and pick you up." Joe pulls out his cell phone and sets up a meeting with Paul Miller for 6:00 p.m.

Paul Miller, Peter Warren, and Joe meet outside the city limits in a small, abandoned house. The place looks like a scene out of a horror movie. The area is covered in weeds up to the windows which have been broken out. The full moon casts long shadows from the overgrown seedless cottonwood trees. The sides of the house have holes and graffiti where the local kids have taken to vandalizing it. Strewn about are beer cans and other forms of debris.

Joe parks by the north side of the decaying building where his car will be hidden by the shadows cast from the house where Joe and Paul take a seat on the steps of the back porch. They sit on a hard cold, slightly wet cement step. Paul and Joe take a seat next to each other, while Peter decides to stand in front of them.

"Well, this place sure seems fitting for what we are about to discuss," says Paul rather uncomfortably.

—◆—

"Hello, Dr. Brinkman," says Skyler, as the doctor enters his hospital room.

"How are you doing this morning?" asks the doctor, as he looks over Skyler's chart.

"I'm feeling pretty good, Doc. Think I may be going home today?"

"Everything looks good, Skyler, but I still want to keep you here for one more day."

A look of disappointment flashes across his face.

"Don't worry, son. I'm just looking out for your own good. I don't want to send you home too early," says Dr. Brinkman, as he replaces Skyler's chart and walks over to check his stitches and his pulse. Satisfied, Dr. Brinkman makes a warm, caring smile at Skyler.

"All seems to be in order. I'll get your discharge papers ready and get you out of here by tomorrow morning."

Skyler's face lights up as he says, "Thanks Dr. Brinkman. I'm anxious to get home and see my friends outside of here."

Dr. Brinkman smiles at him as he walks out the room, leaving behind a very content young man.

———※———

Peter Warren arrives home and, to his surprise, is met by Mary Riggs.

"Hello, Mrs. Riggs. How are you holding up?" asks Peter, truly concerned.

"Hello, Peter. I'm doing much better now. Thanks to your parents. They've asked me to stay with them for a few more days. By then, the police will have no more need to keep the crime scene as it is. Then I'll be allowed to have Skyler's room cleaned so I can go back."

"Good to hear, Mrs. Riggs. How is Skyler doing?"

"Thank goodness, he is doing well. The doctors told me he should be coming home in a few days."

Looking tired, Mary excuses herself from the Warrens and heads for the guest bedroom. She closes the door behind her and lies down on the bed. Slipping off her shoes, she turns on her side and goes to sleep.

"Mom, Dad," says Peter, "I need to discuss something with you. It involves me, Mr. Tingly, and Joe Austin, and what happened at Brinkman Hall."

They sit around the kitchen table and discuss everything that happened to cause Peter to use drugs, attend Tingly's class, and finally, his meeting with Joe Austin and Paul Miller. His parents had noticed a change in Peter's behavior several months before the Brinkman Hall incident. They had discussed the probability of Peter using drugs, but before they were able to confront Peter with this concern, the End Times Association had begun to move quickly. This was a mistake Mr. and Mrs. Warren had made—putting the troubles of the community before their own son. A lesson well-learned, the hard way.

Peter left no detail out or his part in the Brinkman Hall incident or when he told his parents about his meeting with Paul Miller and Joe Austin.

Hours passed as they exchanged information from all they knew about the End Times Association and what part his parents, Michael and Julie, have in this.

They hear Mary Riggs clear her throat as she walks into the kitchen.

"I hope I'm not interrupting anything," Mary says timidly. It is way past dinnertime and Mary was awakened by the rumbling her stomach was making.

"Oh no, Mary. We were just finishing up our discussion. Oh my," says Julie, looking at the clock. "Time just flew by. Michael, Peter, get washed and I'll start dinner."

"Good idea," says Mr. Warren, as he and Peter head for their bedrooms.

"Mary, why don't you sit here and I'll get things started."

"Is there anything I can do to help?" asks Mary.

"Yes," says Julie. "You can start with the salad."

She takes out salad fixings and places them on the counter. Mary smiles and washes her hands in the sink before preparing the salad. Peter and Michael come in, and Julie puts them to work as well.

42

"Well now," says Amon, "this is very interesting news." The fallen angels and the demons, Enepsigos, Belial, Backbiter and Deceit, sit uncomfortably at the large long square table when Amon has a summoned them all in for a conference.

"I understand Chulda has perished and Damian Tingly has betrayed us before they could complete Phase Three: the Downfall. This is very disappointing," says Amon, looking sternly at each one present.

"We have done as you requested, sire," says Allocen, a black-haired, fallen, warrior angel who Deceit had not yet met until now.

"We fought the angels of the Most High God, who, by the command of Michael the Archangel, were ordered to cease and retreat. This enabled us to proceed as far as we could with the phase three plan."

"Yes, sire. We have done our part and are ready to follow through with the plans you have given us," says Belial. "All you have to do is give word, and we will complete our task."

Deceit and Backbiter shift uncomfortably in their seats. They know only part of Amon's plan and are not sure of what he has in store for them, after failing to successfully accomplish their part of Amon's plan to bring down the city where Joe Austin and the others live.

"In two days' time, I want you to complete your task. You have been given sufficient reinforcement. Now go and make me proud," says Amon, as the leader of the six legions of fallen angels rise and take leave of Amon.

"Enepsigos, you will continue to contact Skyler Riggs. Go, and may your mission meet with success."

Enepsigos stands gracefully, and with a nod of his head, he turns and leaves the conference room.

The only ones left at the table are Deceit and Backbiter. Amon stands and walks around the conference table slowly. He clasps his hands behind his back as he continues around the table. The only sound heard is the steady, slow heavy steps Amon makes as he walks back to the head of the table. He stops behind his beautifully carved high back chair. Placing his large hands on the armrest, he leans over the back of the chair and looks straight into Deceit's and Backbiter's eyes.

Deceit smiles at Amon in hopes of lightening the heaviness in the air. Amon returns his smile with more of a sneer than a smile. Deceit slumps into his chair as he lowers his head and looks down.

Pleased by Deceit's reaction, he tests Backbiter who is sitting straight up in his chair looking back at Amon.

"Well, I see your change of attitude has not changed Backbiter," says Amon, little surprised at this. Backbiter says nothing and continues to look Amon in the eye.

You stupid fool, what do you want to do? Get us both cut in half and tossed like garbage into hell?

"Backbiter, continue in your present assignment. Report any changes or news within five hours. I expect there will be some due to the death of Chulda and the betrayal by Tingly," says Amon, as he straightens up and waves Backbiter away.

Deceit lifts his head to watch Backbiter exit all the while hoping he would be allowed to leave as well. Amon pulls out his chair which makes a screeching sound as it is pulled back. Deceit's eyes widen as he straightens himself and prepares for the worst.

"Deceit, I want you to go to Joe Austin's house and learn much as you can from him. He should know by now Tingly and Chulda were the human leaders of the End Times Association. He will be trying to stop the phase three plan from happening. When you have learned what he knows, do what you can to stop him. Call on Belial if you have to. But stop him anyway you can."

"Yes, sire. I will do my best. I know how important this is to you, and I assure you, I will stop Joe Austin from hindering the phase three plan. I surely will…"

"Enough of your rambling," says Amon loudly and sternly, cutting Deceit off midsentence.

"Go and report back as soon as you have stopped the human from hindering our plan."

"Yes, sire," says Deceit, as he pushes his chair away from the table and stands to leave. He waits a few seconds to make sure Amon has allowed him to leave. But being unsure of what to do, he continues to wait for Amon's customary dismissal of him.

With lightning speed, Amon strikes the back of Deceit's head so hard that it bounces off the white marble table. Dazed, Deceit shakes his head and says, "Yes, sire, I'm leaving now."

He stands and wobbles toward the door Amon's office. Once outside, he rubs the back of his head and says, "Stupid idiot, you didn't have to hit me so hard."

Just then, he hears someone clearing this throat. Startled, Deceit turns to see Gusion standing behind him.

"Oh, I didn't see you there. How long have you been standing there?" asks Deceit, frightened that he might tell Amon.

"Long enough to hear you complain about the swat Amon gave you. You know, if I were you, I'd wait to speak my mind far away from here," says Gusion, enjoying the look on Deceit's face.

"Oh, thanks for the advice," is all Deceit can come up with. He turns and quickly makes his way out of the building and takes flight, barely missing a couple of imps who are returning from their assignments.

Deceit flies hard and fast down to earth and lands in the lush green tree behind Joe's house. Thinking he is safe from prying eyes and ears of the unseen, he lets out a stream of profanities directed at Amon and Gusion.

Backbiter sits holding tightly to the limb he is sitting on as he tries desperately to keep from laughing out loud and letting his presence known.

After letting off steam, Deceit jumps down to the ground and walks toward Joe's house and through the kitchen wall. He looks around and sniffs the air in hopes that he will pick up Joe Austin's scent. Unsuccessful in getting a strong scent of his presence, Deceit decides to go looking for him. Backbiter, as usual, follows discreetly behind.

Joe arrives home and sits down at his desk, turning on his computer. He opens up the document he has labeled the End Times. Scrolling to the end, he adds to his notes all he, Paul Miller, and Peter Warren have discussed. Sitting back, he rereads their plan.

"I won't let you bring down any one of us, Joe Austin. I have waited centuries for this opportunity. I am damned to the eternal flames of the lake of fire, and I will take down with me as many of you as I can before I meet with my final destination."

Determined, Deceit retreats into the ceiling awaiting an opportunity permanently disabled from completing his plan to end the phase three plan.

43

"Son, I am very disappointed by your behavior," says Michael Warren. "I thought we raised you with better values than what you have recently displayed."

"Dad, you did raise me better. I am truly sorry I hurt you and Mom. I know I should never have done drugs. But you have to understand, these times are harder than when you and Mom were kids," says Peter.

"Peter, you're right. It is harder than when we were growing up. But that does not give you the excuse or right to do drugs. Son, you're lucky you didn't go to jail for what you did to Joe Austin. You hurt him very badly. It's a wonder you didn't kill him. You could be sitting in jail right now if Joe would have pressed charges. What you did is a very serious thing. And all this was brought about because you were swayed by your drug use and Mr. Tingly."

"Peter, now you understand why we are doing what we're doing. This is for your own good as well as ours," says

Mr. Warren firmly. Mrs. Warren sits next to Peter with a concerned look on her face.

"This may seem a bit extreme to you, but we don't want this to go any further than it already has."

"Dad, I understand. I'll do what you want, especially knowing what I know now."

Both Julie and Lee Warren give Peter a hug. All of them relieved that all their secrets have been exposed, and now they are back to working together as a family and a team.

Peter looks at his parents with shame and regret at what he has allowed to happen. He knows full well he brought all this misery upon himself, his parents, and most of all, Joe Austin.

"Dad, Mom, I am so sorry. I promise I'll never do drugs again. I've learned my lesson."

They look at each other and at their only son. Feeling anger, frustration, and disappointment, mostly at themselves, they decide to put this aside for a better time.

"Son, we'll take this up at a later time. Go get washed up for dinner."

—◦◦◦—

Mary stands in the middle of Skyler's bedroom surveying the cleanup and paint job, as the painter patiently waits for her approval or disapproval.

"Very nice," she says, smiling at the slightly overweight painter. A look of relief crosses his face as he orders his young apprentice to take the paint cans out to the truck. Mary and Mr. Begley walk down the hall and to the front door.

"Thank you for doing a great job in such short notice," says Mary, relieved to have Skyler's room professionally cleaned and painted. She pulls out a check and hands it to Mr. Begley.

"I'm happy to hear your son is coming home soon. If you know of anyone needing a painter, please refer them to us," he says, as he hands his business card to Mary.

"Yes, I certainly will do that," she says, smiling at Mr. Begley as she closes the front door behind him.

Mary locks the door and makes her way to the office and places the business card into her desk drawer. She stands looking out the window, enjoying the view of the flowers now starting to bloom.

She takes a deep breath and turns around and walks back to Skyler's room. Standing in the doorway, she takes one more look around the room. There is no sign left of the terrible incident. She has replaced the mattress and bedding in Skyler's room. The carpet is new. Everything seems to be in order. Her cell phone rings startling her.

"Hello, Mrs. Riggs. This is Dr. Brinkman. I just want to let you know Skyler will be discharged tomorrow.

"Oh, thank you, Doctor. I'm very happy to hear that. What time should I be there to pick him up?"

"Around ten o'clock would be fine. You might want to bring a fresh set of clothes for him including underwear."

"Thank you, I will be there at ten with his clothes."

"Good. Have you heard any news about your husband? The police have already contacted me, and I have agreed to be at his hearing."

"Yes, I have, Dr. Brinkman. I've met with our attorney, and all has been set for the next month."

"I know this has been very hard on both of you. I do hope you understand I'm not coming against you, but your husband needs to get help and frankly so do you and Skyler. If I can be any further help, please don't hesitate to call me."

"Thank you, I will."

With that, they hang up. Taking a deep breath, Mary walks over to Skyler's chest of drawers. She picks up some clean underwear and places it on the bed. Then walks over to the closet and pulls out a shirt and jeans. Leaning down, she picks up a pair of shoes. A glimmer of light catches her eye. She pushes Skyler's clothes aside. Mary drops the clothes she is holding and steps back, putting her hands to her mouth. Staring at the candles and mirror, she picks up the script from the floor and begins to shake. Her face is devoid of color. She drops the script and slowly walks back until she feels the bed behind her. Slowly, she sits down and tries to understand what she has stumbled across. Anger begins to stir in her.

"Why in blazes didn't those idiots tell me about this when they put in the carpet?" she asks herself out loud. Pulling her cell phone out of her pocket, she gets up and hurries to the office. Her hands shaking with anger and revulsion, she

searches for the business card of the carpet company that had
installed the new carpet just a day ago in Skyler's room.

"Sanford Carpet, how may I help you?"

"I need to speak to Mr. Sanford."

"If you tell me the problem, I may be able to help you."

"No, you can't help me. I need to speak with Mr. Sanford
now, and I won't take no for an answer."

"All right, I'll put you right through."

"Hello, Sanford speaking, how can I help you?"

"This is Mary Riggs," she says, trying to keep her emotions
in check.

"I had my carpet replaced a day ago, and no one who
worked on my son's room told me what they had found in his
closet. It was just moved out from the bottom of the closet,
the carpet replaced, and the stuff put right back," says Mary,
her voice rising and her hands shaking.

"Mrs. Riggs, I do apologize, but we are not in the business
of discussing with anyone the things we happen to discover in
our client's homes as we replace the carpet," says Mr. Sanford
in a calm voice.

"Obviously, not all my clients are as conservative as we are.
What they do or have in the privacy of their own homes is
none of our business, unless it is illegal."

By now, Mary has calmed down enough to see his point.

"I hope you don't take this the wrong way, Mrs. Riggs, but
you should contact your pastor. I know if I were in your shoes,
I would certainly be upset as well. I have a daughter about

your son's age. I sure would hate it if she would be involved in something like what I was told they found. As manager and owner of this company, I need to know what they find while replacing carpets in people's homes or businesses. But it's not our responsibility to advise the owners of what others are doing in their own homes. If we find something illegal or highly immoral and it comes to my attention, then I will either talk to the police or the homeowners."

Taking a deep breath, Mary thanks Mr. Sanford. She assures him she will speak with her pastor and Skyler before he comes home tomorrow.

Mary sits at her desk and looks up the number of her church. She leaves a message with the church secretary and decides to speak with the only other person whom she knows can help her at this time.

"Hello, Mrs. Deaton, this is Mary Riggs. How are you?"

"Good, good."

"The reason I'm calling is I need to talk to someone about Skyler. I would appreciate it if we can meet somewhere we can talk privately and openly."

"Yes, I can meet with you now. It'll take me ten minutes to get there."

"Thank you again. I am truly grateful. I'll see you in ten."

Mary hangs up the phone and rushes out the door, locking it behind her.

44

Some friends who helped Joe when he was recuperating from his encounter with Peter Warren decide to meet at the local sports bar and have a few drinks before dinner.

What's the harm in that? It's just a couple of beers.

"That's right, no harm, no foul," whispers Deceit into Joe's ear, as Joe drives to meet his friends.

He tries to shake a most uncomfortable feeling of impending doom. Upon reaching the bar, he runs toward the door, narrowly missing being hit by a car going into the parking lot. Joe is unaware of the close call. He just wants to get out of the rain.

"Hey guys," he says, as he greets his friends who are already seated at a table and have ordered the first round of drinks.

"Hey, Joe! Over here."

They greet each other warmly.

"We ordered you a beer. I know you swore off booze awhile back, but what's a celebration without a couple of bruskies?" asks Tom.

"You're right, a couple won't hurt," says Joe, somewhat uneasily.

They sit and talk about their futures. By now, Joe is very relaxed. His stomach is full and he has had one beer too many.

"Hey, Tom, I've been meaning to call you about Rover and Snowball. Thanks a million for taking care of them."

"Don't worry about it. They're great pets."

"Who knows? They may not want to go back with you," an inebriated Chris says.

"Another round here," says Tom, his speech a little slurred.

"Who wants to share a taxi home, anyone?" asks Tom, as he downs the final and fifth glass of beer. All but Joe decide to share and split the cab fare, then pick up their cars in the morning. None of the four are in any condition to drive.

"Hey, Joe," says Tom, "what about you? You don't plan to drive home, do you?"

"No, I'm going to call my cousin to take me home. She lives a couple of blocks from here."

"Okay," says Chris. "We'll see you at graduation then."

They hug each other good-bye and make their way to the front door. Joe tosses back the last of his beer and pulls out his cell phone. He calls Ann. Voice mail picks up and Joe leaves her a message to call him, but he does not bother to leave a reason as to why or where he's calling from. Thinking Ann will soon return his call, he orders one more beer. An hour goes by and the rain has stopped. Joe pays his bar tab and heads out to the front door.

"Huh, rains stopped. Think I'll wait in the car for Ann to call me back," Joe says softly. He makes his way to his car and gets in.

"Oh, it's cold in here," he says, slurring his speech. He decides to start his car and warm up as he waits for Ann to return his call. The warmth from the car heater relaxes him even more. With his car running, he waits another few minutes, still no call.

"It's already dark, and you're just a few miles from home. Why wait any longer?" says Deceit to Joe.

"Go on, you're okay, you've driven in worse conditions."

Yeah, just a few miles from home. No use in sitting here any longer. He puts the car in gear and heads for home. With oncoming traffic, he is temporally blinded by the headlights of other cars passing by. He slams on his brakes at the last second just as he approaches an intersection. The car behind him also slams on his brakes and skids to a stop inches from Joe's rear bumper.

The lights change and Joe drives on. The driver behind him flashes his lights, turning and waving his fist as he passes Joe. It starts to rain again making it hard for Joe to see. Hoping to find some landmarks to gauge just how far he is from home, Joe spots the only three-story office building on his block.

Relief comes over him. Almost home. He continues to drive at a slower speed, knowing he will soon be home. A minute or two later, he turns onto his street. Driving onto his driveway, he opens the garage door, carefully driving in and closes the garage door behind him.

He enters his house and automatically feels for the light switch. Deceit signals for the imps to cause the lights to go out. He flicks on the light switch, they go on briefly. Joe hears the light bulb make a slight pop.

"Ahhh great," he says, as he makes his way slowly toward his bedroom. He walks into his bedroom feeling his way to the nightstand. He searches the nightstand for his flashlight.

"I sure hope the batteries still work," he says, as he turns on the flashlight. He makes his way to the basement door.

The Lord has allowed Joe's spiritual eyes and ears be opened more than usual. No longer are the imps and demons cloaking themselves from his eyes. They fly around Joe grabbing at him, trying to wound him.

"You know better than to drink too much. You swore off drinking and your old ways. What happened to change your mind?" asks Deceit, his voice mocking him with every sentence.

"Sooo, we meet face-to-face," says Deceit, his hand moving slowly across Joe's face.

"Pity, I have to kill you. You'd of made me a wonderful ally," says Deceit, as Joe stares into Deceit's red eyes.

"I've been following you for quite some time. Almost had you a couple of times, but as always, you manage to escape by the words of your mouth. But those times have ended. Yes, they have."

Suddenly, Joe is hit in the face by Deceit's rough and leathery hand. He falls to the floor, hitting his head against the wall. Stunned, he remains where he is. He starts to feel around the floor for the flashlight. He recoils in fear and disgust as he touches a cold, rubbery, clawlike foot.

"You lose something, pretty boy?" asks Deceit, well aware that Joe can see and hear him.

"Hmm, nothing to say?" he asks mockingly while Joe keeps feeling around the floor for his flashlight, bumping his head on things as he searches.

The stench of fecal matter and sulfur assault his nostrils. His eyes now acclimated to the dark, he can make out the forms of the demons, imps, and other evil spirits. Some are short and stout, others are thin and have long arms and hunched backs. Still others have batlike wings.

"So, pretty boy," says Deceit, as he leans closer to Joe's face, stroking it.

"Cat got your tongue?"

Joe turns his head quickly away, shutting his eyes tight. He calls out to Jesus for help. Instantly, a bright, white light appears and a masculine, tall, beautiful being appears before him. By the light that shines all about him, Joe can make out clearly the demons and imps that seem to fill the room. The angel of the Most High God looks down at Joe and winks his eye at him. Joe stares in disbelief as to what he is seeing.

"Good time for a fight, don't you think?" he asks Joe, who is too scared to say anything.

The angel of the Most High God and the demon square off as the others encircle them, jeering and shouting obscenities at Angelo de Fuego. Joe pulls in his legs and prepares for a fight between good and evil. He makes himself comfortable since there is no way he can avoid it, being he has a front row seat and his escape is blocked.

"Take your best shot, sweet thing. Go ahead. Make my day," says Deceit to Angelo de Fuego who punches Deceit square in the jaw, sending him down to the floor right next to Joe.

"Why, I oughta," says Deceit, as he stands to his feet.

"Attack, you fools! Why do you think I brought you with me as our illustrious leader, Amon, told me to do?"

The imps and other demons attack Angelo with all their might. Clawing, scratching, spitting and biting, they show no mercy. Joe holds his hand over his nose as he tries to crawl to the bottom of the stairs. The room fills quickly with the smell of sulfur and black smoke as many of the lesser demons and imps are disposed of by Angelo de Fuego's double-edged sword.

The fight increases as Deceit calls out for more reinforcements. Angelo fights with such skill; Joe is too intrigued to be aware that Angelo is completely outnumbered by imps, demons, and now several very large, very skilled, and very mean fallen warrior angels. Joe finally snaps and speaks.

"Two can play at this game," he says, as he calls out to the Lord to send Angelo de Fuego more help.

Instantly, there are seven bright, large warrior angels sent by the Most High Guide to aide in the fight against evil. Joe sits watching in disbelief with a mixture of fear and excitement.

The fight goes on for a several hours. Suddenly, the few fighters that remain from the dark side give each other the signal to retreat. They leave battered, bruised, and in need of a quick retreat.

Deceit has long since left Joe's house and gone to lick his wounds safe from harm. The imps and demons have been left to fight bravely, trying to impress each other and make a name for themselves.

"We have been left behind to be made fools of by Angelo de Fuego. Turn, run for safety. We shall deal with Deceit later."

Angelo makes sport of them, smacking them around with the broadside of the sword.

They turn and fly away in a flash, leaving only the scent of sulfur and feces. Joe stands with his back flat against the wall, just a few steps from the top of the basement door. Stunned and not quite believing what he has witnessed, he makes a dash for the top of the stair. He opens it with such force that it slams back into the wall, causing the door knob to punch a hole in the wall.

There is a battle cry of victory from the angels of the Most High God at having again beaten the forces of evil. All the spirits, both good and evil, have departed except one.

Angelo de Fuego stands tall and at ease as Joe circles him. He takes in the masculine, brightly shining creature.

Joe notices Angelo's broad sword which hangs from his wide belt. It burns brightly with fire. Joe dares to touch it with his index finger. Oddly, it does not burn him, rather, it feels bitter cold to the touch. He looks at Angelo in awe of what he is seeing. Angelo smiles at Joe, but says nothing. Stepping back a couple of steps, Joe looks Angelo straight in the eye.

"Who are you?" asks Joe sincerely, wanting to know.

"I am your guardian angel assigned to you at your birth by the Most High God."

"Really?" asks Joe innocently.

"Yes, really," says Angelo, smiling at his friend.

"Have you been around a long time?"

"Yes. I have been around before the world was."

"Oh. Have you seen Jesus, the Father, and the Holy Spirit?"

Angelo de Fuego lets out a booming laugh.

"Yes, of course I have," he answers with a twinkle in his eye.

"Yes, of course you have," says Joe, rather sheepishly.

"How old are you?"

"I have no age. I was created before time was."

"Oh, yes, I suppose you were."

Joe decides his questions are ones he can easily answer himself. He decides not to ask anything else, except maybe one or possibly two more questions.

"How do you get your orders?"

"Directly from the Lord. I do as I have been commanded and assigned to do. If you speak the word of God in faith, then I will do it according to His will."

"One more question, do you have a will of your own?"

"Yes, I do," replies Angelo.

Satisfied with the answers to his questions, Joe decides to keep quiet. Without a word, Angelo disappears as he appeared, leaving only his scent behind.

Joe looks around for his flashlight and finds it quickly. He hurries to the fuse box and flips the switch. The lights go on. Joe runs up the stairs locking the basement door behind him. He locks the doors and windows to the entire house. Shaking from head to toe, he goes into the kitchen and pulls out the strongest drink he has, a Coke. Then he turns on the lights and sits on his favorite chair in stunned silence.

45

Ann checks her phone messages. Seeing Joe has left a message, she decides not to return his call until the following day.

"Gosh, Joe, why didn't you let me know you needed a ride home? I would have come for you right away," says Ann, a bit agitated after hearing that Joe was too drunk to drive but drove home anyway.

"Don't you ever do that again."

"Sorry, Ann, I've learned my lesson."

"Good. Listen, I'm going out of town. I was fortunate enough to get an internship in Maine for the summer. I am so excited. I can hardly wait."

"That's great. I'm really happy for you. When are you leaving?"

"Tomorrow."

"Tomorrow? How come you didn't tell me about this sooner?" asks Joe, a little hurt.

"Sorry. I've been busy with finals, and now that Matt and I are getting serious, it's taking up a lot of my time."

"Good, Matt is a good guy. I hope it all goes well for you and him. Study hard and learn everything you can. Send me a postcard and let me know how it's going for you."

"I will. I have to go now. I have another call coming in. Love you."

———∽∾∽———

It is Tony Watkins wanting to know if it is okay to drop off Joe's pets today. Being that Joe is eager to have Rover and Snowball back with him, he readily agrees. He will be returning them within the hour. So Joe gets up and makes sure everything is ready for his pets. Tony drives up to Joe's house who wastes no time in going out to meet them.

"Hey, Tony, thanks for taking care of them," says Joe, as he opens the car door and lets Rover and Snowball out of the car.

Rover jumps onto Joe almost knocking him over. Not to be undone, Snowball paws at Joe ready to be picked up.

"I see they still know you," says Tony, as he hugs his friend warmly. "Listen, I can't stay. I have to go to my parents' house and help make arrangements for my graduation party. As soon as I find out all the details, I'll let you know. You will come, won't you?"

"I wouldn't miss it for the world."

Rover and Snowball run around the front yard happy to be home. Tony waves good-bye and drives away. Standing in his driveway, Joe watches his beloved pets for a few moments, then he calls to them and heads back into the house.

Once inside, Rover goes from room to room sniffing and getting reacquainted with his home. Snowball lies on the floor and stretches as Joe rubs her belly. Since today is their homecoming, he decides they can have as many treats as they like.

He kneels next to Rover and gives him a big hug and rubs his back, "I've missed you boy and you too Snowball."

Rover shows his affection with a couple of licks to Joe's face, then turns his full attention back to his bowl and happily wolfs down his food. Snowball pays no attention to Joe except for a giving him a meow or two in between bites. *Together again*, thinks Joe, content that he is not alone.

—————

Claire Deaton has invited Mary Riggs to talk and pray for herself and her family. The pies she's made are cooling on the kitchen counter, while the coffee brews.

Deceit has just flown in and begins to look around in hopes of finding out any information that might be of help to him. But before he can, he gets a whiff of the pie and coffee.

He walks across the counter and over to the place where Claire Deaton has placed her apple pies to cool. Bending down, he takes in a lungful of baked pies and freshly brewed coffee. His stomach begins to rumble as he licks one entire pie.

Mrs. Deaton is busy placing the silverware on the table with her back to the counter. She senses Deceit's presence. Slowly, she turns toward the counter and fixes her eyes sternly on the unsuspecting demon who is too busy trying to get a taste of pie to notice Claire's unwavering stare.

Unable to do so, as usual, Deceit continues in vain. Frustrated, he stands looking down at the pie and decides to give it one more try, figuring stranger things have happened. He bends down, his sharp, black tongue sticking out.

Feeling the widow's stare, he slowly turns his head toward her. Their eyes meet. Neither one flinches. At first, Deceit thinks she cannot see him since almost no one else ever has, unless he allows himself to be seen, continues to try and taste the pies.

"Just what do you think you are doing?" she asks Deceit.

Startled, he stops. His tongue almost touching the pie; he straightens up and looks at Mrs. Deaton and says, "Oh, she can't see me. It's just like it was with Tingly."

He bends down again when he hears, "Stop! Get away from there."

"I'm stepping away from the pie," he says, as he walks away with his hands up.

"It's just that it smells so good. I've heard a lot of good things about you, but I never knew that you were such a good baker," he says, hoping she will be distracted enough so he can hide before she banishes him.

He continues to walk backwards on the counter with his hands up. A nervous, little laugh escapes him before he falls off the end of the counter, landing on his rear end.

"Now in the name of Jesus, get!"

Deceit scrambles to his feet and flies out the kitchen window, heading far away from the widow, Claire Deaton, as fast as he can. Backbiter decides to let him go and catch up with him later. *And to think that Amon puts him in charge.*

Mary Riggs sits quietly while Claire Deaton reads to her from the Bible as they sit in Claire's kitchen. Mary takes the words to heart. She understands the importance of keeping intimate contact with the Lord, but also with her church family.

As she drinks her hot, sweet tea, Claire Deaton explains what they have to pray against. She makes sure to explain to Mary that though Skyler and Jason need to ask for forgiveness, she also needs to ask herself. Her eyes tearing up, Mary is unable to look up, her heart breaking. Claire leans toward Mary and holds her hand in both of hers.

With much compassion and grace, Claire says, "Mary, you understand that if you do little or nothing to protect an innocent from harm, you are as much at fault as the abuser. Know that the Lord is always there to help you when you call out to Him. Help comes in many forms and not always the way we think it should come. But it comes in His way and in His timing. That's why it is very important to keep your accounts with Him short and always keep close and intimate contact with Him."

At this, Mary breaks down and cries as she asks the Lord for forgiveness. Mary feels a sense of peace and love flowing warmly throughout her entire body. She takes in a ragged breath and smiles, knowing she is forgiven and much loved. Claire offers Mary some tissue to wipe away her tears.

"How about some coffee? I've made some apple pies. It's one of my late husband's favorites, God rest his soul. He used to tell me when I was his young bride that even his own mother, who by the way, was an excellent cook, could not make an apple pie as good as mine."

She smiles warmly at Mary and pats her hand as she gets up and slices a plump, freshly baked, warm pie. She places them on her grandmother's fine, bone china she uses for her special guests. Mary refills their cups with hot, rich coffee. Both sit and enjoy the delicious food set before them.

46

Skyler has been notified that he will be released the next day. Part of him will miss the kind and caring way the male doctors have treated him.

At least I'll get some peace and not have to worry about getting whipped for a while.

The nurses' aide comes in and takes his vital and records them in his chart.

"You're looking pretty good today," she says with a smile. "Keep this up, and you'll be home very soon."

Skyler smiles at her and asks if he can have a glass of coke. She smiles back and says, "Sure, I don't see any restrictions on your chart. I'll be back soon," she says, as she walks out of the room.

Cute girl. I think she might be a junior at school. I know she looks familiar. I think I'll ask her when she comes back.

"Here you are," says the nurse aide, as she hands over the can of soda to Skyler.

"Thanks."

He takes a long drink. As it goes down his throat, the taste of it gives Skyler another reason to smile.

"What school do you go to?" asks Skyler, taking the nurse's aide by surprise.

"State. And you?"

"Same," says Skyler, adding, "I'm surprised I haven't seen you sooner. Do you like football?"

"Yes, I do."

"Well, I'm the captain of the football team."

"I thought your name looked familiar. I work part-time and go to school full time, so there is little time for any social activities. That's why I didn't know who you were," she says, blushing slightly.

"Since you've taken such good care of me, why don't we go to a movie sometime?" asked Skyler, rather sheepishly.

"Sure, but let's make sure you're completely well before we do."

"Will do," replies Skyler, smiling cheerfully. Just then, Mary walks into the room.

"Hi, Mom."

"I best be going. More people to see, you know," says the aide, as she hurries out the door embarrassed by being caught flirting with Skyler.

"Nice girl, what's her name," asks Mary with a gleam in her eye.

"Ah, I forgot to ask. But I will next time."

Skyler lay comfortably in his hospital bed. His mother has just left, and he is alone with his thoughts. Dr. Bloomington comes in and picks up Skyler's chart.

"Hello, Skyler," he says, as he scans over the chart. "How are you feeling today?"

"Pretty good. Except for my stitches are beginning to itch a lot."

"That's a good sign, son. That means your healing is well on its way. If you keep showing as much progress as you have been, you should be going home in a day or two."

"Really? I hope so."

"Take it easy, and I'll be in to check on you again tomorrow," says Dr. Bloomington, as he smiles and walks out of the room.

His stepmother Mary, has not told Skyler about what happened to his father, Jason Riggs. She thinks it would be better for Skyler if he did not know until after he was home. Skyler wasn't in too big of a hurry to find out about his father.

He lay in bed, relaxed and happy to know he is going to be going home very soon. A few hours later, he is awakened with his last hospital dinner tray.

"Hi, I understand you'll be leaving in the morning," says Kellie.

"Yes, I am. I'm so outta here. I can't wait."

"Gee, we didn't treat you that badly, did we?"

"No actually, I am going to miss my doctors," says Skyler.

"Oh, how sweet."

"Really, they've treated me well and with respect. I'm going to miss that," says Skyler, a little sad.

"Oh, by the way, I didn't get your name. I'm Skyler Riggs."

"I'm Kellie Sanford. Glad to know you."

"Well, now that that's settled, how about giving me your number so I can call you sometime."

Kellie writes her number on a piece of paper towel and hands it to Skyler.

"Don't lose it, now," she says, giving Skyler a wink as she leaves.

"I won't."

Mary knocks softly on the door and calls out to Skyler who is standing next to the window looking out. He turns and smiles at Mary, who is carrying a bag with his clothes in them.

"Doc said I can leave as soon as you get here with my clothes."

"What did they do with your old clothes?"

"Oh, they gave them to the police. They want to check them out for evidence."

Taking the bag from Mary, Skyler goes into the bathroom and changes into his clean clothes. Mary walks slowly around the room wringing her hands. A worried look covers her tired and finely lined face.

Skyler emerges fully dressed, looking like his old self. His long sleeves cover the bandages on his arms. Mary watches him as he sits on a chair and puts on his socks and tennis shoes. She thinks about how she is going to brooch the subject of what she found in his room. This bothers her more than how she is going to tell him about Jason, his father.

A big smile forms on Skyler's face as he stands up ready to leave and go back to life as usual. Without saying a word, they both walk out the door and go down to the parking lot with discharge papers and instructions for his wound care.

"Oh, I almost forgot, we need to make an appointment with Bloomington for follow-up visit."

Mary smiles and nods her head as they head out to their car. As they drive out of the parking structure and head for home, Mary says, "Skyler, there are a couple of things we have to talk about when we get home. One of them is about your dad."

Skyler's mood is so good that even the thought of having to discuss his father does not bring him down. He has not even thought of him for all the time he has spent in the hospital. His thoughts have been on his mother, Ingrid Riggs and Kellie Sanford.

"Mom, I'm hungry. Can we stop by McDonald's and get a burger before we get home?"

"How about the Coffee Cart instead? You need more than a quick burger," says Mary, her motherly instincts taking over her dismay and anger.

"Great, then I can fill you in on the cute nurse's aide I met when I was there," he says with a smile.

They drive on momentarily unfettered by the problems that have yet to be resolved. Mary turns the corner and drives into the parking lot of the Coffee Cart. *I'm going to enjoy this meal and not going to worry about anything else at this time*, thinks Mary, as they take a seat.

———❧———

The skies began to turn dark with clouds rolling in, looking ready to empty themselves of water. Thunder rolls across the sky, sending many scurrying into store fronts hoping not to get wet in the sudden downpour.

Joe hurries across campus, barely making it to the last class of his final semester. He and fellow students shake off the raindrops that have landed on their clothes. Soon the hallway is empty of human life. The floor glistens with rainwater, making it slippery for anyone walking down the halls. The bell rings loudly for class to start. All is as it should be.

Deceit pokes his head into Joe's class. Upon seeing him sitting in his usual, Deceit decides that now is a perfect time to set up an ambush for Joe. He flies upward and into the clouds. There he finds a small group of imps and demons and explains his purpose and plan to advance his position.

"Okay everyone, you have your assignments. Now go to your posts and do nothing until I give you the signal," says Deceit, not completely sure they need follow-through with his orders.

An hour has passed and classes end. Relieved to be finally finished with school and graduating at last, Joe decides he will celebrate with a couple of friends. They hug each other and bid good night to Peter for His wisdom and guidance at this very pivotal time. A special angel of the Most High God is dispatched immediately to assist, protect, and guide Julie and Michael Warren. His name *Metatron* means to "guard and protect."

47

"Hello?"

"Hi, Joe. This is Peter Warren. I had a long talk with my parents last night. We came to an agreement that you, Paul Miller, and the rest of the Warren Group should meet this afternoon at my place. That is, if you're available."

"What time and I'll be there," replies Joe.

"One o'clock?"

"One o'clock it is. Isn't your dad worried about meeting out in the open?" asks Joe, a bit concerned.

"Apparently not. Since the gatekeeper is dead and Tingly is nowhere to be found, the major threat is gone."

"But what about the rest of the association. Won't they try to stop this meeting?" asks Joe.

"That's exactly what I asked my dad. He said time is short, and if they want a fight, they're getting one."

"Oh, okay," replies Joe, a little reluctantly.

"Don't worry. My parents have very strong faith in God. Don't let the enemy get you to doubting His help now."

"You're right," replies Joe, a bit embarrassed by having his doubts exposed.

"I'll see you today at one o'clock at your place. Can you give me your address again?"

Peter gives him his address and then hangs up.

Deceit sits quietly on top of the bookshelves near Joe's desk.

As the notes print, Joe gets up and fixes himself breakfast. While he is busy in the kitchen, Backbiter emerges from his hiding place.

So, their making a move soon. I better hightail it to Amon's and let him know what's going on.

Deceit shoots upward and out of site leaving Backbiter hiding in the wall on the other side of the room.

Backbiter emerges from his hiding place and lands on the desk next to the printer. He positions himself to read the document.

"Hmm, so he is well aware of what is going on. This meeting will produce much needed information to the thwart their plan," says Backbiter. "I better report this to Amon."

Then he takes off through the ceiling and heads toward the compound.

48

Joe has been playing outside with Rover and Snowball all morning long. Lunch time arrives and both the animals head for the back door. Rover paws at the screen door wanting to go in and get fed. Meanwhile, Snowball sits patiently, letting Rover do all the work. Joe looks over at them, smiles, gets up, and lets them in.

"Something tells me you guys got spoiled while you were with Tony Watkins," he says. "I think I'm going to have to put you back on a two-meal-per-day regiment."

The door opens, and Rover runs inside with Snowball close behind. They get to the kitchen and eagerly await their food. Joe serves them both and decides to make himself a light lunch.

After cleaning away the dishes, he goes to his desk, turns on the computer, and opens up the End Times document. He adds more to what he already knows, filling up another page. Leaning back in his chair, his thoughts are on where and how the Warren Group is planning to ruin Chulda's plans. He is brought back to the present at the sound of his phone ringing. It's Paul Miller.

"Hey, Paul, how's it going?"

"So far so good. We're set to meet at Warren's place at seven tonight. You know the address, right?"

"Yes, I do. Who is going to be there?"

"Myself, the Warrens, and a few others that you haven't met yet. About fifteen in all. Do you think it will draw too much attention to have that many cars at his home in the middle of the week?" asks Joe.

"No, not really. Mrs. Warren has her women's group over all the time and there are more of them than us. So I don't think it will be a problem."

"Good," says Joe, relieved to hear that.

"Joe, don't worry about people finding out that we're meeting at Lee's place. The ones you have to be concerned about are the ones you don't see."

Joe says nothing, being concerned about his own spiritual standing.

"Gotta go, see you tonight, seven o'clock sharp at the Warrens," says Paul, a little too cheerfully for Joe.

After hanging up, Joe returns to thinking about the events of the last two days. He begins to pace, thinking out loud, he says, "Well, if I'm not supposed to be worried about humans and what they can do to me, then that means I'm supposed to worry about the spirit world which is unseen."

A shiver runs up his spine as he recalls the events that happened down in the basement.

"Shoot, I rather take on Peter again any day than to meet up with those demons of last night."

His mind goes back to what his father had taught him as a child.

"Now, Joe, remember, demons like to pretend they're shadows, so watch out for them."

He knows there is another truth his father taught him, which he struggles to recall.

He continues to pace as he recalls all but that one particular thing that keeps gnawing at him. Joe decides to let it go for the time being and concentrate on what he has to do now that he has graduated from college. He decides to list them all and check them off as they are taken care of. Joe returns to his desk and opens up a new page entitled Post Graduation Plans.

"I don't think I'll be getting anymore information from this human tonight, so I best go and check up on my cohort instead of hanging around here," says Deceit, as he exits through a window.

49

"Ahhh, it's good to be home again," says Skyler, as he lies down across his bed. Enjoying the feel of his own bed, he briefly forgets what has happened to him. Sitting upright, he takes a look around.

The room seems different somehow. It's been repainted. And my bed feels firmer and the bedspread I know is different. Not bad. As a matter of fact, I think I like it better now than before. I wonder what else is new.

Skyler looks around and sees there are new drapes and new carpeting.

"Oh, crap," he says loudly. "New carpet, that means when the old carpet got taken out, whoever did it found my altar."

His heart sinks as he slowly goes down on his knees and reaches for the candles. *They've been moved. That's the other thing Mom wanted to talk about.* He sits on his heels with his head back and his eyes closed. Skyler falls back onto the floor.

After a short while, he gets up and heads for the kitchen. Mary stands at the stove, heating up water for some tea. She has also taken out a large, plastic tumbler. He knows that whenever she does that, it can only mean one thing—she wants to comfort herself with some port.

Skyler walks up beside her and asks if there is any cake. Much to his relief, she says yes and pulls out two plates and hands them to him. He puts them on the table and gets some napkins.

"Mom, where's the cake?"

"In the refrigerator."

Skyler takes the cake out and notices there are no slices missing. He puts the cake on the table and sits down, while Mary takes out a knife and cuts the cake. Without saying a word, Mary places a piece on his plate and one on hers then sits down herself. She says a short prayer over the food and takes a drink from the tumbler.

Taking a large bite, Skyler smiles at Mary and says, "Mom, this is really good. Thanks for making my favorite cake."

"You're welcome, honey."

Skyler finishes his slice quickly, while Mary refills her tumbler and asks Skyler if he wants more cake. Sitting quietly, drinking her port, Skyler cuts another large piece of cake for himself. He fills his mouth with cake, trying to avoid eye contact with Mary.

"Honey, I've got to talk to you about your father."

Skyler looks at her and takes a sip of tea.

"What about Dad?" he asks, trying to sound nonchalant.

"Dr. Brinkman and Dr. Edelstein talked to me about your dad. Dr. Brinkman noticed the faint scars on your back and confronted your father about them."

Mary gives Skyler a chance to absorb what she has just told him. Skyler looks down, his eyes tearing up. *What else did she tell the doctors*, he wonders.

"Skyler, your father confessed to Dr. Brinkman about abusing you since you were a child. He called the police, and they took him to jail. I decided not to post bail for him. I think he needs to take responsibility for what he has been doing to you. I want to apologize for allowing this to continue. Honey, I am truly sorry."

Skyler looks straight into Mary's eyes. He stares at her for quite a while, trying to absorb it all. Finally, he says, "How long will he be in jail?"

"I don't know. I've contacted an attorney, and he's already spoken with your dad. He said he should be arraigned next month. Your dad may be in jail for a couple of years or more. But during that time, we're going to go into counseling that is as soon as you're feeling up to it."

Skyler sits trying to absorb the news. He is filled with mixed emotions. Part of him is sad that his father is sitting in jail because of him, and the other part is glad because he is getting punished for all the years of abuse he has suffered at the hands of his father.

Mary sits quietly as she tries to read Skyler's face. She does not want to stir up anymore emotions than she already has. But there is still the matter of the candles and parchment she found in his closet. Like it or not, it must be brought into the open and dealt with.

"Is there anything you have questions about? Now is the time to bring them up and discuss them."

Skyler says nothing, waiting for the other shoe to drop.

"Skyler, I found some articles in your closet when I went to pick up some clothes for you to take to the hospital. Can you tell me about them?" Mary asks evenly and firmly.

Skyler takes a long drink of tea and lowers his head and begins to cry softy. Mary gives him a hug and there they stay for a good long while.

50

Joe arrives at the Warren's house shortly before 7:00 p.m. There are cars parked in front of the house and in the driveway. *Well, I better get this done and over with.* He gets out of his car and walks toward the house. Someone calls out to him. It is Paul Miller.

"Ready?" he asks Joe, as he walks to the front door. Joe rings the doorbell.

"About as ready as I'll ever be," he says with a sigh.

The door opens, and Peter greets them both as they enter the house. To the left is the living room where the meeting will take place. Several people are standing around conversing as if they are at any regular social gathering. Someone lets them know there are snacks and coffee in the kitchen. Both Paul and Joe walk over there together.

A large pot of freshly brewed coffee is on the counter, along with water bottles. There is a hot pot of water for tea which is placed next to a tray with several types of teas, as well as artificial sweeteners and sugar. There are two plates full of assorted cookies and a large platter of sliced fresh fruit. Next to that is a platter of deli meats and sliced bread. A stack of napkins and plastic forks and spoons are held in separate cups. The smell of fresh coffee fills the air giving the atmosphere a sense of comfort, which lessens the stress of what they are here to meet about and discuss.

Both Paul and Joe take their cups of coffee and plates laden with cookies, fresh fruit, and a couple of sandwiches into the living room and find a place to sit. Thirty minutes later, the meeting is called to order. Everyone seated comfortably, the meeting is called to order.

"Now you are all well aware of why we're having this meeting. For the sake of those who are new, I would like, at this time, to have everyone introduce yourselves, starting with myself. My name is Lee Warren, and I am the head of the group known as the Warren Group.

"We have been operating as a team for two years now. Our mission is to bring down the group of people who call themselves, the End Times Association. They have put into place a widespread plan called Phase Three: the Downfall. It was put into action a couple of weeks ago. Their mission is to get control of the city by means of our youth. They educate them in the occult without them realizing it and through key people, pillars of the community as it were, in all walks of life. Their goal is to take control of the community, state, then the nation, state by state. No need to tell you that our goal is to prevent this from happening. So if anyone of you feel you are not prepared or willing to give what it takes to accomplish this, by all means, you are free to go. There will be no ill will, nor any recriminations or retaliation."

Everyone looks around and mumbles softly to one another, hoping no one will leave. When it seems as if they are all going to stay, a young woman, professionally dressed, gets up and excuses herself and leaves. Then two more get up and leave. Mr. Warren reminds everyone that they have every right to leave, and if anyone else chooses to leave as well, may do so at this time. Everyone looks around the room, but no one else leaves.

"Good, now Julie, why don't you go next?"

Julie Warren introduces herself and states what role she will take. Finally, the last one introduces himself, and the meeting takes on its first subject on the agenda. Hours pass as the group works out a counterplan to eradicate the End Times Association. At the end of the meeting, each one is well aware of what role they are to play in all of this.

"Okay, everyone, you all know now what your job is and who to contact in case something goes wrong. We will have someone else come in to assist you should you need it. Thank you very much for coming and for your commitment to see this thing through. Now before we leave, I'd like to say a short prayer."

At the end of the prayer, amens are heard almost in unison. Everyone bids each other goodnight and thanks their hosts for their honesty, perseverance, and hospitality.

Joe walks out with Paul. They wish each other well as they make their way back to their cars. As Joe drives home, he is glad to know he is not alone in this fight. He feels a sense of security as he enters his home. Rover ambles over to Joe, who gives Rover a pat on the head as he heads straight for the bathroom. He readies himself for bed and finally pulls back the covers. Climbing into bed, he lets out a long sigh. He is soon asleep. Rover comes in followed by Snowball, and they both lay down at the foot of Joe's bed.

51

It has been a long night for everyone, even for Deceit, Backbiter, and Enepsigos. Deceit has been busy going back and forth between the Warren and Riggs's residences. He has been trying to listen in on all the plans they have laid out to correct the situation the dark forces have created.

Skyler lets his stepmother, Mary know just what he thinks about her failure to protect him. In return, Mary lets him know just how sorry she is for allowing the abuse to go on for such a long time.

Skyler explains why he had the altar set up in his closet, and he even tells Mary all about the Daughters of Amon and what they had promised to do for him when he paid them the two hundred dollars they requested.

They have come to an agreement that no good has come about by meeting with the Daughters of Amon and his encounters with Enepsigos, who masqueraded as Ingrid, Skyler's biological mother.

Together, they've taken out the items that formed the altar and placed them in a box and sealed it with tape. Mary calls Claire Deaton to let her know what she and Skyler have done and asks her how they are to properly dispose of the items.

She asks Mary if she will bring the box to her house to dispose of it correctly, for she knows the items are now cursed and are a homing device for demons and imps. For the first time in his young life, Skyler feels truly at peace.

Mary and Skylar arrive at the widow Claire Deaton's house, with the box in hand. They make their way to the front door and ring the doorbell twice before the door is opened.

"Hello, welcome," says the widow. "Please do come in. I'm so happy you're doing well Skyler. And Mary, you look well rested."

They walk in and are directed straight to the backyard. In the middle of the modest backyard is a metal trash can. She asks Skyler to put the sealed box into the container. She then pours a generous amount of lighter fluid over the box, along with a small bottle of oil she has prayed over and blessed. She hands a box of matches over to Skyler.

Taking a match from the box, he lights it and tosses the match into the metal trash can. The box ignites quickly into flames. Mary, Skyler, and Claire Deaton pray as they watch the box and its contents go up in flames. Soon it is reduced to ashes. He pours a pitcher of water over the ashes to make sure the fire is put out completely. Then he empties the wet ashes into a plastic bag and throws the bag into the trash can to be picked up the following day.

"Well, thank God that's done. How about we go inside for some carrot cake and coffee?"

"That sounds good to me," says Skyler, eager to have some of the delicious carrot cake the widow Claire Deaton is well known for.

———❧———

Deceit decides to stop and take some time from his work. Not wanting to have any distractions, he flies up into the atmosphere and looks for a place to land. A piece of an old, long since forgotten, space satellite floats by. He goes after it and lands on top.

Making himself comfortable, he lies down placing his scrawny hands on his belly and crosses his legs. He looks up at the beauty of the outer atmosphere. The stars shine brightly, giving off different colors of light.

As he floats around, he is struck by the marvelous wonders of the works of the Creator. The sounds emanating from the planets sound very much like music. Marveling at the beauty of the planets, the stars and the galaxy, he listens to the distant sound of angels singing. Yes, even out here, he can hear their beautiful voices sing praises to the Most High God. *I tell you that, if these should hold their peace, the stones would immediately cry out.*

Every so often he likes to come up here, closer than he should, to see the beauty of the Creator's handiwork.

Sometimes, he foolishly flies close to heaven and watches as the angels of the Most High God fly down to earth. Seeing them makes his heart ache in such a way that he swears he will never to do it again.

He remembers the great war when Lucifer, as he was known then, was thrown out of heaven with one third of all the angels. His fall from grace was long and hard.

"Oh, if only they knew what is in store for them that believe in Him and make Him their Lord and Savior. Such wondrous things, such joy, peace, and delight, ever to be with Him for all eternity," says Deceit wistfully.

"What a fool I have been, oh, such a fool. Now, I have hell and damnation to look to for eternity."

A small piece of meteor rock floats by, hitting his floating oasis and brings him back to the business at hand. Deceit looks around quickly to see if any fallen angels or other spirits, good or bad, have seen him. To his knowledge, no one has.

"Okay, now what have I learned about the meeting held today at the Warren house. They have set into motion their counterplan to thwart ours. What part of it shall I disclose to Amon and what part do I keep to myself?" thinks Deceit out loud.

"Skyler Riggs no longer lives. I am not sure why he was attacked nor by who. If I find out what happened, then I can use that information to possibly work it into my own plan.

"Oh, but some of these humans are more bold and more full of faith than I thought they were. Just when you think you've got them where you want them, they go and repent of their sins. Then they are forgiven and given guidance to accomplish the will of the Most High God. That is never good for me."

Deceit lies on the space junk and continues to sort out fact from fiction. He has only part of the Warren Group's plan and also the completed plans of young Skyler. He continues to float around the earth, opening his eyes occasionally to see the angels of light speeding down to earth. Deceit has decided what he will tell Amon and what he will withhold.

He takes his time in standing up and stretches himself to his full height. If only he could eat and drink, he would take more of these little respites.

He takes one more look around and heads back to headquarters and to report back to Amon.

Since the Warren Group has met, all is in place to get the ball rolling. First is to identify all officers of the law who are involved with the End Times Association. Thankfully, there is only one. Gary Holmes, a new recruit who unwillingly tips his hand at a local bar. Two members of the Warren Group have suspected him for a while and have gotten close to the officer through social media on the internet.

He is supposed to be the mole, but due to his young age and lack of good judgment, he is easily taken down and taken into custody after getting drunk in a bar and starting a fight.

Later, he will be charged with aiding and abetting in the delinquency of a minor. He has a history of being a partier and trying to solicit underage girls. But due to the changes to the legal system brought on by the Warren Group, he and others deemed willing to undergo psychiatric and rehabilitation therapy, along with Christian fundamental teachings, will be reviewed for possible parole when their parole review comes up.

The next plan of action is to shut down all of Mr. Tingly's teaching of the occult at the college and to bring legislation to allow Christians the same freedom others already enjoy.

Skyler walks up to Kellie Sanford's front door and rings the bell. After a few moments, the door opens and there stands Mr. Sanford. A nervous Skyler smiles and greets Mr. Sanford who opens the door and invites Skyler in. Mr. Sanford calls out to Kellie. When Skyler sees her, he is struck by how different she looks outside the hospital.

The three of them sit down in the living room and get to know each other a little better before Skyler escorts Kellie to the movies.

Deceit stays outside on the sidewalk, unwilling to risk a fight with the formidable, guardian angel of the Lord of Hosts that is stationed at the front of the house.

Skyler and Kellie leave with Deceit, staying at a good distance from them since a very large angel is assigned to each one of them. Deceit decides he will cut his losses and let Enepsigos tangle with them at his convenience.

—⟞∿⟝—

Laura Parson sits on a bench near the fountain across from the bank, a man standing several feet away looks right at her. He nods his head slightly as he leans down and picks up his briefcase and walks past her. She in turn picks up her purse and follows him at a distance.

The soft material of her dress flows gently around her as she makes her way across the street and into the bank. She heads for the counter where the mysterious gentleman in his navy blue, pin-striped suit and expensive loafers is filling in a deposit slip. Laura walks over next to him and also begins to fill out a deposit slip. The envelope which he has taken out of his briefcase is lying between them. He picks up his briefcase and heads toward a teller. After making his deposit, he leaves, not acknowledging Laura.

She discreetly picks up the envelope he has left behind and goes to another teller at the opposite end of the bank. She deposits into her account the contents of the envelope. Five thousand dollars even. Taking her receipt, she leaves the bank. Once outside, she pauses to look at her watch and places her bank receipt into her purse. A slight smile forms on her full lips as she puts on her sunglasses and walks back to the office.

—◦◦◦—

Joe picks up the phone and dials a number.

"Hello," answers a young woman in a rich, full voice.

"Hi, this is Joe. Did you just get home from work?"

"About half an hour ago," she answers.

"So, you haven't had dinner yet?"

"No, I haven't. Does this mean you're going to take me out to a scrumptious dinner?" asks Laura Parson, knowing the answer.

"Yes, I am. Where do you want to eat?"

"Stephanos."

"Pick you up around seven?"

"Yes, I'll be waiting," she replies.

"See you then." Joe smiles as he hangs up the phone.

Stephanos. Something special must have happened for her to suggest Stephanos. I wonder what it is, thinks Joe, as he heads for the bathroom to take a shower and shave.

Maybe she just wants to finish up the work week with a special dinner because she won a tough case. Yup, that must be it, thinks Joe as he pats on a light cologne.

As he drives to Laura's apartment, he thinks about how they first met.

He was on his way to meet a friend for lunch when he saw her sitting near the fountain at the plaza downtown.

Her shoulder-length, chestnut brown hair glistened in the noonday sun. Her brown eyes were covered with expensive, designer sunglasses as she sat gazing out at the fountain in front of the bank.

Her fair skin was turning slightly pink as she finished up her lunch. Her well-shaped legs were crossed, showing them off. Her feet were covered in fine, soft, leather designer shoes. Taking in a deep breath of fresh air, she put away her leftovers and napkin into her lunch bag. It had been such a long time since he had free time to ask anyone out. He was not about to miss out on this golden opportunity. He walked over to her and introduced himself. They sat talking for a few minutes, getting to know a little about each other. She looked at her watch stating she had to go to the bank before having to go back to the office and accepted his invitation to meet her the following day for lunch.

Arriving at her apartment, Joe walks up the short flight of stairs and down the hall to the end unit.

Why does she chose to live here when she could easily afford a nicer apartment, even a nice house if she wanted to, he thinks as he rings the doorbell. He only has to wait a few seconds before Laura opens the door. She is dressed in a black pant suit with a white silk shirt. She looks more like if she is going to court than to an expensive restaurant like Stephanos. Joe hopes his expression of disappointment does not show. He was looking forward to nice leisurely dinner in a romantic restaurant with the woman he loves.

"Hi," she says, smiling cheerfully at him.

"Hi," replies Joe, as he leans in to give her a kiss. She turns her head at the last second and he winds up kissing her cheek. Without a second thought, Laura motions to Joe to leave. She picks up her purse from the end table next to the front door and walks out closing the door tightly and locks the dead bolt. She starts walking down the hallway at a pace too quick for his liking. They usually stroll down the hallway and take their time in getting into car.

"What's the hurry?" asks Joe, as he closes the car door behind her. She just smiles at him through the window and does not answer as he slides into the driver's seat. He starts up the car and they drive away.

Laura turns up the radio and punches the button to the preset, soft jazz station. Neither one says a word all the way, leaving Joe to ponder just what is going on. He gets out of the car and walks over to her side to open the car door for her as he always does, but she is already out and closes the door before he reaches her.

Ohhh, something is wrong here. She's never acted like this before, thinks Joe as he follows her in.

"Good evening, Ms. Parson," says the host, as he greets Laura. "Good evening sir, right this way please," he says, as he takes them back to a more private seating area. Turning to Laura, the host asks her, "The usual?"

"Yes please," she says, as the host places the menus before them.

"Would you like something from the bar, sir?"

"Just mineral water, please," replies Joe politely, trying not to show his surprise at the way he greeted Laura. As far as he knows, she has only been here twice before, both times with him.

A waiter appears with a glass of white wine for her and mineral water for him. She takes the glass and drinks in the clear, cool liquid.

"Mmm, I needed that," she says, as she takes another long drink of wine. She places the glass down. Holding the stem of the wine glass, she smiles sweetly at Joe.

"So, how was your day," she asks Joe, who is in the middle of drinking his water. He takes his time in replying, not sure of what to say.

"Oh, it was a long, full day. I've finished the design I've been working on for several weeks on a limb for a young vet who needs a new leg," replies Joe with much satisfaction in his voice.

"That's nice," says Laura, as she turns and scans the room.

"Are you expecting someone?"

"Oh, no, no, just looking around to see who's here, that's all," she replies, not seeming to care what Joe thinks. He discreetly looks around the room, not sure who he is looking for. The waiter returns and asks if they are ready to order.

"Yes," says Laura, without even looking at the menu. She places her order and Joe requests the same, also without looking at the menu.

Laura continues to drink her wine as she openly scans the room, occasionally making small talk with Joe. The dinner arrives and Laura begins to eat before they give grace, which she usually gives.

This is too weird. What in the world is going on here? She's acting really strange and out of character.

Dinner progresses in a dull and boring fashion. Laura has left the table several times during the meal. Each time to return looking disappointed.

"Would you like some dessert?" asks Joe, knowing full well her answer will be no. Without further ado, Joe catches the waiter's eye and asks for the check.

As they are walking out, a tall, attractive man of about forty years of age helps his date—a lovely, blonde-haired woman—get out of the car and go into the restaurant. The valet drives up in Joe's car and holds the door open for Laura. Joe generously tips the valet and gets into the car. Laura is already buckled in and looking a bit angry. At this point, he feels it better not to ask her what is wrong. Up until now, things were a bit strange, but not strained.

Laura looks out the window all the way to her apartment. The silence is thick enough to cut with a knife. Arriving at her apartment, Laura tells Joe not to bother walking her to the door. Her tone says she is quite serious and will not be swayed.

"Thanks for a lovely dinner," she says tersely and slams the car door shut. Joe watches as she hurries up the stairs and down the hall to her apartment. He sits in his car for a moment trying to understand what has just transpired this evening.

"Forget it, I'm going home," he says, putting his car in gear and drives away. As he opens the door to his own house, he is greeted by Snowball and Rover.

"At least you're happy to see me," he says, as he turns and locks the door. He glances over at the grandfather clock.

"Eight thirty, that's one for the books," he says aloud. He changes into his pajamas and decides to go to bed early.

"No use in worrying about it."

52

The following day, Joe sits at his desk checking his e-mail for any mail he might have received from Laura. Not finding any, he shuts down the computer and walks over to the living room.

Thinking out loud, he says, "Okay, what do we have here? Laura was expecting to see someone at dinner last night. Two, why did she scarcely speak to me during dinner? Three, she's been there before, obviously many times without me. Four, she drank almost an entire bottle of wine by herself, something I have never seen her do before. As a matter of fact, she almost always drinks white wine and only a glass at most. Five, she seems to know the man who arrived with a woman just before I got my car. Six, she didn't answer my call when she got it. What's more, she always returns my calls the same day. Finally, who was it that picked her up in a limo?"

Joe paces as he ponders the stream of events. He decides to call her.

"Hello?" answers Laura, trying to sound cheery.

"Hi, Laura. Are you busy?"

"Well, no, not really. I just have a few errands to run, and I want to get them done early," replies Laura.

"Okay, when would be a good time to call? I need to talk to you about something."

"Joe, I really am busy, and I will continue to be busy for the next few days. I have a situation going on, and I need to take care of it as soon as possible. I'll call you when I get some free time and we can talk then. Gotta go now, bye."

Joe is left surprised by her abruptness. *What is the world is going on here?* He wonders.

Nothing seems to be going right. Could it be that she has found someone else and that's why her behavior has been so strange of late? Or is it that things are getting stirred up again in the spirit.

Joe decides to seek the only one who can help answer these questions. He begins to pace in front of the sofa and prays earnestly for answers. Rover and Snowball have already made themselves comfortable in their usual places to watch Joe as he paces while saying his prayers. Since the final battle with End Times Association, not a day has passed that he has failed to pray for strength and guidance.

He questions God about Laura and why she has acted so out of character. He pours out exactly how he feels and what he thinks the problem may be.

Who was that man in the Jag? Her mood turned sour after seeing him and the lady he was with. Could it be she's in love with him and is jealous of the other woman? Joe, now you're just grasping at straws.

He goes outside and lies down on the hammock to rest his body as well as his mind.

Deceit comes down from his hiding place and lands on the foot of Joe's hammock. He sits their looking at Joe, thinking and doing nothing for a while.

That's a first, thinks Backbiter, as he watches Deceit from his hiding place. *Wonder what the fool is planning this time. Probably more of the same.*

"You better sleep now, while the getting is good. Because soon, your life is going to take another major change, and this time I'm going to win," says Deceit to Joe, as he l sleeping.

53

Deceit takes flight and heads out into the lazy afternoon. First, he heads out to Laura's apartment. He pokes his head through the back wall and sees she is not there.

Nothing to be gained here, he thinks as he flies out the back window and to Stephanos. The aroma of the cuisine travels up his nose, making his severely empty stomach rumble. He lands on a table for two who are enjoying fine wine and a steak lunch. Deceit leans over the plate of one unsuspecting diner and takes a deep breath.

He opens his mouth wide and places his black, rubbery lips on top of the wine glass. Sticking his tongue deep into the wine, he hopes to taste what he cannot have, but desires with all his being.

Frustrated he can't drink even a single drop, he leans back, clears his throat, and spits into the glass. He walks around the table stepping on the bread and salad, then he remembers why he is there.

A few tables away from the one he is on, he sees John Langer who is conversing with a lovely, blonde woman.

"Well, I'll be a monkey's uncle. These two are in love," says Deceit rather loudly.

"The human, Laura Parson, has a thing for this man."

Deceit lets out a high-pitched laugh.

"Oh, I couldn't of planned this better myself," he says, rolling around the table as he continues to laugh heartily. He stops and strokes his chin as he takes a good long look at Langer.

"I must find out who this human is and exactly what kind of a relationship he has with Laura Parson. Oh yes, this is the break I have been waiting for," Deceit says, as he shoots up and out in search of Gusion. Backbiter is not far behind.

Amon has kept Backbiter on this assignment to tail Deceit. He knows what kind of demon he is dealing with and he knows Deceit will not stop until he gets the desired results. That is, of course, when it suits his purpose. He has vowed to bring Joe Austin down regardless of the cost to him. Amon has already struck him in the face for failing so miserably in this assignment. This is something he never wants to repeat again.

Deceit heads straight toward the west end of the compound. He lands gently to the left of the giant pillars in the courtyard next to Gusion's office. This is only his second time here. He makes his way to the beautiful, arched windows which lead to Gusion's office. He looks around to see if Gusion is there. He is not there.

Deceit decides to make an appointment with Gusion's assistant. He turns and bumps right into Gusion, falling flat on his back. Deceit stares up at him, his eyes wide as saucers as he scrambles to his feet.

"Oh, mighty angel of Satan," he says, curtsying deeply before Gusion, "I didn't see you standing there."

Gusion looks down at Deceit with a look of amusement.

"I'd ask you what you were doing, but I already know."

"Oh yes, you would, wouldn't you," replies Deceit with a nervous little laugh.

"I have come as you know to inquire about Laura Parson. She is a human woman that is seriously involved with Joe Austin. But I suppose you know of him."

"I do. He's the human that brought you and the End Times Association down, but a scant seven years ago," replies Gusion, looking at Deceit's cheeks turn a darker shade of black with embarrassment.

"Well, yes, I suppose you could look at it that way."

"Now, tell me what it is your desire to know about Laura Parson."

Deceit explains mostly everything he wants to know about Langer and Laura Parson.

Gusion calls out to his assistant and requests some information he has complied on Laura Parson and Langer.

Without delay, Gusion's assistant disappears down the hall. He returns shortly after a minute or two and relays his information to Gusion in hushed tones.

Meanwhile, Deceit walks around looking over the beautiful courtyard with his hands clasped behind him. He tries to listen in on the conversation between Gusion and his assistant, but to no avail.

"Good, and get me the information on the others I requested."

Gusion's assistant rushes out of sight to gather information on the names Gusion has requested.

"Come in to my office and take a seat. I will be with you shortly," says Gusion.

Deceit walks into Gusion's office and is taken aback by the beauty of it. Unlike Amon's, this office has a multitude of artwork and statues.

The chairs are blue in color and ornately carved out and decorated with silver. The room is large and Gusion's desk is also blue and ornately decorated with silver. His chair has a high, padded back and padded arms covered with white silk cloth. There is a large, square blue and silver rug with a beautiful pattern. The crystal chandelier gives off a multitude of colors against the blue of the chairs.

Deceit pulls back one of the two chairs which are placed in front of Gusion's desk. There is no sound to be heard. Deceit takes a seat and makes himself comfortable.

"Now this is what I call an office," he says softly.

"Why Deceit, after all the things I've heard about you, I would never have thought you had such refined tastes."

The sound of Gusion's voice startles Deceit to where he jumps high off his chair and actually pokes his head through the twelve-foot-high ceiling.

Gusion laughs at the sight of Deceit pushing himself with both hands against the ceiling, trying to get his head free of it. Giving the final push, Deceit breaks free and crashes down, narrowly missing the chair. Gusion sits and motions Deceit to do the same. Deceit picks himself up carefully, and with as much grace and dignity as he can muster, he sits himself down.

54

John Langer decides to call Laura Parson later that day. He has known for some time that she might be in love with him, but thought it was just an infatuation. Figuring after Laura got close to Joe Austin, this infatuation would finally be over. He was flattered at the thought of a beautiful, younger woman so interested in him. But after carefully infiltrating the Warren Group and gaining the trust of Lee Warren, Langer was not about to throw away all his hard work over a pretty face.

Langer is tall with dark brown hair and with graying temples. His steel gray eyes are set in a handsome face, which lends to the allure of the physically fit attorney.

His wife of fifteen years met him when he was a young assistant to one of the up-and-coming older attorneys by the name of Lee Warren. He had met him in Washington after he applied to the position Lee Warren had vacated when he had taken a position with the newly appointed attorney general of the United States at the start of the new administration.

Langer had worked long and hard to keep his secret and nothing and no one was going to mess this up for him now.

"Hello, this is Laura Parson speaking."

"Good afternoon, Laura. This is John. I'd like to get together with you at the park sometime today. We need to get things straightened out."

"Oh, you sound so serious," replies Laura. "I'm free now. How about we meet in half an hour and go for a run around the park?"

"Half an hour it is at the start of the running trail," answers John and hangs up without saying good-bye.

Gee, that sounded serious. Could it be he's still upset about running into Joe and me at the restaurant. I know he loves me, only his wife won't give him a divorce.

Laura hurries to change into her deep purple sweatsuit and pulls her hair back into a ponytail. She hurries out the door, hastily locking it behind her.

Joe finishes cleaning the shed and gathers what he has to donate to charity and puts them into the trunk of his car. He decides to go to the park after donating his items.

He comes across the box with the games in it, one being the Ouija board. Placing all but the Ouija board box in the donation pile, he opens it up and looks through it.

Seems harmless enough. But he decides to burn it instead of giving it to some unsuspecting soul. He has long known that the "game" is nothing short of a hand into the occult.

Without any hesitation, he pulls out a metal trash can and empties it out into a large plastic garbage bag. He throws the board into the metal trash can and pours lighter fluid over it. He strikes a match, but it goes out almost immediately. He continues to do so until his match folder is empty.

"This is ridiculous," he says aloud, going into the house to get more matches.

Upon returning, he tries again to light the match. After four tries, he gets frustrated and goes into the house again and brings out the fireplace lighter. As he turns the lighter on, he notices the flame waver as if someone were blowing on it. He cups his free hand around it and lights the game board. It explodes into flames, emitting an excess of black smoke which smells strangely like sulfur. It burns completely, leaving nothing but foul-smelling ashes.

It's been quite a while since he has been able to rest and enjoy his weekends alone. Laura and his work have taken up much of his time.

Since Laura has been acting so strangely of late, I think I'll call her tonight and see what's up with her.

Joe loads up Rover into the back seat of his car. Not wanting to be left behind, Snowball climbs over the side yard fence and runs after Joe, meowing as loudly as she can.

"Ohhh, Snowball," says Joe, as he picks up the still meowing cat. "I'm sorry, sweetie, come on get in." Joe opens the car door and puts Snowball in.

With her ears still pinned back, she looks at Rover with such a look as to cause him to lie down and put his head on his front paws. It does not take long for both Rover and Snowball to get over their emotions and enjoy the trip to the thrift store and park.

Joe puts a leash on both and lets them out. Once they hit the ground, they both take off in different directions. With a firm tug, Joe gets them going in the same direction where he is headed.

Deciding to make sure the fire is completely out, Joe turns on the water and hoses down the contents of the can. The smoke stops with what sounds like a whimper, sending shivers down Joe's back. He throws the wet ashes into the half-filled trash bag and seals it quickly.

Deceit sits to the side of the can trying to catch his breath. He has blown out all the matches Joe has tried to light the board with.

"I'm too old to be doing this," he says, still trying to catch his breath. Then he quickly looks around to see if any other spirit had heard him finally admit he was old and ready for their final destination. Deceit is many things and one of them is vain.

Unbeknownst to him, Backbiter has been watching Deceit trying to blow out all the matches as quickly as they are lit.

But halfway through the second matchbook, Deceit has run out of air, so he starts to put the fire out with his fingers.

Backbiter holds his tongue as he watches this comical sight. Unable to contain his laughter any longer, Backbiter flies up into the air and lets out a howl of laughter. Then he flies back in to the full, leafy tree in Joe's backyard.

By now, Deceit has regained his ability to breathe regularly again. He flies up and around the backyard hoping to catch sight of the spirit which was originally assigned to the Ouija board. He wants to ask them a few questions pertaining to what they had seen, heard, and learned about Joe and any others who might have come in contact with it.

Backbiter watches in amusement as Deceit flies around the yard, stopping occasionally to ask a rock or a bush if they were the spirit assigned to the board.

Since Deceit has no knowledge of Backbiter spying on him, the unexpected sound of laughter frightens him to the point he is unable to move. Backbiter being aware of this, decides he will try and make a bigger fool out of Deceit, now that he has the chance.

Backbiter climbs to another branch and starts to make strange noises and hisses. He jumps from limb to limb delighting himself at the cost of Deceit.

By now, Deceit is so shaken. He jumps up as hard as he can and heads upwards passing through a flock of birds flying across the midday sky. This unexpected pass is all that is needed to scare Deceit into screaming in terror and flying away as fast as he can, not caring where he goes or where he winds up.

Seeing this, Backbiter is laughing so hard, he falls out of the tree, landing directly on top of the demon who was originally assigned to the Ouija board. The demon lets out a howl of pain that makes Backbiter scream as well, and the two demons flee in opposite directions, leaving Joe to finish his task in peace.

They make their way to the dog park, and Joe leaves Rover there to play with other dogs. Then he and Snowball go for a leisurely walk around the park.

Laura and John have been running for fifteen minutes and are in front of a clump of trees and shrubbery. John pulls Laura behind the bushes.

Without any hesitation, Laura throws her arms around him and starts kissing him. John quickly grabs her by the arms and pulls them from around his neck.

"Don't you ever do that again," he says, his steel grey eyes burning furiously as Laura, taken by surprise, meekly moves her arms away from him and steps back a couple of steps.

"Listen, and listen well. We are both professionals and have a job to do. This sort of behavior has got to stop now. Understood?"

"Yes, but—"

"But what?"

"I thought you loved me too. The way you were so sweet to me when we first met and when you avoided me completely at dinner the other night. I thought you were trying to get me jealous by the way you were acting with that woman."

"That woman, as you call her, just happens to be my wife. I love her, and I have no desire to hurt her or leave her, ever. Do I make myself clear?"

"Yes, yes you do," says Laura, looking down not wanting to let him see the tears in her eyes.

"Listen, I don't like being hard on you, but you must understand that I am close to getting vital information that should put a halt to the new legislation that will surely pass. This will give all Christians the same rights as the non-Christians have now. I hope you realize that if this key legislation goes through, we're in for it."

"Yes, I do understand. I might be young and a bit new at this, but I know how important this is to us."

"Fine, now that we've cleared the air, I see no reason to meet again under any circumstances other than professionally and at our drop-off meetings," says John, a bit softer than before.

Laura let her arms drop to her sides as she watches him jog away. Anger begins to rise deep within her, forming a hard shell around her heart. Taking in a deep breath, she closes her eyes for a moment and lets her breath escape slowly.

She walks out from behind the bushes and starts to walk to her car when Joe spots her.

He calls out to her, but she is too far away to hear. He takes his cell phone out and dials her number. Laura stops and looks at who is calling. She sees Joe's name come up and continues to let it ring as she gets into her car and drives away.

Joe keeps the phone to his ear, but decides not to leave a message. He stands momentarily, as Snowball sits quietly next to him.

He leans down, picks up Snowball, and walks over to the dog run. He calls out to Rover who is roughhousing with some other dogs. Joe calls him again, and Rover runs toward Joe.

"Having too good a time to pay attention to me when I call?" he asks Rover, who is wagging his tail so hard, he knocks Snowball over who is standing next to him.

Joe laughs as Snowball rolls a couple of times before stopping. Indignant, she pins her ears back and tries to swipe Rover missing his hind end.

"Now, now," he says to Snowball, as he picks her up and pets her head.

Rover could care less about her. He is still high on having a romp with some of his buddies on a sunny afternoon.

On the way home, Joe thinks about what happened the night before and why Laura did not answer his call just a few minutes ago. *Something strange is going on here, and I'm going to find out just what it is.*

Joe picks up the phone and dials Laura's number. This time, she answers.

"Hi, how are you?" says Joe, deciding not to let her know he has seen her at the park.

"I'm great, how about you?" answers Laura cheerfully.

"Just thought you might want to have a late dinner?" he asks, trying to sound normal.

"Oh, no thanks. I've been working on a case here at home. I haven't even been out at all today. I think I'll just stay home and take a long hot bath and rest up for Monday."

"Really? You don't want to go out? Well, okay" says Joe. There is a long pause before anyone speaks again.

"Are you okay? Is there anything wrong? You weren't yourself the other night."

"Yes, I'm doing great. This job just takes it out of you, you know."

"Okay, I'll let you go then. Have a good night."

Joe hangs up and decides he is going to confront Laura face-to-face. He gets cleaned up and heads out the door.

Parking a ways down the street, he heads toward Laura's apartment. As he is crossing the street, a dark-colored limousine drives up and stops in front of her apartment. As Joe gets closer, he sees Laura rushing toward the limousine. She gets in the backseat and the limo speeds away, leaving Joe standing in front of her apartment complex staring after her.

"Would you like something to drink?" asks the older gentleman sitting next to her.

"Yes, I would."

"What would you like?" he asks calmly.

"Grey Goose, if you have it."

"Certainly," he says, as he pours a drink for her. Laura takes it and downs it immediately. The man sitting next to her looks mildly amused and offers her another drink of vodka. Again, she takes the drink and downs it quickly.

"I see you did need that drink after all," he says calmly, as he takes a wine glass and pours out some wine for himself.

"Now, Miss Parson, it has come to my attention you are having a bit of trouble with Mr. Langer. Do you mind explaining it to me please?" he says, as he drinks his wine, savoring it slowly.

"No, I'm not having any trouble with John, I mean Mr. Langer. It was just a misunderstanding, that's all."

"He didn't seem to think so. Otherwise, why would you be here with me?"

"Look, I appreciate all you have done for me, paying for college and law school, but really this 'thing' between Mr. Langer and I is over. Nothing more to discuss. I might have overstepped my bounds, but I'm back on track. No need to worry."

"Oh, but I do worry. I have invested a lot of money in you and have set you up with a monthly allowance so you may be able to be live very well. You need to look the part in order to play the part. Now I know you've been under lot of stress lately, but I figured with a romantic outlet with your handsome beau would be of aid to you. He is a key player in opposition to us, you know. I'd hate to have to replace you at this time. Once you become his wife, you will be in a unique position to influence him like no one else can."

"Yes, sir, I understand, but you see…"

"No, my dear, I don't see. I have been getting mixed reports on you, and that is why I have taken time away from my lovely island home to make sure all is running smoothly, and no major mistakes take place at this crucial time."

"I have been loyal and I have done everything you've asked of me and more. I don't see why you have to take the word of Mr. Langer over mine."

"But, my dear, I'm not. John was not the one who contacted me. Either you do your job, which you have been generously compensated for, or we will be forced to replace you. Do I make myself clear?"

"Yes, you do. I do have one more question to ask," says Laura, as Mr. Tingly sips the last of his wine. He looks over at her and nods his head indicating she can ask.

"If it wasn't Mr. Langer who called you, then who was it?"

Mr. Tingly tells the driver to return to Laura's apartment and refills his glass, not answering her question. Laura sits quietly looking out the window of the limousine.

So, he won't tell me. Fine, I'll just have to find out for myself.

The limo arrives at Laura's apartment and as soon as she is out, Mr. Tingly closes the door for her and the limo drives off leaving Laura looking after it. Fully persuaded that the matter with Laura is under control, he decides to return to his island retreat.

55

The phone rings and Jessie picks it up on the first ring.

"Hello, this is Jessie, how can I help you?"

"Son, this is your mother."

Immediately, he knows something is very wrong. His mother seldom calls, much less, calls him son.

"Your father died last night and the funeral will be in a couple of days."

"What? What did you say? Father's gone? What happened?"

"Well, if you would stop asking so many question, I'll be able to answer you. Why didn't you call or visit? He had been sick for months, and you never even called or came to visit him. He was calling out for you just before he died. But no, you were always too busy to come and visit. Now look, your father's gone and I'm left all alone."

Jessie is too stunned, not only by the news of his father's death, but by the way his mother has turned her anger and loss of her husband on him. He never had a close relationship

SUSAN B. A. HOFMANN

with either of his parents, but to be accused of not caring was almost more than he could bear.

His mother is still raging on the phone when he says, "Mother…Mom, please calm down. I called many times before, but both you and Dad were either out of town, or something else kept you and father from talking to me. Mom, please."

"I just got in from the funeral home, and I'll fill you in on when and what day the funeral will be. I'll have your old room ready for when you arrive tomorrow. Good-bye."

With shaking hands, Jessie calls the airport and makes flight arrangements for the flight home. His next call is to his employer, Joe Austin, at Austin Robotics. He lets him know his father has passed away, and he needs to take some personal time off to attend the funeral and to help his mother with his father's estate. He will take all his vacation time and hopes to be back at the end of three weeks or perhaps sooner.

Joe is sympathetic to Jessie's plight and understands fully just how Jessie must be feeling at the loss of his father.

"And remember, just call and let us know if you need any more time. Take as long as you want. If there is anything else I can do for you, please let me know. I'll have my secretary call for a temporary replacement for you while you're away. And don't worry about your job. You'll still have it when you're ready to return to work."

"Thank you, Mr. Austin. I really appreciate this. I'll be back as soon as I can."

"Don't worry about it. I hope all goes well for you."

Jessie collects his lunch box and makes a call to his backup at the office. He explains the situation to him and as soon as he comes in, Jessie leaves and heads for home. In need of a strong drink, he changes his mind and decides to get that drink and something to eat. He drives to the Coffee Cart.

Tingly arrives at the same time. Heading toward the restaurant, he sees Jessie and sees by the expression on his face, all is not well with him. Deciding to talk with Jessie, he walks toward him. He figures Jessie has already lost his job and that's why he looks so down. But before he can reach him, Jessie is met by a couple of ladies from the church in the parking lot. Tingly does not want anyone to know he knows him. So he decides to eat at the café on the outskirts of town.

"Hello, Jessie," says Claire Deaton. "It's good to see you again. How have you been?"

All he can do is to look into her eyes, his chin quivering.

"Why, Jessie, what's wrong?"

All he can do is weep, with both hands covering his face. Both ladies hug him from both sides. Jessie, now overcome with emotion, rests his head on the shoulder of Mrs. Deaton and begins to sob. They remain there for quite a while, both ladies praying silently.

56

Time has passed since the downfall of the End Times Association. The Daughters of Amon have disbanded. Sara Cunningham a.k.a. Chulda is deceased, and Damian Tingly has long left the country. The university has replaced Tingly's classes with Christian studies.

Samantha and Mia's untimely and vicious deaths have long since been considered cold cases, and their files are stored in a warehouse, where they gather dust, waiting for the time when they will be solved.

Jason Riggs was found guilty of child abuse and has served his time. Jason, his wife Mary, and son Skyler faithfully attend church and their court ordered family counseling.

Skyler has graduated college with a degree in psychology and has taken a job with the city to help counsel abused children.

Mr. Warren has been elected attorney general. Julia, his wife, works tirelessly alongside others to help those who are homeless.

The widow, Claire Deaton, is on her second year as head of the church afterschool program. The volunteers who help her range from high schoolers to grandparents. Much has been gained through their help in care of children and babies whose parents must work and simply cannot afford child care. Here they all enrich each other's lives by helping and caring for one another and by teaching Christian values to the young.

The city has grown in community services and projects involving substance abuse, child abuse, and mental health to keep the many streets and parks around the city safe and clean. Alongside the church, they help the elderly and disabled in many ways, as well as to keep their yards and homes clean and in good repair.

Angelo de Fuego's true identity is still unknown to Joe Austin. The now disbanded Warren Group members continue in their current professions. Paul Miller has been promoted at his job and is looking forward to his upcoming nuptials.

Ann and her husband Matt are expecting their second child, a boy, in June. Marriage has softened her temper greatly, and she is now a stay-at-home wife and mother, happy to raise and care for her family.

Tony Watkins and the others in Joe's small circle of tight friends have all gone on to work in their chosen professions, keeping regularly in touch with each other.

These are just a few of the projects that have taken root since the dismantling of the End Times Association.

Joe Austin's company, Austin Robotics, has grown considerably since the attempted takeover several years earlier by Damian Tingly and two others. Life for this city has improved greatly and is now considered one of the flagships of economic and social growth, as well as in green industries.

Deceit flies around the city, deeply disappointed in the failure to bring down this jewel of a city. His plan to be promoted, took a downward turn, but Deceit has formed another plan to rise again to his former station. Knowing how to deceive humans throughout the centuries, he has learned one thing for sure—when times are tough, many rely on their own wits and seek help from the dark forces, while the pesky Christian seek help from the Most High God.

"When will humans ever learn that we on the dark side are here to cause problems? We kill, we steal, and we destroy. That is our mission. If humans ever learn to first ask help from the Most High God, they would not be so easily deceived and lulled into complacency and be led into trouble, thereby rendering us, impotent. For many, it is too late. When will they ever learn? Time is getting short for us and for the world. So therefore I will go forth and go to hell, then into the lake of fire in a blaze of glory."

57

Joe Austin, the widow Claire Deaton, and other prayer warriors continue to pray. They have not yet felt the release to stop. If they could see into the spirit world, they would see their guardian angels along with several other angels surrounding them, some with their swords ready to strike at any foe who might come to cause them any harm.

Among those praying are Peter, Julie and Lee Warren. Next to them are Mr. and Mrs. Densmore and Laura's parents, Mr. and Mrs. Parson.

Laura paces as she feels a heaviness upon her. Unable to stand it anymore, she decides to seek help in the only place she knows where she will not be turned away.

She leaves her apartment in such haste that she does not even bother to lock her door. Arriving at the church, she parks her car just a few parking spots away from Joe's. Hurrying inside, Laura sees the faces of her parents, Mr. Delmore and Joe Austin. Surprised, she hangs back and slides on to the last bench of the church. No one has noticed her since they are deep in prayer.

Laura sits quietly taking in what is before her. She begins to shake as she realizes her parents have given themselves over to Christ. She is not surprised to see the Densmores or the Warrens there, not even Joe. That is to be expected, but her parents who disowned her years ago and had come to know the Lord as their Savior was not what she had expected. She had expected them to contact her when they became Christians, but they did not. This she could not comprehend.

Surely, they would have contacted me as soon as they had converted.

Laura sits listening to the others as they pray alongside Joe. This is what she has been waiting for since she had become a Christian herself, for her parents to come around as well.

"My Lord, I am so sorry for turning away from you. I am so sorry. Please Lord, forgive me," says Laura softly, as she lowers her head and cries as only one who truly repents can.

The others see her, but do not recognize her since she has her head down. They just assume she is another member of the congregation who has come to pray along with them. As they pray, they feel the burden lift from their hearts and begin to feel joy.

Laura also begins to feel her soul being unburdened as well. As if orchestrated, all present, except Laura, begin to shout for joy. Some run around the church with their hands in the air. Others kneel, looking up to heaven and raise their arms with absolute joy on their faces. Some like Joe and Widow Deaton lie on their faces giving homage to God, thanking him for the victory.

"Laura, honey, is that you?" says Mrs. Parson, as she walks closer to her.

Laura lifts her head and looks into the face of her beloved mother. Without hesitation, she jumps up and runs to her with outstretched arms. They embrace as Mr. Parson walks quickly down the aisle where Laura and her mother are. Without saying a word, Mr. Parson hurries over to them. Laura opens her eyes and sees her father standing behind her mother. They look at each other momentarily before they hug each other as tears flow freely down their faces.

Joe stands next to Claire Deaton and smiles. Joy fills his heart as he sees Laura walk with her arms around the waist of both her parents as they walk out the front doors of the church.

He turns to Mrs. Deaton and smiles as he hugs her and thanks her for being such a strong, godly presence in his life.

"Would you like to have coffee and a slice or two of apple pie?" she asks, holding Joe's hand with both of hers.

"I would love to," replies Joe, as he waves good-bye to the others.

"Well, son, how about we go home?" asks Mr. Warren, as Mrs. Warren and Peter come and stand next him.

"Hey, Mom, is there any pie left that Mrs. Deaton gave us the other day?" asks Peter with a smile.

"I believe there is. Mr. Delmore, would you like to join us for a late night snack?"

"I sure would," he replies, as they make their way out the door of the church.

58

M r. Tingly has returned from his island home once again. He has been given a new assignment. It was a simple matter and dealt with quickly. Curious as to the state of the portal, he decides to make a visit before returning home. He waits till midnight to return.

The place had been put up for sale soon after the untimely death of Sara Cunningham, known as Chulda, the gatekeeper, to her peers. This is something that had been bothering him since it happened. He had been toying with the idea of possibly buying it himself. But before he could inquire about the property, it was taken off the market.

As Tingly decides he will open the portal, an uneasy feeling comes over him. But the urge to do so is too strong. As he draws closer to the portal, he hesitates. Keeping a strong grip on his emotions, he takes a deep breath and stands firmly; his feet solidly planted. And raising his arms, he calls out to the spirit, Gusion. The portal opens. Gusion and two other spirits appear—Enepsigos and another being he has never seen before.

Tingly's heart begins to beat faster as the three assemble themselves before him. They take a few steps toward Damian Tingly, as he takes several steps back.

"Why have you opened the gate to the portal, Damian Tingly? We have no business with you at this time. As the successor to the former gatekeeper, you know to guard the gate and open it only after you have received word from Amon to do so," says the unknown spirit.

Tingly is too afraid to speak. He stands frozen, staring at the three, formidable, fallen spirits of the underworld that stand directly before him.

"Speak now or we shall do the speaking for you, Damian Tingly," says the unknown spirit in a low and menacing voice.

Tingly opens his mouth in hopes something will come out. Much to his surprise, it does. A loud, high-pitched scream that originates deep in his soul.

"Please, do not harm me. I came here to see if anyone had opened the portal since Chulda had opened it prior to her death. Since I was appointed the new gatekeeper, I decided to open it tonight myself and seek the wisdom of Gusion. There have been a few problems here in the city since my departure. They were minor and were dealt with immediately upon my return," replies Tingly, his voice shaking along with his knees.

"Damian Tingly, you do not have to open the gate to hell in order to get me to visit with you. Yet you have. Do you not know that we are not at your back and call just to get some insignificant information which you could have been easily obtained by simply having a séance?"

"Yes, but I did want to see if there had been any activity since my departure," replies Tingly, well aware he is rambling on.

The three spirits come close to each other and speak in a tongue unknown to Tingly. They seem to come to some agreement and step back to their original positions.

"Enepsigos, Gusion, and I, Baal, have come to the agreement that you have overstepped your bounds, and that we will no longer need your services as the gatekeeper."

Tingly turns white with fright still unable to move. Baal steps toward him and raises his hand toward Tingly. Just then, a brilliant flash of white, blinding light appears, surrounding them all.

Enepsigos, Gusion, and Baal turn around in fright, as they see the warrior angels of the Lord of Hosts, surrounding them. The few daring imps and demons which climbed out of the portal when Tingly had first opened it now try to scurry back in as they see the angels of the Most High God surround the trio of spirits as well as the human, Damian Tingly.

With their swords drawn, the angels of the Most High God let out a battle cry and attack.

Enepsigos is the only one able to escape back through the portal and come out at another portal miles away, which a new coven of six young people have just opened.

Baal and Gusion both call out to other the fallen warrior angels to assist them. Suddenly, there is a legion of fallen warrior angels engaged in hand-to-hand combat with the angels of the Lord of Hosts. The sound of swords clashing and the battle cries is deafening.

Tingly tries to crawl away as the battle rages on. The sparks and tongues of fire from the clashing swords fly in all directions. He is burned in several areas of his back and head. But being in near state of shock, he is unaware of the severity of the burns and cuts he is receiving from both the good and the fallen angel's swords. All he can think about now is to get away with his life and limbs intact.

He continues to crawl away as he has the opportunity to do so. Finally, he gets his chance to run as the angels take to the air. Not hesitating, Damian Tingly stands to his feet and runs for his life. As he reaches the back of the mansion, he stops to catch his breath. The smell of sulfur is strong in the air, making it hard for him to breathe.

He makes his way around the side of the building and to the front porch where he slides to the floor and sits, trying to compose himself and catch his breath.

As he rests, he looks at his watch by the light of the brilliance of the angels themselves. His heart sinks. His driver will not return for him for another half hour. His heart beating faster, Tingly stands to this feet and walks down the few short steps to the driveway.

If I start running now, I should be well away from this horrid place. Yes, that's what I shall do. Run for dear life.

Tingly takes off running toward the road.

"Damn, that Chulda, why did she have to have such a long driveway," he says, as he stumbles and falls on his way down the long, dark, winding driveway.

"Where do you think you're going?" says Deceit, as he stands in front of Tingly, blocking his path. Tingly stops abruptly. Deceit slowly walks toward him.

Tingly opens his mouth, but this time nothing comes out. The stench coming from Deceit makes the already weary Tingly nauseous. Puffs of black smoke ooze from the wounds he has received during the battle.

Deceit had been following Tingly when he had overheard Tingly telling his driver not to stray too far away that evening because he wanted to make one last stop at the portal before leaving.

"You have cost me dearly, Damian Tingly," says Deceit in a voice that shakes Tingly to the core.

"I thought I had an ally in you. But I see all I have is a quivering mass of human jelly. You are not fit to be the gatekeeper. You're nothing more than a second rate consolation prize."

Tingly lies on the ground listening to Deceit as he slowly walks around him.

"I wonder why they picked you for such a position. I would've made a far better gatekeeper than you, you miserable human."

The sound of battle has diminished greatly, but the stench of sulfur has increased. Deceit turns to look to see who is left standing. Unable to see clearly through the dense cloud of sulfur and smoke, Deceit walks back to the portal.

Tingly stands to his feet and leans over with his hands on the tops of his knees, breathing hard as he tries to catch his breath. He can see the headlights of a car heading his way. Without hesitation, he runs to the middle of the street and begins to wave his arms.

The limousine comes to a stop a few feet in front of Tingly. With great urgency, Tingly gets into the backseat of the limo and orders the driver to leave as fast as he can and return to the villa. Without delay, the driver makes a U-turn, running over bushes and rocks as he turns and speeds away.

A lone figure stands in the middle of the dark street in front of Chulda's former house and says, "This is not yet over for you, Damian Tingly, not by a long shot."

NOTES

Hebrew Female Names Source—20,000-Names.com: meaning and origin: Chulda: Variant spelling of Hebrew *Chaldea*, meaning "mole" or "weasel"

Angel-art-andgifts.com/angel-names.html

www.angelghosts.com/fallen_angel_names_htm2012

FALLEN ANGEL NAMES

The following list is of traditions as fallen angels' names gathered from different religions, mythologies, and lore. These angel names are of those angels considered to be of a bad nature and not good angel names.

Enepsigos. F.A. who appears in the shape of woman.
Gusion. F.A. who can discern the past, present or future.
Satan. Christian F.A. whose name means "adversary."

Allocen. F.A. who is a duke in hell.

Eligor. F.A. who appears as a good knight with lance.

DEFINITION OF TERMS

Repent. To feel regret; to turn from sin and do oneself to the amendment of one's life; to feel regret or contrition. To change one's to feel sorrow, regret or contrition.

Contrite. To grin, bruise, to rub felling or showing sorrow and remorse for sin or shortcoming.

Penitence. Sparrow or sins or faults

Penitent. To cause regret, fell regret, felling or expressing humble or regretful pain or sorrow for sins or offences.

Portal. Portal, city gate, porch, entrance: a grand or imposing one to the whole architectural composition surrounding and including the doorway and porches of a church.

Port. A gate, door portal, passage.

Prayer and repentance. Pray and repentance will be keys in releasing the glory. When Jesus was baptized, he accentually identified with man's sin and repented for us through the act of water baptism when He fulfilled that at of righteousness. "The heavens were opened…" (Matt. 3:16)

The Lord is calling His people to focus prayer and personal as well as identification repentance (Matthew 3, Daniel 9–10, Nehemiah 1) in order to "open the heavens."

From 11-9-2011

http://www.elijah list.com/words/display word/1109

Nebuchadnezzar-ing of Babylon Jeremiah 21:2
Lord of Hosts 1 Samuel 1:3
Luke 19:40

CPSIA information can be obtained
at www.ICGtesting.com
Printed in the USA
LVOW04s2054120816

500060LV00016B/190/P